The Vanishing of Lord Vale

The Lost Lords
Book Two

Chasity Bowlin

Dedication

To my wonderful husband for inspiring me, for pushing me, and for doing the laundry and the dishes while I get lost in the world I made up. Thank you.

Books from Dragonblade Publishing

Knights of Honor Series by Alexa Aston
Word of Honor
Marked By Honor
Code of Honor
Journey to Honor
Heart of Honor

Legends of Love Series by Avril Borthiry
The Wishing Well
Isolated Hearts
Sentinel

The Lost Lords Series by Chasity Bowlin
The Lost Lord of Castle Black
The Vanishing of Lord Vale

By Elizabeth Ellen Carter
Captive of the Corsairs, *Heart of the Corsairs Series*
Dark Heart

Knight Everlasting Series by Cassidy Cayman
Endearing
Enchanted

Midnight Meetings Series by Gina Conkle
Meet a Rogue at Midnight, book 4

Second Chance Series by Jessica Jefferson
Second Chance Marquess

Imperial Season Series by Mary Lancaster
Vienna Waltz
Vienna Woods
Vienna Dawn

Blackhaven Brides Series by Mary Lancaster
The Wicked Baron
The Wicked Lady
The Wicked Rebel

Highland Loves Series by Melissa Limoges
My Reckless Love

Clash of the Tartans Series by Anna Markland
Kilty Secrets

Queen of Thieves Series by Andy Peloquin
Child of the Night Guild
Thief of the Night Guild

Dark Gardens Series by Meara Platt
Garden of Shadows
Garden of Light
Garden of Dragons
Garden of Destiny

Rulers of the Sky Series by Paula Quinn
Scorched
Ember

Viking's Fury Series by Violetta Rand
Love's Fury
Desire's Fury
Passion's Fury

Also from Violetta Rand
Viking Hearts

The Sons of Scotland Series by Victoria Vane
Virtue

Dry Bayou Brides Series by Lynn Winchester
The Shepherd's Daughter
The Seamstress
The Widow

Table of Contents

Elizabeth Masters has put her scandalous and painful past behind her. She's taken a position as companion to the tragic Lady Vale and her primary duty is to dissuade the woman from believing that everyone from the butcher's delivery boy to the ostler at an inn is her missing son. But a late night visit to an alleged mystic in the city of Bath results in near tragedy as Elizabeth is nearly abducted by ruffians waiting for them outside. They are rescued by a handsome and mysterious stranger who calls himself Benedict, the very name of Lady Vale's lost son.

Benedict has his own reasons for being in Bath—to locate his missing sister and see her safe once more. Waylaid by a pistol ball from the men who attacked Miss Masters, he finds himself dependent upon the assistance of Lady Vale to rescue his Mary. In exchange, he must consent to her investigation of his past to determine if he is, in fact, her missing son, an unlikely scenario in his mind.

As their investigation unfolds, it becomes clear that the danger they face, the attempted abduction of Elizabeth and Mary's disappearance are all connected to the fateful night twenty-four years earlier when Lady Vale's son was ripped from her arms, never to be seen again. Forced to work together, Benedict and Elizabeth cannot fight the attraction they feel for one another. Yet with every piece of evidence uncovered, the truth of Benedict's identity threatens their burgeoning relationship... and the danger that brought them together looms larger at every turn.

Prologue

London, 1796

THE ELEGANT TOWNHOUSE in Grosvenor Square had recently been refurbished and expanded, the viscount having annexed the abode to its left through what was rumored to be less than pleasant persuasion. It was now the largest home on the square. The Georgian facade, precise and symmetrical, faced the street much like a haughty dowager, daring any and all to defy the propriety demanded by its esteemed location. From the outside, with its trappings of wealth and privilege, it was a thing of beauty. But it hid dark and ugly secrets within, much like the man who owned it.

"I ain't never seen a 'ouse that big," one of the men said. Large and rough spoken, with broad shoulders and a barrel chest, his cockney heritage was evident in his speech. The man removed his hat and scratched his shaved head, courtesy of the prison he'd recently been discharged from. Shaving the heads of inmates was the best way to curb infestations of lice and other vermin.

"It ain't so big, Henry," Alfred, the smallest of their crew, said. Short, wiry and deceptively strong, there was a coldness in his eyes that was very different from his companions.

Fenton Hardwick cursed his luck to have joined up with two such dimwitted criminals. "Do not use names, you fools! Our goal is to get into that house, get what we're looking for, and then be gone from it without anyone being the wiser."

"You sure they're gone from 'ere?" Henry asked. "Don't seem right that a body with a warm hearth and a nice young family would be out and about, not on Christmas like!"

"I'm certain of it. I heard it from Lord Vale himself," Fenton snapped. The man had told him where they'd be, where to find the item in question, though in somewhat vague terms. He owed Fenton and this was how the debt would be paid. Better spoken than his friends, from a far different background, they had little understanding of how the upper echelons of society worked. Though given his own poor dress at the moment, he would be hard pressed to convince anyone that he was more well-versed in the ways of that world. "I was standing in the mews right behind the house when he told the driver to have the carriage readied… that he and his lady would be attending the theater!"

"Toffs is strange," Henry said, shaking his head.

"Don't much matter. We'll get in, get the goods and be gone," Alfred said. "Then we're all square like wiv' the boss and can get on with honest work. Now 'ush up and let's get on wiv' it."

In the darkness, with the mist and smog shrouding the muddy streets, they slipped toward the house and the back gate that Henry had disabled earlier. It hadn't taken much effort to break the locking mechanism on his way out after he'd delivered a load of meat to the kitchens. Now, they'd slip inside, up the stairs, and directly into the lady's chambers. They'd retrieve the item the "boss" wanted and, perhaps, help themselves to a few trinkets to ease their way into a life of, as Alfred had said, honest work. It was The Season, after all. She'd have all her best jewels and fripperies about. They could take what they liked and sell it to the highest bidder.

As they entered the garden, a loud chorus of singing erupted from the servants' quarters on the lower floor. It was the perfect cover. With his hand wrapped in heavy cloth, Henry gave the glass farthest from the servants' hall a tap. The pane fell inward, but the sound of it was muffled by the carpet and masked by the revelry inside.

"Check the corridor. Make sure no one is coming to investigate the noise," Fenton urged. They had a sound plan, a free pass as it were, in and out of the house, yet he found himself unaccountably nervous.

Alfred rushed ahead to do his bidding, watching through the narrowest crack in the door. Several moments passed and no one appeared. "We got the all clear," he said.

Opening the door fully, he stepped out into the hall and the other two followed suit. They made for the back stairs. Henry's sister had worked as a maid there once, until Lord Vale tried to put his hand up her skirt. She'd only been too happy to give them the information they asked for about the layout of the house.

Once on the upper floors, the house was unnaturally quiet. With all the servants below, enjoying their Christmas feast, and the lord and lady of the manor out for the evening, the grand house was like a tomb.

"Gives me the shivers, it does," Henry said crossly. He might have been the biggest of them, but he'd always been more heart than brains, not to mention the fact that he was often gutless. Were it not for his compatriots goading him on, he'd have been more than content to continue delivering luxurious cuts of meat to the wealthy toffs his butcher employer served.

"Only a 'ouse," Alfred replied. "'Tis the people inside it we've most to fear from. Let's keep it moving. I don't want to still be standing 'ere, yammering on about it, when the lord and lady decide to come back 'ome."

"The master's chambers will be at the end of the corridor. You go there and get anything he might have of value. There will be coin, jewelry, gold buttons off his coats. Cut every last one of them off. I'll head to her ladyship's rooms and see what she might have laying about." He hadn't told the others about the book. That was an agreement between him and the "boss" only. Fenton turned to Henry and added, "And you stay here. If anyone comes up those stairs, you come find me. Understood?"

Henry nodded his understanding and Fenton continued. "And cover your faces. In the off chance someone returns, we can still make our escape if they cannot identify us!"

Dutifully, the other men pulled up the cloths tied around their necks so that the lower halves of their faces were covered and each one headed out in the direction they'd been given. Henry took up sentry in the hall, monitoring the stairs. Big as he was, he managed to blend his hulking shape with the shadows.

Shaking his head at the conundrum of his large but dimwitted companion who could seemingly vanish in plain sight, Fenton headed toward Lady Vale's rooms and the riches that awaited him there.

"I DON'T WANT to sleep in my room. I want to sleep in yours… there are beasties in my room."

Sarah, Lady Vale, smiled down into the upturned and cherubic face of her son. In this one thing, she thought, she'd done something right. Her husband might find fault with her in every other regard as a wife and as a woman, but she'd provided him an heir and never had a more beautiful boy graced a family than her dear Benedict. Brushing the blond curls from his furrowed brow, she shook her head.

"There are no beasties, Benedict. There is nothing in this house that would harm you!"

"Maisy said there was," he protested. "She said there were all sorts of nasty things going on in the corridors. Said it were nothing but evil."

"It was nothing but evil," she corrected automatically. "You mustn't repeat things you hear from Maisy as the girl is full of superstitious nonsense and her grasp of the language is utterly atrocious."

"What's atrocious mean?" he asked, hugging the small, wooden horse that was his favorite toy.

"It means awful." And there were awful, evil things occurring in the corridors. But she couldn't possibly tell her son that his father was the perpetrator of them. James seemed to feel that any female servant was fair game for his unwanted advances. She'd made it a point to stop hiring pretty girls and, instead, only hired those who were significantly older or who would be willing to tolerate his advances for whatever reward it might bring them. It was a lowering thing for any woman to look at the servants in her own house and wonder which one was warming her husband's bed for the night. Of course, she was relieved when anyone warmed it other than herself, so there was also a strange sort of consolation in it. "And Maisy didn't mean evil like monsters or beasties. She was talking about people playing pranks on one another. You've nothing to worry about, darling. I promise."

"Please, Mama?"

Her heart melted, as it always did. He was so sweet and she'd be lying if she said she didn't find comfort in the weight of his little body snuggled against her own. Benedict was the only child she would ever have. His delivery had been a difficult one and she'd been told that more children would be impossible. James had raged against her, claiming she'd done it on purpose. Even the doctor, a long acquaintance of her husband, had been mortified.

Sarah looked down at her son and thought of another purely selfish reason to let him come with her to her bed. If he was sleeping beside her, no matter how drunk and ill-tempered James was upon returning home, he'd not disturb her or the boy. She'd avoided his advances on many a night by allowing her poor, dear child to be her shield. It wasn't something she was proud of.

James was out with his mistress, but that meant nothing. He might still come home determined to prove the doctor wrong, to prove that he was virile enough to get her with child regardless of what all the best medical professionals had told them.

"Very well," she agreed. "You may come with me and you may sleep in my room tonight, but only because I'll be lonely for you if you're not there. Not because there are any beasties!"

The smile that spread across his delighted face warmed her to her toes. She'd never thought it possible to love as strongly or as fiercely as she loved her child. Lifting his little body into her arms, she carried him much as she had when he was an infant. It was highly unfashionable for a woman of her standing to be so involved with the day to day care of her child. The standard, of course, was for the child to be turned over to nurses and nannies and for the mother to continue all the same amusements that had comprised her life before marriage and children. But she had no interest in balls or musicales. She had no interest in going about in society and pretending to be happy when married to a monster. Her happiness was found in moments like the present, with the weight of her sweet son resting against her, his head tucked beneath her chin.

As she traversed the corridor, a feeling came upon her. It was one of dread and fear, and one that she typically associated with the presence of her husband. But it was only past ten and she knew that he would not be home till the wee hours of the morning. Continuing on, her slippered feet moved silently over the rug that blanketed the parquet floor. Yet the feeling remained.

"Mama, I don't feel good," the boy complained.

"Benedict, I need you to be very quiet," she said softly. The certainty that they were not alone in the hall had hit her forcefully. While her eyes could not penetrate the darkness, while there appeared to be no visible proof that they were not alone, she would not be foolish enough to ignore the feeling and place them both at risk.

Had he hired someone to kill her? It would not have surprised her. She was more surprised that he'd waited so long. A wife that could not produce children was not worth having. But annulling their marriage was not a possibility, not without rendering the heir he did have illegitimate. Stepping back, she retreated slowly toward Benedict's room. If she could get inside it, she could duck through the adjoining nurse's room and get to the servants' stairs.

Before her hand closed over the knob, a great hulking shape emerged from the shadows. She screamed and Benedict followed suit. The man, for surely even gigantic as it was, it could be nothing else, clapped her on the head, sending her hurtling to the floor. Dazed as she was from the blow, she could see Benedict lashing out at him, kicking and wailing. The man closed his hand over her son's mouth, his big hand covering almost the entirety of the boy's face.

"Go quiet like an' I won't 'ave to 'urt 'im."

She labored to decipher the cockney accent, but nodded just the same. She'd agree to anything to see Benedict spared.

"Get up and go to your room," the man directed.

Sarah did as she'd been bid, struggling to her feet. Dizziness swamped her and she had to place her hand against the wall to remain upright as she followed his directive. She glanced back at Benedict who was wide eyed, kicking and struggling in the large man's hold. He would injure himself or, perhaps far worse, anger his captor. In the hopes of appeasing him and sparing Benedict the man's temper, Sarah rushed to comply with his edict. Once at her chamber door, she opened it and stepped inside. Another man awaited them within.

"Bloody hell! You weren't supposed to be here!" he hissed. "You were supposed to be out with your husband."

"Who would have you told you such a thing?" she asked. "I never attend balls, and most certainly not with my husband."

"Seems I was misinformed," he answered, before turning his gaze to his larger companion. "For pity's sake, you're suffocating the boy!"

The large man immediately removed his hand and Benedict gasped and coughed. Terrified, Sarah turned to him and took him from the large man, holding him close to her. The man had let him go without a protest. For the moment, she didn't feel they were in immediate danger. Even the man's rough treatment of Benedict seemed to be incidental to his size and not intended to do harm. Deciding to face the matter boldly, she offered, "If your intent is robbery then, by all means, take whatever you want. I will not stop you and I will not raise the alarm. So long as my son remains un-harmed, you may do as you please. But touch him again and I will scream down the entire house."

"We're not here to harm anyone," the more well-spoken of the two said. "By all rights, you should have been out and the boy should have been abed. We're only here to take what's owed us."

"Then be done with it," she snapped.

"It'll be much faster with your help," he said. "The sooner we're out, the sooner you can feel safe again." The last was said with a sneer, like he was aware of something she was not.

With Benedict still in her arms, clinging to her tightly with his tear-stained cheek pressed to her shoulder, Sarah walked to her dressing room, opened the secret panel in the wall and revealed her jewelry collection. "Take whatever you want and then leave."

"We'll take a few, just to tide us over," the man said, reaching in and indiscriminately grabbing several pieces which he then shoved into his pockets. "But we're looking for the book."

"What book?" she shot back.

"The one your husband said was hidden in this house!" he snapped. "Don't play stupid with me! Where else would he hide it but in this chamber?"

She laughed bitterly. "My husband never enters this chamber. I cannot tell you where he hid it!"

"He said it would be here!" the man snapped at her.

His tone was sharp, snappish, and yet there was fear buried within it. She knew what fear was. Her husband had done his best to acquaint her with it from the day of their wedding forward. To the burglar, she said, "Then he lied. If you are acquainted with my husband at all then surely that cannot be a surprise."

"That book was promised to someone... and if we don't deliver, it'll go badly for us all. Very badly, indeed. That includes you and your husband. If you've any inkling where it might be," Fenton said softly, "then you need to tell us now."

"I know nothing of the book you speak of. My husband rarely visits my chambers and I rarely leave them," she insisted. "We may be wed but, in truth, we live very separate lives. If he told you it was here, then you, like so many, have been misled by him."

He looked at her, his gaze raking over her figure. "I find that difficult to believe."

Sarah blushed. "The birth of my son was difficult. I can bear him no more children, thus I no longer serve a purpose for him. Perhaps this book you speak of is hidden in his mistress' rooms instead of mine.

You should look there, though given the vast number of them, it could take you the better part of the night."

FENTON EYED THE viscountess coolly. There was something about her that sparked his pity and, yet, he tamped it down. A man in his position could not afford any emotion so soft as pity. It would only be his downfall. "If I understand correctly, then you are of no value to him?" When she remained silent, he snapped, reached out and grabbed her arm, twisting it painfully until she cried out and sank to her knees, still holding the boy tightly to her. He didn't want to hurt her, but he would if it came to it. Whatever sadness might lurk in her pretty eyes, it was her life or his. "Answer me!"

"No," she replied softly. "I hold no value for my husband!"

"But the boy does," he mused. "He's the heir after all."

"No! No!" she shouted. "I won't let you do anything to him!"

"Subdue her," Fenton snapped at Henry as he shoved her away and grabbed up the crying child.

She fought like a demon. Kicking, clawing, scratching. There were moments when, as Fenton watched, the small, struggling child in his arms, he thought she might very well best Henry. At one point, she did escape the larger man and dragged herself over to him. She clawed at him as he made his way toward the door, ripping at his clothes and very nearly pulling the child from his arms. Whatever else could be said for Lord Vale, when he'd chosen the mother of his child, he'd chosen well. Her devotion to her son was surely without equal. But devoted or not, Henry was a beast of a man, large and strong. He claimed her once more, picking her up easily and carting her back toward the bed. When attempts to simply hold her failed, the giant of a man cuffed her ear and sent her sprawling to the floor. Before her head could have even stopped spinning, she was back on her feet.

"Bind her. Use the ties from the bed curtains and get her under control," Fenton hissed. "We haven't time for this nonsense!" She shrieked again like a banshee. Even with the commotion of the servants celebrating below stairs, it was unlikely that such commotion would go unnoticed for long. Removing his neckcloth, a garment curiously fine for the rest of his tattered clothing, Fenton approached her and shoved it into her mouth. He tugged at the sash of her wrapper until it came free and tossed it at Henry. "Use that to finish gagging her. Now, Lady Vale—Sarah, I'll promise you this, so long as you cooperate, and so long as your husband sees the book delivered into our hands, no harm will fall on this boy. It's not my wish to harm women and children, but my life is on the line, and I'll not sacrifice it for the lot of you. Do you hear me?"

She nodded, her face pale in the moonlight and her wide eyes brimming with tears, as Henry finished securing her hands. "Don't like this none," Henry groused. "Don't seem right, it don't! I don't 'old wiv' roughin' up women and babes!"

"Shut up. Get Al—get your partner and let's be gone before we're discovered," Fenton said, barely catching his slip in time. He looked back at Lady Sarah, Viscountess Vale. "For what it's worth, I am sorry. You do not deserve any of this, but your husband is at fault, madame. We are but the instruments of the downfall he has wrought." To the boy, he whispered, "If you're not quiet, if you let out a single peep as we leave this house, I will come back here and I will do far worse than just tie your pretty mother up? Nod if you understand me, boy!"

The little boy's soft curls bobbed as he stared up at Fenton and nodded his head. Lady Vale turned her face away, weeping silently. Fenton continued, "We're going on an adventure. You keep quiet, your mother remains unharmed and you'll have lots to tell her when you return home. Yes?" The boy nodded again and Fenton gave one last look at the slumped and shaking shoulders of the viscountess sobbing in the darkness as he slipped from her chambers and into the shadow-shrouded hall.

He didn't notice the absence of his pocket watch, that it lay on the carpet of the chamber he'd just exited, engraved with his damning initials.

Chapter One

E LIZABETH MASTERS EXITED the shop on Pulteney Bridge and smiled. It had been a frivolous purchase, a length of ribbon that she would never dare to wear in public. The lovely emerald hue was far too eye-catching for someone who did everything in her power to blend with the wallpaper. She had reason enough to want to vanish, she reflected bitterly. A woman in service could not afford to draw too much attention to herself but, beyond that, it was imperative for her position that no one recognize her from her previous life. Being a companion required being respectable above all things. And as her past forays into society had marked her as rather fast and imprudent, she had created as much separation from those days as possible.

Moving to Bath, as different from her bucolic upbringing in Hertfordshire as one could imagine, and leaving the all too brief acquaintance of the glittering gaiety of London behind, she'd set out to be very different from how she'd begun. Once she'd seen how tarnished and ugly London and its society truly were, it had allowed her to see herself in a new light and to make the changes necessary to become a better person.

Parties, balls, and endless frivolity had masked a deeper unhappiness inside her, a need for approval and attention that had left her easy prey to certain unscrupulous men. It had been a hard lesson learned, but she was the better for it. If her newfound life of piety and hard work did not bring joy, it was because she still needed to attend to the flaws in her own character, she reasoned. She was still allowing frivolous things to hold too much importance in her life. Even with that assessment ringing in her head, she continued to clutch the paper-wrapped length of ribbons as tightly as a child with a prize.

Stepping off the bridge, she crossed toward St. Michael's Abbey and the nearby Pump Room. Lady Vale had excused her during her daily appointment to take the waters and Elizabeth had been unable to resist the length of green satin that had been calling her name for days. Every time she'd passed the shop window, she'd stared longingly at it. Now it was hers, to be hidden away in a drawer or pinned to some of her underthings as her own little secret vanity.

A feeling of unease stole over her and she glanced over her shoulder to see a large man leaning against a stone railing that overlooked the weir. He was roughly dressed, which was unusual as they were in a more fashionable part of town. Since he leaned nonchalantly there, he clearly was not a workman or in the employ of someone. He appeared to be quite at his leisure. He also appeared to be intently watching her. Immediately on guard, Elizabeth didn't dare take her eyes off him.

Still looking over her shoulder, she was caught unawares when she walked directly into another person. Elizabeth stumbled, dropped her paper-wrapped package and her reticule and nearly fell on her bottom. She would have, had a pair of strong hands not grasped her upper arms and steadied her.

"Oh, dear heavens! How terribly clumsy I've been," she muttered apologetically.

The man had stooped to retrieve her things as well as his hat which she'd sent flying. Only the top of his golden head was visible to her, but she heard the smile in his voice, as he spoke, "There is no need to apologize. You appeared to be quite deep in troubling thoughts."

"Not so troubling really," she denied. "Nonetheless, I do apologize, sir. I have quite made a cake of myself."

He rose then, hat in one hand, her reticule and packaged ribbon in the other. Hand extended, he offered her items back to her, but it took

Elizabeth a moment to quite make sense of what was happening.

The stranger she had inadvertently accosted wasn't simply a handsome man. He was, in fact, the most beautiful man she'd ever seen. Every feature was chiseled, patrician perfection. And when he smiled at her, her heart thundered violently in her chest. It appeared all the work she'd done to distance herself from the shallow and vain creature she'd once been had been undone with a single glance at what surely was a model for Adonis.

"Forgive me, sir," she finally managed. "I don't mean to stare but you seem quite familiar to me." It wasn't untrue. There was something familiar in his face, but it wasn't that which had prompted her to stare. Rather the sense of familiarity had been borne of the fact that she could not drag her gaze away from him in all his golden perfection.

He laughed then. "I don't think we've met. We hardly run in the same circles, now do we?"

She blushed, humiliation burning inside her at the gentle rebuttal. Based on his clothing and deportment, it was obvious he was a gentleman. Given her drab attire, there was no mistaking that they were not of the same class. But that was what she had striven for, was it not? To disappear into the drudgery of a not-quite-a-servant's life that was, to her, her lot forevermore.

Finding her voice, she replied as coolly as she dared, "Certainly, you are correct, sir. Thank you and good day."

He frowned. "I've insulted you and I assure you it was purely by accident… I don't mean to imply that I move in exalted circles, miss. Quite the opposite. I only look like a gentleman. I am not one. And regardless of your current employment, I daresay you are always a lady. Good day to you."

Elizabeth watched him walk away and wondered what sort of man would dress so finely, speak so eloquently and display such pristine manners while referring to himself as not a gentleman. He was puzzling to be certain, but handsome puzzles that piqued her curiosity and her attraction were a recipe for disaster. She could not afford to be intrigued by him. She could not afford to do anything that would sway her from her current bleak but proper course.

Looking over her shoulder once more, she saw that the large workman was gone. "I am letting my foolish imagination get the better of me," she muttered and turned to make her way toward the baths. It had been a curious day to say the least. Given the appointment she had arranged for Lady Vale for later that evening, it was only destined to grow stranger by the hour.

BENEDICT WATCHED THE woman from a secluded doorway. Concealed in the shadows, he watched the large man lumber away, taking a set of stairs that would lead down to the river. It had been the rough-looking man who'd first caught his attention. The ruffian matched the description he'd been given by the porter of the man he'd seen following Mary only a week earlier. In the square, surrounded by fashionably dressed ladies out to shop, pay calls and take the waters, he'd stood out like the proverbial sore thumb with his rough clothes and rougher appearance.

As Benedict had observed him, it had become glaringly apparent that the man was actually watching someone else. He'd kept his gaze glued to a small storefront. When the woman had emerged, dressed in her drab brown with her tightly-coiffed hair, he'd noted that the large man relaxed immediately. She was his quarry, there was no doubt.

Reflecting on the woman, Benedict had determined two things about her immediately. Underneath her drab costume, and he couldn't help but feel it was, indeed, a costume—an affectation for whatever reason—she was far lovelier than she wanted anyone to realize. She'd also been attuned to the danger that the other man posed. Which begged the question of why she would be familiar with such? Had it been a simple instinctive response, like a rabbit running from a fox? Or did she know him?

The large man emerged again from the stairs he'd taken. Had he ducked out of sight to answer the call of nature or to report his findings to someone else? Benedict considered his options. He could follow the woman and assume that the hulking goon was, in fact, hunting her, or he could follow the goon and see if, perhaps, he'd been wrong in assessing the situation.

The woman piqued his interest. She was a study in contradictions and he had always enjoyed a puzzle. But she was also a distraction, and one that he could ill afford. Following her could confirm whether or not the other man was a threat to her and, by extrapolation, had been a threat to his sister. But if he was wrong, if the lumbering oaf watching her had simply been a coincidence, he would have lost his advantage there. As the miscreant was the more likely source of information if he was to locate Mary, Benedict bid a mental farewell to the vexing woman who had nearly upended them both and followed the thug.

Chapter Two

THE HOUSE WAS in a less than fashionable neighborhood but not so much so that they felt unsafe arriving there via sedan chair. A discreet placard in the front window declared that *"Madame Zula Is In"*.

"Lady Vale, I think this is a terrible idea. What do we really know of this woman other than the glowing recommendations of those women at the Pump Room?" Elizabeth asked, eyeing the narrow street with skepticism.

"I have very little expectation from this evening, Miss Masters. You needn't distress yourself so. I've no intention of turning over the family fortunes to a mystic. You must think me as cabbage-brained as Brandon does," Lady Vale said haughtily as she disembarked from the sedan chair.

"Not in the least... I simply have concerns about this neighborhood. It is barely respectable, after all," she protested.

Lady Vale scoffed. "We're in Bath, Miss Masters, not London. Nothing ever happens in Bath!"

Elizabeth thought of the hulking beast of a man she'd seen earlier that day and the sense of danger she'd felt from him. She refused to let her attention wander to the handsome stranger she had bumped into. "Let us at least get inside quickly before we tempt fate any further!"

Climbing the steps as the sedan chairs were carried off by the strapping porters, Elizabeth raised the simple iron knocker. There was a lighter silhouette on the door beneath it. No doubt the brass one that had been there originally had been stolen.

The door opened and the same handsome young man she'd encountered two days earlier opened the door. He stared past her to Lady Vale and frowned. "You were to come alone to the appointment, Miss Masters."

"There has been a change of plans," she said. "I have decided to allow my employer to use the appointment in my stead. May we come in?"

His frown deepened, but he stepped aside and opened the door wide. Once inside the foyer, the scent of incense and herbs was cloying.

"I will need to speak with Madame Zula," the servant said. His tone revealed his agitation far more so than his words did. But his demeanor remained stiff and somewhat uncertain.

"Certainly. We shall wait here," Lady Vale said. "Naturally, Madame Zula will be compensated for the inconvenience."

He disappeared behind a heavily-lacquered pocket door. Stepping closer to it, Elizabeth peered through, heedless of Lady Vale's hissed protest.

She couldn't see Madame Zula as the settee she occupied faced away from the door, but she could see the servant bent low, whispering into the woman's ear. It was a strangely intimate conversation and Elizabeth found herself shying away from it. The man was clearly more than just a servant to Madame Zula.

"That was impossibly rude," Lady Vale whispered. She followed up her momentary censure with the question, "What did you think of her?"

"I couldn't see her. But I think she is very familiar with her servant," Elizabeth answered.

Lady Vale's lips parted in surprise. "Oh, I see. Well... that is neither here nor there, is it?"

Nothing more was said as the servant returned. He eyed them both suspiciously but stated, "Madame Zula has agreed to the change in scheduling... though typically, she would refuse a client for such an abuse of her goodwill. I assume that you have an item for her to use during your reading, madame?"

"I have brought something," Lady Vale said.

The servant nodded again and stepped aside, opening the pocket door for them and letting them pass into the parlor.

The room was bathed in dim light, the lamps shuttered to prevent their glow from penetrating the deep shadows of the room. As they entered, making their way toward the small settee that faced the fireplace, they were both somewhat shocked at the appearance of Madame Zula. She was younger than anticipated though still significantly older than her servant and lover. None of that detracted from her dark beauty, however. Dusky-skinned, with almond-shaped eyes set off by thick lashes and winged brows, she looked every inch the gypsy she claimed to be.

Madame Zula remained seated, her hands folded in her lap, her turbaned head bowed, and a serene expression marked her countenance. Her manservant had entered behind them. The improbably handsome servant began rearranging the room to suit a gathering of three rather than two. She wondered that he seemed to do all the tasks of footman, butler, assistant and secretary as he walked over to a small table and wound the mechanism on a clockwork music box. The tinny notes filled the room, eerie and even somewhat discordant.

"Madame Zula is in a trance-like state… calming the mind before she breeches the spirit world. When the music stops, she will awaken," he explained in a pleasantly deep voice filled with just a hint of an Irish accent. "You may speak to one another, but do so softly and please do not attempt to engage her until she acknowledges you."

"Certainly, sir," Lady Vale answered in a cool but not clipped tone.

Like so many things about Lady Vale, her reply was all that was ladylike and dispassionate. Most of the time, it was a facade that she carefully maintained. There were moments when it slipped, when Elizabeth could glimpse the carefree and beautiful girl that her employer had once been but, more often than not, those slips only revealed a woman who lived daily with grief and uncertainty.

It was not the first time they had visited a mystic, fortune teller, soothsayer or other variety of charlatan. They were so commonplace that Lady Vale could manage to approach even such metaphysical attempts to locate her lost son with an outwardly objective aplomb that was both admirable and worrisome. But Elizabeth knew the truth. She often heard her mistress weeping at night, sobbing into the darkness. The loss of her son haunted her.

"Have you the item?" Lady Vale asked after the manservant left the room.

Elizabeth nodded. "Yes, your ladyship. I have it with me." She was well acquainted with the routine, of course. This was not the first mystic that Lady Vale had employed in the search for her missing child. Unlike many of them, Madame Zula came highly recommended. But then, when a psychic told people precisely what they wished to hear and proved herself by revealing sensitive information that could be easily ascertained by greasing the palm of a disgruntled servant, it wasn't difficult to gain recommendations, Elizabeth thought bitterly. She had no belief at all in the nonsense such performers, for that is what they were surely, spouted.

For herself, Elizabeth put no store in such things. But if it brought Lady Vale some measure of comfort to do those things, it was certainly not her place to object. Employed by Lady Vale's brother-in-law, the Honorable Branson Middlethorp, Esquire, it was not her job to prevent such activities, only to accompany Lady Vale and report back should any of her endeavors become too costly, either emotionally or financially.

Madame Zula opened her eyes. Her gaze traveled from Elizabeth's face to Lady Vale's. It was obvious that she recognized Lady Vale immediately. Everyone did, after all. People whispered about her everywhere they went.

"I understood that the appointment was for a Miss Masters. I was not aware there would be other guests," Madame Zula said with a hint a censure in her voice.

"I scheduled the appointment for my employer," Elizabeth said. "In order to avoid gossip and speculation, I felt it best not to have her ladyship's name associated with such activities. I'm certain you understand." It had also been a calculated effort on her part to reduce the amount of foreknowledge the psychic might gain about Lady Vale's situation.

Madame Zula inclined her head. "Certainly, Miss Masters. You are most welcome, Lady Vale. Might I ask what position Miss Masters occupies for you? Maid, secretary?"

"Companion," Lady Vale corrected.

Her tone implied the truth of it. *Keeper.* That was how she viewed Elizabeth, and that was unlikely to alter.

"Of course," Madame Zula said, her voice pitched low and nonetheless dramatic for it. "Forgive my misunderstanding." She reached for a small bell on the table beside her. It tinkled lightly and the young, obscenely pretty servant entered again. They whispered to one another for just a moment before he nodded and left. Only a moment later, he returned with another chair which he placed at the table that occupied pride of place in the room.

"Please, we will sit at the table, no? It is much easier to do what must be done there," Madame Zula continued, gesturing toward the elaborately-draped table that now housed three heavy chairs.

Or easier to conceal a person or a mechanism beneath the elaborate table-cloth in order to further her charade, Elizabeth thought. As the wisest course of action was to keep her opinions to herself, Elizabeth simply followed Lady Vale and Madame Zula to the table. After both had seated themselves, she followed suit. She had a moment of envy for the lovely cloth that covered the table. Alternating panels of rose velvet and silk, it would have made a lovely gown.

It had not escaped her that she was the most poorly dressed person in the room. In another life, long before her circumstances had been so irrevocably altered, she had danced and laughed and worn pretty gowns. There had been color and gaiety but, through her own idiocy, it had all gone away.

Now, her brown, dowdy dress was a sort of armor that she had donned. An outward symbol to others of her lowered status and a reminder to herself not to allow her own vanity to sway her.

Working first as a governess, then as a companion, she had quickly realized that she was trapped in an in-between world, not unlike the spirits Madame Zula claimed to commune with.

Neither servant nor gentry, the rules of society prompted her to be present at functions without ever participating. But that put her in the field of vision of unscrupulous men whose attention she did not want. Dressing in drab colors, scraping her hair back into tight and hideous chignons that left her head aching, as did the unnecessary spectacles perched on her nose, provided the only form of protection available to her. They were also a constant reminder to her of just what her own vanity and recklessness had cost her. In order to survive her posts and her newly lowered position in the world, it had been imperative to make herself appear as unattractive as possible.

While protecting her virtue, or at least what remained of it, was certainly of vital importance, there were moments when she missed simply being pretty, when she missed laughing at a ball and slapping a man's arm with a fan when he was too forward. She hadn't been a raving beauty to attract all the beaus, but she'd had her share. It was rather telling that they'd all vanished when it became apparent she had no dowry or estate to bring with her into a marriage, all but one. His intentions, however, had proven to be much less than honorable.

Madame Zula placed her hands flat on the table and dropped her head forward onto it, moaning strange syllables under her breath. Forcing herself to pay attention, to focus on their surroundings and what might be happening, Elizabeth put away her moment of self-pity. She had a job at least, a position that paid fairly well and that allowed her to go to bed each night without placing a chair against the door for added security.

"Spirits, I ask for your guidance... give me your voices that I may provide answers to this poor woman... answers not held within this realm," Madame Zula called out dramatically, her voice rising like any veteran of the stage. "Come to me. Fill me with your knowledge!"

Elizabeth did not roll her eyes. In point of fact, she was perfectly still, focusing solely on the woman speaking. There was something strangely compelling about the performance, about the way her voice rose and fell, the deft and yet delicate movements of her body as she swayed in her chair under the alleged influence of the spirit world. Mesmer, Elizabeth thought. She had studied information about his technique, about animal magnetism. Was it possible that Madame Zula was a practitioner?

"Give me the item you have brought with you," Madame Zula instructed, holding out her hand, palm up. Her fingers moved in a rhythmic fashion, one that drew the eye and invited the observer's focus.

Taking the small pouch from the pocket of her gown, Elizabeth opened it and poured the contents into the woman's outstretched hand. The simple pocket watch made her pause. Why on earth would Lady Vale's son, a lad of only four when he vanished, have a watch?

Madame Zula, lifted the item, examined it closely. Her face seemed to pale in the candlelight. "This item belongs to the person you wish to contact."

Lady Vale smiled but it was not a friendly expression. "That item belongs to someone I very much wish to speak with."

Madame Zula rubbed her thumb across the initials etched rather crudely on the casing. She gave a jerky nod and closed her hand tightly around the watch. Her head dropped forward, moving side to side almost like a dance. "Yes, yes! The spirits are whispering, talking amongst themselves... deciding if we are worthy of their assistance."

Elizabeth looked to Lady Vale, curious. The woman was again impassive, but there was a gleam in her eye. What was she about, Elizabeth wondered? Had she known all along that the woman was a charlatan, and the fob was simply a way to prove that? Whatever was happening, it seemed that Lady Vale was playing a game of her own with the mystic.

Not for the first time, Elizabeth reflected that there was no reason for Mr. Middlethorp to employ her to ensure that Lady Vale would be safe from those who would exploit her. The woman was as cunning as any of those attempting to make her a mark in their confidence games.

"Your son is not with them, my lady," Madame Zula said. "He is not part of the spirit realm, but there are others there who know of him, of his fate." A soft whispering sound filled the room, low and inaudible, it could have been the buzzing of insects on a summer day, but it felt infinitely more sinister than that.

Elizabeth felt a chill run through her, but she forced it away. The hair on her arms rose and she felt a strange urge to flee. Reasoning it out, Elizabeth reminded herself that the woman could easily have found that out via news sheets or through simple gossip. It was common knowledge, after all, that Lady Vale's son had vanished after a trio of assailants entered their London home and made off with him. It was equally common knowledge that, despite all evidence and logic pointing to the contrary, Lady Vale still believed him to be alive.

"Go on," Lady Vale said softly, bowing her head ever so slightly. A breath shuddered from her, another visible crack in her otherwise cool facade.

"They took him into the darkness, and then panic set in." She paused dramatically and lifted her gaze to Lady Vale. "How he cried for you!"

Cold fury washed through Elizabeth. It was blatant manipulation and nothing more. She parted her lips to speak, but Lady Vale gave her a sharp look and a shake of her head.

"Go on," Lady Vale said to Madame Zula. "I never imagined that my sweet boy did not mourn after he was taken or that he was not afraid, even if he was too young to fully understand what was occurring. Continue, Madame. I will steel myself to hear it!"

Madame Zula eyed Lady Vale for a moment, her expression displaying a grudging respect before she dropped her head and continued. "What were they to do with a small boy? A trio of bandits and a towheaded child would draw too much attention," the woman said. She looked up sharply, "An adventure he promised."

Lady Vale's hand stiffened in hers and her breath rushed out in a low hiss.

"He was so brave, to go with them... to save you," Madame Zula continued.

Her voice was different, distant it seemed, Elizabeth noted. She'd cocked her head to the side as if listening, as if someone whispered in her ear. It made Elizabeth's blood run cold. She glanced at Lady Vale and saw the woman's face had paled considerably. Her posture had stiffened, her back completely straight, but that did not hide the tremors that wracked her.

"They gave him to a couple... a man and woman who had no children of their own," she intoned dramatically.

"Where?" Lady Vale demanded.

"The couple was traveling—no... they were travelers. Not gypsies, but wanderers. There were in the north."

"The north?" Elizabeth snapped. "As that leaves the entire countryside of England, all of Scotland and a portion of Wales to consider, do you think, perhaps, you could narrow it done somewhat?"

Madame Zula moaned loudly, her head dropping forward onto the table. When she spoke again, her voice sounded strange and even terrifying. "He has suffered, this boy! And he has done awful things to survive... terrible things. He is not the man you would have raised him to be, Lady Vale. If you continue your search, it will only break your heart!"

Lady Vale's expression shuttered and she answered simply. "I have no heart left to break so it does not matter."

The strange whispering sound grew louder and it felt as if the very air around them was charged somehow, like a summer's day before a storm. Forcing herself to be rational, to disavow the theatrics and atmosphere to focus only on the facts, Elizabeth dissected what had been said. Anything that the woman said that was based in fact was largely recited conjecture from newspapers. Anything else was simply a guess or creative storytelling. How many articles, all collected over the years and stored in a large book in the library by Lady Vale, had posed that theory? It was ludicrous. Everything was blamed on gypsies, stolen children most of all.

"Is he well?" Lady Vale asked.

Madame Zula smiled but it was a sad and wistful expression. "He is healthy, but he is not happy, my lady. He's haunted by ghosts of his past… faint memories of a life that was before, and from… they were not kindly people, those who raised him. He suffered at their hands," Madame Zula said, seemingly reluctantly. "You should leave him to his fate. Some things, once separated, cannot be made whole again!"

Lady Vale drew in on herself, seeming to shrink in her chair under the weight of that cautionary statement. It mimicked an argument Elizabeth had overheard between Lady Vale and Mr. Middlethorp. He'd said essentially the same thing, that if her son were still alive, to introduce him to a life so removed from what he knew would likely break him.

Elizabeth shifted in her chair. Her leg brushed against something that was not the table at all. Her suspicions confirmed, she rose to her feet.

"That is enough!" Elizabeth said. Without warning, she yanked the rose-colored silk free of the table, exposing the small-framed man who sat beneath it, blowing into a strange instrument that produced the whispering sound they had heard. "How dare you use this woman's grief to exploit her for your own financial gain?"

"And is that not what you do, my dear?" Madame Zula demanded, all pretense of her vaguely but unidentifiable European accent gone. She sounded Cornish, in fact. "If the lady weren't grief-stricken and likely to be taken in, you'd not have a job, now would you?"

Those words wounded her because they were true. Were Lady Vale not such a tragic figure, her own situation would be infinitely more dismal. "True enough… ah, but there's the word. True. Truth. Honesty. Lack of pretense. Those, *Madame Zula*, are clearly concepts you struggle with! Consider yourself lucky that we will not call the watch… but you will leave Bath and never importune this fair city again with your lies, your schemes, and your charades."

Lady Vale rose. "There is no need to take on so, Miss Masters. I was well aware that Madame Zula was a fraud. Your man should be more careful about brushing the skirts of ladies beneath the table."

Madame Zula sat back, smug and strangely serene. "All that you see here is theater, mere trappings. People do not wish to believe that there are those like myself walking amongst them. These props, if you will, allow them a sense of security because they provide an illusion of separation, that I am far removed from their mundane lives. But mark me, Miss Masters, and you, Lady Vale, my skills are real, my visions are real." She waved her arm around the room, highlighting the strange jars filled with macabre things that defied description and the shuttered lamps and dark, dreary fabrics. "All of this… it's what people want, what they expect from someone who lives on the veil as I do. I spoke the truth to you, my lady, regardless of what your companion believes. And I will continue to speak it now. Your son is nearer than you think. He hovers on the edges of your world and will come to you in the most unlikely of ways. As for you, Miss Masters, I applaud your protectiveness toward your mistress. I hold no ill will toward you for your accusations."

"How very magnanimous of you! I cannot tell you how relieved I am to hear it," Elizabeth said sarcastically. The woman's theatrics had been far easier to tolerate than her current smugness.

"And on account of my admiration for your character," Madame Zula said with a smirk, "I will give you my insights free of charge… your life is about to change dramatically. All that you know, all that you believe, and everything that you have envisioned for yourself will crumble away and leave you fumbling in the darkness for your way. There are other options, but only if you have the courage to take them. Mark my words, Miss Masters, you've no notion of what awaits you beyond these walls."

"That's it?" Elizabeth asked. "My life will change… both bad things and good things await me beyond these walls? Opportunity and, perhaps, a tall, dark stranger will knock upon my door? Given the quality of your theatrics, I would have thought your content would be slightly more original!"

"Think what you will, my dear, and you also, Lady Vale. But I know my own truth, even if it is beyond your scope of understanding," Madame Zula continued. "And if you have need of me further, I will be here. I've nothing to fear in this city and you cannot make me leave it. Should you need me again, let us not stand on pretense… my name is Zella Hopkins. Madame Zula will be reserved for those clients who need the drama in order to believe."

Infuriated by the woman's smugness, Elizabeth turned to her mistress, "Let us leave here, Lady Vale. I will secure sedan chairs to see us home as the hour has grown late."

"You may go, Miss Masters, but there is more that I have to impart to Lady Vale that is not intended for your ears," Madame Zula said.

Elizabeth's lips parted in an expression of surprise and then she laughed bitterly. "You are a cheeky one, aren't you?"

Lady Vale nodded. "Please, Miss Masters. I can't imagine that there is anything she could say to me that would change my opinion at this moment. But if she wishes to speak privately, it certainly can do no harm. After all, in spite of her earlier deceptions, Mrs. Hopkins has been remarkably forthcoming now."

"Miss," the woman corrected. "I never married. More's the pity."

Elizabeth considered her options. She wanted to protest but had no grounds for it. Lady Vale had acquiesced easily enough to the notion that the woman was a charlatan. If she wished to extract her pound of flesh, Elizabeth could not deny her that. But if she was entertaining the notion that the woman was being truthful in claiming that her abilities still had merit—well, that was something else altogether.

"I will be back inside as soon as I have secured the sedan chairs," she uttered softly, and shot a warning look to Madame Zula out of Lady Vale's sight. With a swish of her dowdy skirts, reminiscent of a time when she'd worn silks and satins of her own, she turned on her heel and exited the parlor.

Chapter Three

BENEDICT REMAINED HIDDEN in the shadowy alcove of a doorway as he eavesdropped on a conversation between clearly unintelligent criminals. They made no attempt to keep their voices lowered or to be circumspect in plotting out their crime.

He'd been following the big brute for most of the day, until he'd joined up with his colleagues, for lack of a better word. A more sorry lot he couldn't recall ever laying eyes on. Still there was something about the one seemingly intelligent individual in the sad trio that seemed strangely familiar to him.

"How long you reckon they'll be in there?" the first one asked.

"Don't rightly know. Never been to a mystic 'afore."

"Mystic my eye!" one of the other men replied. "She's no more talkin' to spirits than you or me! You know that as well as I do. She's got her part to play and so do we!"

"What you think she says to all them fancy society birds? What could a fine lady like 'er want with a mystic?"

The first one guffawed, clearly amused at his own thoughts. "Probably wonderin' which lover's bed she left 'er jewels in! Either way, she weren't supposed to be 'ere."

The third man approached the others from his place of concealment and cuffed the other two on the ears. "We're not here for her. It's the other one, the younger woman that should be of interest to you. We've been paid to take her and take her we will! Now keep your eyes open and your mouths shut!"

Benedict had arrived after them and not seen the women who

entered the mystic's home. They'd given up following his little brown bird earlier in the day so he had no fear for her safety.

Why did bands of miscreants always seem to run in trios, Benedict wondered? Still, it was of note that the men were waiting outside the very address he'd come to Bath to investigate and that they were speaking of abduction as if it were a commonplace activity for them.

That address, Madame Zula's, was the last place Mary had been seen, the last place anyone could place her before she'd simply vanished without a trace. And now they were discussing having been paid to take a young woman emerging from that very home. It didn't bode well. Thinking of the fate that might have befallen his sweet sister, his blood ran cold and a quiet rage filled him. If she'd been harmed, and the miscreants in front of him had been a party to it, he'd see them all pay.

The door opened and a woman emerged. It was too dark and he was too far away, at first, to see her clearly. But as she descended the steps and entered a small pool of light from one of the gas lamps, he bit back a curse. With her dowdy dress and hair, it was impossible to mistake that it was the same young woman he'd met earlier in the day, the one who had piqued his interest so greatly. Fear gripped him as he thought of what might happen to her if the gang of ruffians succeeded.

"That's her!" the leader of the group of ruffians murmured.

"Why would a toff pay so much for a mousy little thing like 'er?"

"Not our business why he wants her, just that he does," the man in charge said. "They like virgins, these toffs, and, from the looks of her, I'd reckon her to be one."

The first man to speak, the one who was so clearly amused by his own wit, chortled again. "If he wants virgins, I can get 'em for 'im. I had two of 'em last night. Was wiv' the same two the night before. They're all virgins if it'll get 'em a bit more coin!"

The woman turned in the direction of the sedan chair house at the end of the street and the three men sprang into action. One of them jumped out, grasping the woman around the waist and hauling her back toward the small alleyway that had housed them.

She might have dressed like a little brown bird, but she fought like a tiger, Benedict thought as he crept forward. With three of them to fight off, he needed the element of surprise. The woman kicked out again, catching her second assailant squarely in the bollocks. Her brief, satisfied smirk showed him that it had not been an accident. She'd meant it and, while he admired her spirit, he knew that was not an insult that would be easily forgiven.

Even as he thought it, the attacker rebounded, rising up from his pained crouch, and drew back his hand. The sharp report as the back of his hand connected with her cheek echoed through the fog-shrouded street and she staggered, clearly rattled by it. She stumbled against the side of the building, sinking down onto her haunches, dazed.

"Do not mark her! You fools!" The third man boxed the ears of the man who'd struck her. "If you damage her, then we do not get paid!"

The largest of the men picked her up easily and tossed her over his dauntingly broad shoulders. She rallied then, beginning her struggles anew. Her kicking feet had no sway over him. The ineffectual beating of her fists on his broad back was equally ignored.

Creeping closer, Benedict lashed out with the sword stick he carried, sending the first man to the ground. Bringing his clasped hands crashing down onto the man's head, he rendered the thug unconscious and then turned toward the others.

The man in charge eyed Benedict cautiously even as he withdrew a brace of pistols from his cloak. "Take her on! We can't afford to lose her!" he shouted to his compatriot.

What happened next left Benedict reeling. The man fired one pistol, but not at him. Instead, he shot his unconscious companion in the head and then raised the second pistol to point it at Benedict.

"You've no cause to involve yourself in this," the man warned softly. "Walk away now, let us have the girl, and you can survive the day unscathed."

"I wouldn't even if I could," Benedict replied just as softly. The man fired, and Benedict dove to the side. The bullet grazed him, taking a large furrow out of his shoulder. Even as he tucked and rolled, he retrieved his sword stick. On his feet again, he disarmed the man with relative ease despite his injury. He might have been in charge of the operation and had no doubt committed any manner of crimes in his life, but the man was not a trained swordsman who had what it took to fight someone to the death. That was clearly evident when he turned and ran.

With only one of the villains remaining, Benedict turned. The larger man was nearing the street from the small alley they'd dragged the woman into. While she wasn't a heavy burden, she was a highly uncooperative one and had thus slowed the man down considerably. As Benedict approached him, the man turned, cursed, and without warning, tossed the woman at Benedict, sending them both sprawling to the dirt.

Benedict shuffled her off him. He didn't take the time to check for injury. It wasn't because he didn't care, but because he needed information and the only source was getting away. The man in charge was long gone, and would likely not have talked anyway. The other underling was dead, no doubt a precaution to keep him from speaking, and the brute strength of the band was all that was left.

Taking a run at his retreating back, Benedict managed to take the man to the ground. Only the blade he held pressed to the man's beefy neck gave him the advantage, as the man had him in weight by at least three stone and was nearly a head taller than his own six foot frame.

"You took another woman from this address… where is she now?" Benedict demanded.

"Don't know!" the big man muttered. "Never tells us where he takes them after!"

Them. There was more than just one. "She was blond, very petite… was she injured? Did you hurt her?"

When the larger man was slow to answer, Benedict struck him. "Answer me!"

"We never 'urt 'em. Get less money that way!"

"The people in this house," Benedict demanded, "are they involved?"

"I ain't talkin' to the likes of you!" the man shouted.

The door to the house opened again and a woman screamed in alarm. That distraction cost Benedict. As he turned his head in her direction, the giant reared up and sent him staggering backward with one punch. He was no match for the man, not with his limited reach. The second blow sent him barreling into the steps of a neighboring townhouse, striking the corner of one of the stairs. His last sight, before the world went dark, was of the giant of a man who held the secret of what had happened to his sister running full tilt into the darkness.

ELIZABETH RUSHED FORWARD toward Lady Vale. With her dress torn and her hair having pulled free from its chignon, she looked like a wild woman. She was shaking, out of breath, and felt, for the first time in her life, in danger of swooning. Fear had left a sharp metallic taste in her mouth, or perhaps it was blood from where the other man had slapped her. Her mind raced and she couldn't quite make heads or tails of her own thoughts.

"Are you hurt, dear?" the older woman asked.

"A few bruises but nothing serious, I think," she answered, hating the tremors that wracked her voice. "Thanks to him. He saved me. I don't even know where he came from. I exited Madame Zula's and headed for the sedan chair house and those men accosted me. They dragged me into that alley and I cannot bear to think what might have happened had he not intervened!"

Lady Vale's expression changed, growing darker. "Did they… that is to say, Miss Masters—Elizabeth, if they violated you, you must tell me. There are steps that can be taken."

Elizabeth blushed. "No. There wasn't time for that."

Lady Vale shook her head. "You'd be surprised how little time it does take for some. What shall we do with him?"

"We cannot simply leave him here, bleeding in the street," Elizabeth worried. "What if they come back?"

"That's hardly likely, but I agree. His heroics deserve something more than to be left lying bleeding in the dirt!"

Just then, Madame Zula's, or Miss Hopkins' as she'd asked to be addressed, manservant appeared in the doorway. "We heard screams! Are you injured?"

"You mean Madame Zula does not know?" Elizabeth fired back quickly. Calming herself and her temper, she added, "We are not injured but my rescuer is. Can you obtain a hired carriage for us?"

"Madame Zula has a carriage. It will be readied for you," he said as he disappeared into the house.

Elizabeth dropped to her knees beside the fallen man. Gingerly turning the man onto his back, she gasped in recognition. His perfectly-chiseled features, features that would have set any young woman's heart to racing, were still emblazoned upon her memory from their earlier encounter. He'd been charming then and now, coupled with his heroic actions, was it any wonder that simply looking at him made her already thundering heart flutter? But they had not introduced themselves earlier as it would have been impossibly forward to do so. He lay there bleeding at her feet and she did not even know his name.

"Sir?" she queried. "Sir, can you hear me?"

He moaned, turned his head and opened his eyes. Behind her, Lady Vale gasped. The sound drew his attention and he looked toward her mistress, but his injuries and the darkness they wrought claimed him again. His long-lashed eyelids fluttered closed again.

"We must get him home. He will be attended by the finest doctors in Bath," Lady Vale commanded.

While Elizabeth was certainly grateful that her mistress felt so inclined, she could not help but find it curious. "That is most generous, my lady. Thank you."

"No, my dear. Thank you. Whatever happened to put you in harm's way has returned my son to me... that man, lying there on the dirty street, wounded in such heroic action, is my Benedict."

Elizabeth blinked up at Lady Vale. Words escaped her as she tried to envision how on earth she would explain that to her employer, Lady Vale's brother-in-law. One disaster had bled directly into another it seemed.

Chapter Four

INSIDE THE TOWNHOUSE, Zella Hopkins dropped all pretense. Her voice came out harsher, her true accent more pronounced and significantly less genteel. "Damn you, Dylan! Damn you! You know that we never book appointments without being certain who will be attending!"

"She never said anyone else was coming with her," the young man insisted. He reached for her, his hands stroking her arms gently, dropping lower to take her hands in his.

Abruptly, she pulled away. She wasn't truly angry with him, but she was frightened. Failure was not an option. The consequences would be swift and ugly. "Did you ask?"

"She came in alone," he protested. "I asked her if the appointment was for her and she replied, 'who else would it be for'! What was I supposed to think?"

She wrung her hands as she paced the length of the room. Despite her diminutive stature, her strides were long, her movements brisk. "This is a disaster. We've lingered too long here."

"We've had better luck here than anywhere. The number of young, gullible women in this city is rivaled only by London! We're better off here, in fact, because they are more gullible. Women in London are too suspicious, too aware that things like this can happen!"

"And if any more women disappear in Bath, how long do you think it will take them to become just as suspicious here?" she fired back.

"We promised him the girl. It has to be her. He was very clear about that. What do we do? If we don't deliver her to him—"

Fear had been her constant companion and, to some degree, she was accustomed to it. But it made her heart ache to hear it in his voice. She turned toward him, reached out her hand and cupped his face. "My handsome love, do not fret so. We'll get him the girl but, in the meantime, we'll give him a peace offering. She may not be the one promised, but you'll find one. Go to the taverns. Find one young enough to still be moved by your pretty face, and pretty enough that he won't mind she's not an innocent."

He gripped her hand, holding it tightly to him as he turned to kiss her palm. "It won't cancel the debt."

"No. It's simply an olive branch to appease him. One to keep him happy until we can deliver what we promised... Miss Masters. We'll need to work this very carefully. And above all, we need to find out who her dashing hero was."

"I saw him. Earlier in the day, he was walking up and down the street, paying particular attention to our front door," Dylan said. "If we're lucky, he'll die from his wounds and cause us no more problems."

"I doubt we're that lucky. It doesn't tend to favor people with souls as dark as ours," Zella answered in a hushed tone. "We can only assume that he's connected to one of the others. After you've procured the girl, find Fenton and ask him what the man said. We need to know who he is and why he's asking questions."

"When this is over and we're free of him—"

Zella placed her fingertips to Dylan's lips, marveling as she always did that he could have been blessed with such beauty. It was a pity his wit was not so worthy of exultation. "We will never be free of him. And thank heavens for it. As long as we are useful, we live. The moment he no longer has need of us, then we'll simply vanish... and there will be no one to ask where we've gone. Do you understand that, Dylan? We're in this for as long as he lives or we die."

THE ROOM WAS pitch black when she awoke. The darkness was so deep and impenetrable that she couldn't see her own hand in front of her face. Swallowing a moan of despair, forcing herself to work through her fear, Mary sat up on the narrow cot that was her only respite from the cold and damp that surrounded her. She couldn't even be certain she was alone. Was it preferable to be alone in the darkness? What if she wasn't alone? What if whoever or whatever was in the darkness with her meant her harm?

Summoning her courage, she called out tentatively, "Hello? Is anyone there?"

Her own voice echoed back to her, distorted and strange to her ears. Alone then, she thought grimly. Perhaps it was for the best. Blinded as she was by the inky blackness surrounding her, she would never be able to differentiate friend from foe.

She moved her hands experimentally and found that the bonds she'd worn before were gone. Though sore and tender to the touch, her wrists were now free of the ropes that had held her fast the last time she'd awoken. Her ankles were freed, as well. She took neither as a good omen. If her captors believed there was any possibility of escaping whatever dungeon currently held her, those bonds would never have been removed. Despair welled up inside her, but she tamped it down. She would not give up and she would not give in.

"I'm not like other girls," she said softly, her voice little more than a whisper. "I survived the Masons and their torment, didn't I? I can get through this, too! I'm not going to just sit here and wait for whatever fate they have in store for me."

With those hollow words of encouragement ringing in her ears, Mary struggled to her feet. She swayed, still dizzy from whatever substance had been on the foul smelling cloth they'd held over her mouth and nose as they dragged her to a waiting carriage. Using the edge of the cot as a guide, she followed it to the wall. With her hands pressed against the wet and sometimes slimy feeling stone, she inched carefully, one painful step at a time, around the periphery of the room. The aches and pains of having been manhandled, bound, tossed in a carriage and then dragged into whatever pit she currently found herself in had taken a toll on her.

Her foot struck a loose stone on the floor and she gasped with the sudden agony of it. Disoriented by the dark, stiff and sore from being bound for so long, she lost her balance and pitched forward onto the hard floor. The rough stones scraped her palms and the jolt of it made her shoulders ache. Tears threatened, but they were a useless indulgence. Forcing them back, swallowing past the lump in her throat and the metallic tang of fear, she rallied.

Struggling once more to her feet, she placed her abraded hand against the wall and moved forward again. More carefully than before, she patted the ground in front of her with her foot to ensure that the way was clear.

The texture of the wall changed, giving way from stone to wood. It wasn't quite relief as Mary was unwilling to give herself leave to hope just yet. But wood meant a man-made structure, and a man-made structure meant there was likely a door or window. Based on the absolute blackness around her, she had to assume that she was underground or hidden away well within the confines of another building.

Running her fingertips up and down the boards, she kept moving until she encountered the rusted metal of a hinge. Taking a deep breath, she sighed into the darkness and let the feeling of relief swarm her for just a moment. Whether she could get out or not, at that time, remained a mystery. But at least there was a way out and now she knew where it was.

More investigation revealed a second hinge and several inches further, she encountered the heavy latch. It was locked, of course. She hadn't expected anything less. Sinking back against the wood, she allowed herself a moment's reprieve. After catching her breath, she reached up to her hair, hoping against hope that one of her pins had managed to snag in the tangled mass. Luck, in that respect, was with her at least. Plucking the one remaining pin from her hair, she carefully lowered herself to the floor once more and began working on the lock.

A soft shuffling noise sounded on the other side of the door and Mary stilled immediately. She dared not even breathe. After what seemed an eternity, when no other sound was heard, she leaned forward again and pressed her face against the wooden door, listening for any hint of who might be on the other side.

Suddenly and without warning, a fist pounded heavily on the door causing her to jump back. She landed on her bottom, terrified and feeling as if she were being toyed with.

"I hear you in there, little mouse!"

The words were called out in a soft sing-song fashion, taunting and cruel. "Who are you?" she shouted back. "Why am I here?"

"You'll find out soon enough, my little mouse," the man answered in that same childish fashion. "All in good time."

Mary could hear him laughing as he moved away. She wouldn't give up. She would find a way out of that room and a way to avoid whatever fate her cruel captor had in store for her.

Chapter Five

*T*HE HEAT IN *the small loft where he and Mary slept was unbearable. The air was so thick it felt like it was closing in around him. As he rolled onto his back, praying for a breeze to flutter through the opening in the wall that had never held a single pane of glass, Benedict imagined what it would be like to swim in the big pond on the estate where he'd gone with his father to deliver coal just that morning. The cook had given him a biscuit and it had been the sweetest treat he'd ever had in his life. He'd tried to save some for Mary but it had crumbled to nothing but crumbs in his pocket by the time they'd made it home.*

Closing his eyes, Benedict imagined the cold, clear water closing around him, gliding over him as he cut through the pond. Fish would dart and dance around him, and the blessed coolness of it would soothe away the heat that left him sweating on the thin straw mat that was his bed. His father had gone to the village with the money he'd been paid for delivering the coal. If they were lucky, he would stay there all night.

Benedict continued thinking of the pond until, soon, he was dreaming of it, drifting into sleep.

"You're a sorry excuse for a son. All you do is take, take, take. You eat our food, you sleep under our roof, you do nothing to earn your keep!"

The kick to the gut had him gasping and rolling away from the heavy, booted foot. He didn't move quickly enough though. It came down on his head with just enough pressure to pin him to the floor.

"I could crush you, boy! Like a damned bug," he slurred.

Benedict had learned early on that when his father's words were sharp and clear, life was smooth sailing. If there was even a hint of slur, it was best to hide. But he'd been lax, he'd fallen asleep before his father had returned home and hadn't heard the loud greeting he'd called out to the house.

The weight of the booted foot increased as he applied more pressure. The pain of it was excruciating. "You're worthless, boy! Worthless. If I thought it'd end my misery, I'd put an end to you right here!"

"Stop! Stop it! You're hurting him!"

The soft, sweet voice of his baby sister registered through the haze of pain and fear. He tried to call out, to stop her, but he couldn't even form the words. Abruptly, the boot was removed. Another kick to his ribs had him gasping as his father walked away, directly toward Mary.

"Run, Mary!" he managed to shout. She looked at him then, just past their father, but it was too late. The slap sent her sprawling, her little body flying nearly across the room. It wouldn't be enough. Even as he thought it, he saw their father take a step toward her fallen form. She wouldn't survive the kind of beating he routinely received.

Benedict dove toward the bed, his hand slipping beneath the hay-stuffed mattress and closing over the blade he'd hidden there.

⁂

"WHAT ON EARTH must he be dreaming to have him thrashing about so?"

Elizabeth pressed a cool, damp cloth to his brow and sighed. She didn't know, nor could she even imagine. From the violence of his response, his nightmares must be terrible, indeed. "I could not say, my lady. The laudanum may be making them worse, but given the fervor with which Dr. Nichols dug out the pistol ball, I cannot imagine how much pain he would be in without it."

They'd managed to get him into the house with the help of servants. Two strong footmen had carried him up the stairs while yet another had been sent to fetch the doctor. That had been hours earlier. It was now well past midnight and they were both teetering on the brink of collapse.

Pressing another damp cloth to his brow, he stilled at the touch, turning his face toward her palm. Elizabeth took a moment to study his face, the sheer perfection of planes and angles that resulted in something that was so much more than simply the sum of their parts. She could admit that she'd never seen a more handsome man. And whether it was simply his physical beauty, or the heroic manner in which he'd rushed to her rescue, or his flirtatious and easy manner from the square that afternoon, she didn't know. Whatever it was, she felt drawn to him, connected to him in a way that left her feeling incredibly unsettled and far more invested in his welfare than she should have been for a stranger.

To find herself attracted to a man, one who might not even survive his current injuries, was only further proof that the weakness of character which had lowered her position in society remained intact. It was not the first time in her life she'd found herself drawn to an inappropriate man. God willing, it would be the last.

As Elizabeth wrestled with her conscience, Lady Vale continued her pacing. Her voice quivered with emotion and she was clearly overwrought with the situation. There was no swaying her. She was completely convinced that this stranger was her long lost son. "No. He must have it. I don't want him to suffer physically, but it is so difficult to see his mental anguish. What must have happened to him after he was taken from me? What is it that haunts him so?"

Elizabeth did not reply immediately. Instead, she carefully composed her reply so as not to overset her mistress. The doctor had come, removed the pistol ball and stitched the wound. Afterward, he'd left them with his final statement being that it was in the hands of God. He clearly had not appreciated being called out so late at night. She had thought, at his callous statement, that Lady Vale was going to rip the man's head off and beat him with it. She did not want to invoke a similar response by pointing out that the injured man might not be Lady Vale's son.

As to what haunted the man so, she could not dare to guess. The way he thrashed and cried out hinted at a violent past. When he tensed at her touch or flinched away from her, it led her to assume others had not touched him with care and kindness. As Lady Vale had already reached that same conclusion, stating it again would hardly be beneficial. Still, it struck a chord inside her, it raised tender and protective feelings that she did not fully understand. Having been foolish in the past, she'd learned to guard her heart against all men, especially handsome ones.

As she studied his face, Elizabeth had to grant that the similarities between the unknown man and Lady Vale were striking. Every time he opened his eyes, Lady Vale grew more convinced that he was her missing son returned. Despite their physical similarities, Elizabeth could not quite put her faith in that theory yet.

Taking another look at him, she catalogued his features. Ostensibly it was to identify points of similarity. She vowed to herself it had nothing to do with her own selfish desire to study his form.

While the planes and angles of his face were harder and more chiseled by virtue of his sex, he did possess the same startling pure bone structure and patrician features as her ladyship, and same oddly hued blue-green eyes. He was her masculine counterpart in appearance. Still, the coincidence of it all bothered her. From running into him in the square that afternoon, to her being attacked outside Madame Zula's and his well-timed rescue as he rushed to her aid there, in full view of Lady Vale, was all entirely too convenient. That all of it followed Madame Zula's predictions as well as her cryptic statements about the disappearance of Lady Vale's son—it was all tight and tidy and all the more suspect for it.

"Lady Vale, I know that you believe him to be your son, but… he has not spoken of his life, of his childhood. It is very possible that he is not," Elizabeth protested softly. "I will grant you that the resemblance is uncanny, but we should not make any assumptions until he is awake to confirm or refute them."

"He is my son!" Lady Vale stated firmly. "I know you think me a lunatic, as does Branson. That is why he set you to watch me, after all!"

Elizabeth dropped her gaze. "No, my lady, he does not think you a lunatic and neither do I. Mr. Middlethorp hired me to act as your companion because he felt your search for your son made you vulnerable to those who might exploit your grief!"

Lady Vale halted her pacing long enough to throw her hands up in the air and glare in Elizabeth's direction with righteous indignation. "And you eagerly reported it to him any time my search employed unorthodox methods! I'm not a child, nor am I fool... yet for most of my life men have treated me thusly!"

"I only reported to Mr. Middlethorp when I feared for your safety or for the security of your fortune," Elizabeth protested. "And I say this to you now, not because I do not wish for him to be your son, or because I do not wish for you to have such a joyous reunion, but because if it is not true, your heart will be broken all over again. I only want you prepared for the eventuality rather than buried under disappointment if your belief proves false!"

A low groan from the bed silenced them. Those familiar blue-green eyes opened. They were clearer than before, more cognizant of the present.

"Sir, you've been shot. Please lie still and have a care for your stitches," Elizabeth murmured softly.

He grimaced and then, slowly, brought his gaze to her face, focusing intently. "Little brown bird," he murmured softly and then, once again, he drifted into unconsciousness.

"He may be developing a fever," Elizabeth said.

Lady Vale wrung her hands. "What on earth happened outside Madame Zula's, Miss Masters? Why were those men lying in wait and why was he there?"

"Perhaps we should ask Madame Zula," Elizabeth said. "I heard him questioning that brute of a man. He spoke of another woman who had been taken from there, from the very same address. Perhaps we need more information before we proceed."

Lady Vale nodded. "I may detest Branson's interference in my life, Miss Masters, but despite how you came to be a part of my household, there are times when I am quite relieved to have you present. You do have a remarkable clarity of mind, girl."

Elizabeth shook her head in denial. Her mind felt anything but clear. Buzzing with her own wayward thoughts, with the confusion of the events and with the strange feelings that now consumed her for the man in her care, it was praise she did not deserve. "It was not so clear earlier. I might have helped him more… perhaps even prevented him from being wounded so gravely."

Lady Vale placed a comforting hand on Elizabeth's shoulder. "You could not have done more… not against three attackers. It's a wonder that he is not more seriously injured. As for you, thank God he prevented them from making off with you. I shudder to think what fate might have awaited you at their hands."

Elizabeth had been pondering just that same question. "I believe they meant to turn me over to someone else. While I was raised within the ranks of the gentry, I have been on my own for enough years to understand the dangers of unscrupulous abbesses and the lengths they will go to in order to procure innocent young women for their clients. It is my understanding that women of breeding are even more highly sought after by certain gentleman."

Lady Vale did shudder then, visibly, and then for both their sakes, changed the subject. "What on earth should we do for him now?"

"At this point, I cannot tell if it is the blow to the head, a developing fever, or simply the loss of blood that is rendering him senseless. So long as he continues to wake every few minutes, I suppose we can let him rest without it doing any harm. You should rest as well, madame. I will sit with him a while longer and if I become too tired, I will rouse one of the maids."

Lady Vale nodded. "I believe that I will write to Branson. I will not say anything about my suspicions regarding his identity… but I will tell him that we have brought the man who rescued you to my home to recuperate. Otherwise, Calvert will tell him and then heaven knows what that man will embellish it with."

Lady Vale had often accused her of being a spy but, in truth, it was Calvert, her butler, who reported with the greatest frequency to Mr. Middlethorp. He also greatly exaggerated the degree to which Lady Vale's continued search for her missing son put her in the way of danger. What the man's agenda was remained to be seen.

"I think that is a wise choice," Elizabeth conceded. "I will say nothing to the other servants about your theory regarding our mysterious hero… at least not until he rouses enough for you to speak with him and ascertain if it is even possible."

Lady Vale gave a curt nod. "That is fair enough, I suppose. You will wake me if he worsens?"

"Yes, my lady."

Lady Vale nodded again and then swept from the room with a swoosh of her elegant skirts. Again, it stirred memories she'd thought long buried.

"I used to do that," Elizabeth confessed to the unconscious man. "I moved with all the winsome grace my tutors had drilled into me and I tried so very hard to make up for in elegance of bearing what I might lack in true beauty. Sadly, I was never quite as successful at making a grand entrance or exit as her ladyship is. But I was the belle of a few balls, back when such things mattered."

How she missed dancing, she thought. The lift and fall of the music as she swayed in her partner's arms to a scandalous waltz, the rush and exuberance of a country reel—it had been two years since she'd danced but, in some ways, it felt like a lifetime. It was one of the many things she had set aside, forfeited, along with her virtue. There was no place in polite society for a woman who was known to be fast. Oh, she could have easily been someone's mistress or joined the ranks of the demimonde, but it hadn't been money or even passion that had prompted her fall from grace. It had been her own foolish belief that she was in love and that Freddy had loved her in return. The truth had been bitter medicine.

Forcing her mind away from such dark thoughts, she continued in the vein of her earlier comments, talking nonsense to him as the fever burned. Leaning over, Elizabeth touched his brow, stroking his overly-warm skin and wondering what strange circumstances had brought him into their small world.

Chapter Six

"*I*T WILL BE *an adventure.*"

Those words echoed in the recesses of Benedict's dreams. That phrase had haunted him throughout most of his life, both waking and sleeping. He didn't know where it had come from, or why it sounded with such ominous frequency in his head, but it was there, inescapable and panic inducing.

Forcing his eyes to open again, he found himself staring up into a sweetly feminine face etched with concern. She was lovely, her face softened from sleep, hair slightly mussed, and her lips pursed with worry.

"What will be an adventure?" she asked. "Why would you such a thing?"

Memory of those men grabbing at her, attempting to carry her off into the darkness, flared in his mind. "You're safe. They've gone?"

"They're gone. We're all safe," she whispered soothingly. "You need to rest."

She touched him again, cupping his face tenderly. He turned into it, savoring the softness of her touch, the sweet scent of her skin and all the comfort she offered with a gentle touch. It soothed him to his soul and he, once more, fell into the dark abyss of unconsciousness.

Benedict drifted there for a while, in and out of consciousness, existing in a strange melange of past, present and fantasy. It might have been only moments or it could have been hours. One minute he was ducking blows from the miserable sot that was his adopted father and the next he was listening to the soft, sweet voice of the woman that had soothed him. At other times, he was chasing Mary, always behind her, always losing sight of her just as she rounded a bend, hearing her call out for him and never reaching her.

It was from one of those terrifying and frustrating visions, of chasing Mary down darkened streets only to watch the shadows swallow her up, that he sat bolt upright in bed. He took in his surroundings cautiously, not entirely certain of where he'd landed himself. The room was beautiful and luxurious, but didn't have the overdone decor that he'd come to associate with bawdy houses and hells. Which meant he was in a private home and it belonged to someone wealthy and refined.

Pale light streamed between the drawn curtains, indicating that it was early morning at the very least. Turning his head and ignoring the pain it caused, he noted the woman sleeping in the chair next to the bed. She curled into herself, sitting on her hip with her knees drawn up. Her chin was tucked against her chest and her hair had long since escaped the confines of the tight chignon it had been in when first he'd seen her. He remembered her instantly, of course—the one he'd mistaken for a servant, the one who'd fought so fiercely. The one who, with only a brief exchange in the square, had captivated his attention and stirred his lust.

Guilt clawed at him. He was there to find his sister, to discover what awful fate might have befallen her. It was not a proper time to indulge in a flirtation or embark on an ill-fated affair. The woman was a distraction that he could not afford.

Outside, the sun notched higher in the sky, filtering through the curtains and falling on the strands of hair that curled along her neck. Noting the fine texture and how it shined in the light, he snorted.

"Little brown bird, indeed."

It didn't resemble the feathers of a sparrow so much as rich sable. She was lovelier and far younger than he'd first realized.

Even as he thought it, her eyelids fluttered open and she turned in his direction. Her eyes were the same bright blue as a cornflower.

"You're awake," she stated redundantly. Her voice was low and husky from sleep, but her words held the clipped precision that he'd worked so hard to copy. Whatever her present circumstances, she'd been raised as a member of the gentry at the very least.

"Yes, as are you. You are unharmed?" he queried.

"Thanks to you, yes, I am unharmed," she replied, tucking her chin to her chest and looking up at him through lowered lashes. It was not intended to be a flirtatious gesture, of that he was certain. It was artless and effortless from her, but it was a look that courtesans and members of the demimonde practiced routinely to perfect. On her, it was all the more compelling for having not been intended.

"You were not so lucky, it would seem," she continued. "A pistol ball to the shoulder and a nasty lump on your head were your rewards for all your dashing heroics… but at least you're speaking sensibly now. You roused several times during the night, muttering naught but nonsense."

Benedict wondered at what he might have said, at what he might have revealed. It pained him that she might have some insight now into the ugliness of the world from which he'd come, but there was naught to be done for it. Instead, he turned his attention to the matter at hand. "Who were those men? Have you ever seen them before?" he asked.

"I'll answer your question if you answer mine," she fired back. Her chin was up, her back straight, and wherever it had been hiding moments earlier, she'd found her confidence it seemed.

"And if I choose not to?" he challenged. It was rude, impossibly so, and went against everything he'd learned about behaving like a gentleman. But he couldn't afford to nurture any tender feelings or attraction between them. If she disliked him, if she thought him arrogant and rude, all the better. She'd keep her distance and he could attend to the things he had to do.

"Why would you? You risked your life to rescue me, but I have sacrificed greatly in caring for you since, sir. We are not enemies," she stated simply. "Bath is not so large a city. But it is large enough to question crossing paths with someone twice in one day when that person has so vehemently denied that we could ever move in the same circles."

Benedict was forced, in that moment, to reevaluate his opinion of her. She'd been called a brown bird and he'd likened her hair to sable. But there was no mistaking that behind her gently pretty face was a cunning and wicked mind.

"You're not a brown bird at all. I think perhaps you are a fox."

She cocked her eyebrow at him. "Perhaps I was wrong in thinking that your hours of insensible gibberish were at an end."

"Ask your damnable questions then," he said, with grudging respect and no small amount of ire. He hadn't time to be intrigued by a woman. There was too much at stake. "We'll see how insensible I am."

"What is your name?" she asked.

"Easy enough. Benedict Mason."

She tensed, her eyes narrowed, and she was silent for a moment before asking, "Mason is your family name, then?"

Her response to that question was a curious one and, before long, he'd know the why of it, he determined. "I have no family name. Mason was my adopted father's some time occupation, and mine, too, as a boy. If he had a surname he never disclosed it, likely because there was a bounty attached to it."

She paled considerably, her eyebrows arcing up in surprise and her delicious, little mouth forming an "O" of surprise. No doubt his disclosure of his base upbringing and his family's likely criminal history had put her off for good. Still, he couldn't stop looking at her, and he couldn't completely ignore the temptation to reach out and touch her hair to see if it felt as silky as it appeared. The loose tendrils curled around her face, softening it and highlighting just how young she actually was.

Upon closer examination, it was apparent that she wasn't simply pretty as he'd first thought. With her alabaster skin, deep blue eyes, and delicate features, she was quite a beauty. It was no great mystery why a woman would go to such lengths to disguise it. Before their fortunes had turned and Mary had been able to avoid employment, she'd often done the same. His brown bird's dress marked her as a companion or governess, perhaps even a lady's secretary. Women in service of any kind were targets. Blending into the furnishings was the best way to avoid unwanted attentions.

"I see," she finally managed. "And where was this that you and your adoptive father worked as masons?"

The way she said adoptive triggered a warning bell for him. She was after something and he wasn't about to give it to her without knowing why. There were secrets in his past that could see him destroyed, and Mary, as well. It would take more than her pretty face to get at them.

"My adoptive parents rarely stayed in one place for very long. They weren't truly gypsies as they move about by choice and not because a drunken sot made an ars—a cake of himself in front of the entire village. We moved every season it seemed... that would be seasons and not the Season. I've no doubt you know the difference," he replied with a sharpness to his tone that belied just how tiresome he was finding it to speak of his family.

She sat back in her chair, her face a mask of serenity, as if he hadn't just bitten her head off. "I see. And you are well acquainted with Miss Zella Hopkins, are you?"

He frowned. "Who is speaking insensibly now? I know no one of that name. Now, it is my turn to ask questions... who were those men and have you ever seen them before?" he demanded again.

"I've never seen them before yesterday. They did not introduce themselves as they attempted to abduct me... more's the pity. Why were you at that address?"

Benedict debated how much to tell her, how much information to put forth when he had no idea what the outcome would be. There was still something about her that he did not quite trust. She had an agenda that he could not begin to fathom. Ultimately, he elected for the truth albeit a vague version of it. "Because I am looking for someone and that is the last place she was seen. When I crossed paths with you in the square, I was following them. And again last night. I have reason to believe that those men were responsible for her disappearance. Had I not intervened, I fear you and she would have suffered a similar fate, whatever it may be."

"It's Mary you speak of, isn't it?" she asked.

He tensed. "How do you know that?"

She shrugged. "You had rather violent nightmares during the night, no doubt from the laudanum. While you were talking in your sleep, you said her name. Several times, in fact. You must care very deeply for her."

"I do," he agreed. "She's been missing for a week now. And it's imperative that I find her before something awful happens."

"Well you're in no shape to do anything about it at the moment," she said pragmatically. "Another run-in with those ruffians and you won't survive it. You're as weak as a kitten."

It was the truth, of course, but he resented it greatly. He had other questions. Things he needed to know that would not wait. "What is that house? Who lives there and what is going on in it that my—that Mary would have been there?"

"That house belongs to Madame Zula... a mystic," she explained as she rose from her chair. Her movements were stilted at first, no doubt her body stiffened from the awkward position she'd slept in. But gradually, she began to move with more ease, each motion a study of grace and economy.

"A mystic?" he prompted, wondering what on earth a woman as seemingly pragmatic as she was would be doing there. He knew immediately why his sister had gone, of course.

"She tells fortunes," she said, tossing the words back over her shoulder. "And contacts deceased loved ones. She claims to help people find the truth in whatever they seek. Personally, I believe her to be nothing more than a charlatan. She insists that, in spite of the theatrics employed to lend atmosphere and panache during her *salon,* her gift is quite real."

The disdain in her tone was telling enough. Whatever she had been there for, Benedict reasoned, she was not a believer. And he wouldn't have thought that his sister would be, but then he knew just how desperate she was.

Mary was looking for her family—and for his. Neither of them knew exactly what circumstances had brought them into their adoptive parents' care. Over the last few years, she had become obsessed with finding the truth, with discovering where they belonged, as she'd put it. She believed, and perhaps rightly so, that they had not been given into the care of the horrible couple who had raised them, so much as they'd been stolen away by them. He didn't know and, frankly, he didn't care. His childhood was an aspect of his life that he was only too happy to close the door on forever.

"And what truth were you seeking at Madame Zula's?" he asked.

"None. I was not there for Madame Zula. I was accompanying my mistress, Lady Vale, who has lost her son."

The explanation was pat but, again, her tone alerted him to the fact that there were things left unsaid. "You are an unusual creature— I'm sorry. I don't believe I know your name."

"You do not. I've never given it to you… but as we are beyond the point of formal introduction, I am Miss Elizabeth Masters," she replied, even as she rose from the chair. "I'll see about getting you something to eat from the kitchens. I imagine you must be famished at this point."

He was. Before he could reply, the door burst open and an older but still beautiful and undeniably elegant woman rushed in. There was something hauntingly familiar about her. A tune played in his mind, a soft and sweet melody that he could only barely recall.

Those sorts of phantom memories haunted him—occurring at random times, sparked by things he could not fathom. Unfortunately, those memories never provided enough clarity for him to follow up on them.

"How is he? Is he recovered from the fever yet?" the woman asked, her voice tight with concern.

Miss Masters dipped a curtsy. "Lady Vale, good morning. Our

patient is awake and coherent. The fever still burns, but not as severely as before."

The woman seemed to simply melt. The tension left her body in a wave and she placed her face in her hands and wept.

Benedict's eyebrows shot up in both surprise and alarm. It was quite a dramatic response to his recovery from someone he'd only just met. As a general rule, he had little to do with ladies beyond his sister. The women of his acquaintance were of an *earthier* sort. Was this what a fit of the vapors actually looked like?

"Please, my lady, sit. You are overwrought and this is not good for your health," Miss Masters said, helping the other woman to the chair she'd only recently vacated.

"I am terribly sorry to take on so," Lady Vale offered after she'd taken a moment to collect herself. She approached the bed and took Benedict's hand in her own, holding it far more tightly than necessary. "I'm just so greatly relieved to know that you will recover. I simply cannot imagine what I would have done otherwise."

"I daresay you would have recovered admirably from the shock," he replied. "I must thank you, Lady Vale, and you, as well, Miss Masters, for taking it upon yourselves to provide aid when I was injured."

Lady Vale smiled beatifically at him even as she dabbed tears from her eyes with a delicately embroidered handkerchief held in her other hand. "As if I could do less for you, my sweet boy! I am overjoyed to have found you again."

It was the last word and the wealth of enthusiasm in her statement that pricked his curiosity. "Again?"

"Yes… again," she repeated, more insistently. "What do you call yourself now?"

She was mad, he decided. Utterly and completely mad. It was a pity and a shame. "Benedict Mason," he answered. "Lately of London."

She dropped her head again, but did not give in to tears the second time. When she lifted her gaze to him again, she was smiling through her tears. "I cannot tell you what it means to me that you've kept the name I gave you!"

Benedict looked to Miss Masters. It seemed she was the only one in the household possessed of both a sound mind and body. "Madame, forgive me, but I fear you must have me mistaken for someone else."

"I do not," Lady Vale insisted very firmly. "You are my son. You are Lord Benedict Middlethorp, Viscount Vale. You were taken from my arms when you were only a small boy, and I have devoted my life to finding you!" Her voice broke on a sob then, though a smile still curved her lips.

Benedict looked at her and recalled a trip he'd taken abroad. He'd gambled his way through Europe, a scoundrel's version of the grand tour, financed by fleecing foolish young men who drank too much and bet too freely. It hadn't all been games of chance and wicked women. He'd used that opportunity to study and better himself, to learn about art, to be tutored in dueling and finance. In one of the homes he'd frequented, there'd been a painting of Saint Theresa, her face lifted to the sky in adulation. To say that there were similarities to that portrait and Lady Vale's current expression was to put it mildly.

"It's just as Madame Zula said it would be!" she said tearfully. "You've been returned to me!"

"That woman!" Miss Masters said. Her ire was obvious in both her tone and the murderous expression that crossed her face. "She is naught but a charlatan! It's all parlor tricks and theatrics, Lady Vale!"

"Then explain to me how she predicted that he was closer to us than we realized?" Lady Vale demanded, her eyes bright and her tone sharp. "And all that she predicted for you came to pass as well! She said that your life was about to take an unexpected turn and you were nearly abducted right there on the spot, only to be rescued heroically!"

Miss Masters eyed Benedict warily. "Perhaps Madame Zula knew I was about to be abducted because she was involved in arranging the entire thing! Have you considered that he is a fraud, that they are colluding with one another in an attempt to swindle you?" Realizing what she'd said, she closed her lips firmly together and turned to him.

"Forgive me, Mr. Mason, I do not mean to offend. I speak in hyperbole simply to make a point."

"I am not offended," he replied easily. "It would be foolish of you not to take such things into consideration. I have found you, in our short acquaintance, Miss Masters, to be many things... but foolish is not one of them."

She stared at him for a moment longer and, as if uncertain of his motives, finally looked away and continued to make her case to the madwoman who was her employer. "Lady Vale, while I am greatly appreciative of his assistance in saving me from a fate I cannot even begin to imagine, that does not necessarily mean that he is a man to be trusted... for all we know those three ruffians, this man, and Madame Zula could all be part of some elaborate charade!"

He realized that, on some level, he should be offended, but he was not. She had a suspicious turn of mind and he found himself not only intrigued by her thinking, but also curious about her past and what might have introduced her to the kind unscrupulous behaviors that would allow her to think so badly of others.

Still, there were more pressing matters to see to than dissecting his pretty fox's storied past. While her statement was untrue, at least for his part, it was still quite plausible. Given that he was now certain Lady Vale was unhinged, it seemed that dissuading her from that belief was the best course of action even if it did require besmirching his own character. Wisely, Benedict held his tongue.

"He would hardly allow himself to be shot in order to gain our sympathy, Miss Masters," Lady Vale insisted. "He could have died from such a wound!"

"Perhaps, things went awry, my lady. Perhaps, the larger man didn't know his own strength and did greater injury to him than anticipated. Perhaps, in the fog, the shooter's aim was off and he actually hit his target rather than missing him as planned," Miss Masters continued. "We cannot jump to conclusions."

Lady Vale whirled toward him then. "You are my son. I would know, wouldn't I? Do you not think that a mother would recognize her own child?"

Seizing that moment to insert himself into a conversation that appeared to be bordering on utter chaos, he used his most soothing tone to address Lady Vale. "Madame, I cannot say what a mother would and would not do. What I can tell you is that I believe you to be mistaken about my identity. I am not your son. It's impossible for me to be your son."

"Why is that?" she demanded. "You were so very young when you were taken! A boy of barely four, you would hardly remember anything of that life as a grown man... and with the trauma endured from the abduction, it's hard to imagine what that might have done." She stopped there, giving in to tears as she sobbed brokenly, clearly haunted by the memories of what she had endured and the long decades of grief since.

He was distinctly uncomfortable. Her words sparked something inside him, some desire for it to be true, he realized. What would it be like to be mothered by someone who so clearly loved and held her child in such esteem? The woman who'd raised him had barely bothered to acknowledge his existence beyond boxing his ears or screaming at him that he'd ruined her life.

Rousing herself, Lady Vale came to her feet once more. "And somehow, I will prove it to you both!"

"I don't—" Miss Masters' protest was cut off sharply by Lady Vale.

"You may be employed as my chaperone in these matters, Miss Masters, but this is still my house and until Branson elects to lock me up in Bedlam, I will do as I please!" Lady Vale's sharp reply brooked no argument.

Realizing that Miss Masters was not in a position to speak reason to the woman, he felt compelled to attempt it himself, yet again. "Lady Vale," he began, "I think it's highly unlikely that if I were your long lost son, our paths would have crossed in such a fashion. Surely, you must realize how farfetched all of this appears?"

She stood her ground, meeting his gaze directly. "Who am I to question the auspicious contrivances of fate, Benedict? It's brought you back to me... and of all the boys and men who have approached me over the years, claiming to be my son in order to gain access to the title and associated wealth, no one has ever looked the part as much as you. Perhaps you are not my son, but I must exhaust every possibility. Surely, you understand that?"

He wasn't without sympathy for her, but he was also on a mission himself. And Mary's disappearance could not simply be ignored while he allowed her to pursue what was likely a pointless endeavor. "I do understand that, madame. But the events that led me to be at that address are pressing. I cannot simply halt my own search for a missing woman to appease you."

"You are in no position to argue. Weak as you are, what would you possibly do if you found her?" Lady Vale demanded. "I have investigators at my disposal, dear boy. You will set them to looking for whoever this woman may be. I assure you that they are competent and will find whatever information is available. While they take up the search, you will remain here to recuperate and we will explore the possibilities of your identity together!"

"So competent that in nearly two decades they could not locate your son?" he queried. "I cannot risk it."

With that pronouncement, he pushed back the covers and struggled to a sitting position. He was still weak and the room spun hazily around him as he forced himself to his feet. He could hear Lady Vale crying out in alarm. Miss Masters stepped over and blocked his path with outstretched arms.

"Sir, your health is still in too fragile a state for this! You must return to your bed at once!" she insisted.

He glared at her. "If I'm a kidnapper or a criminal, why should that matter?"

"Those were merely examples of why we should not rush to any conclusions, sir. They were not accusations!" she insisted. "Please return to the bed while you can still do so under your own power!"

"I must find my—I must find Mary. She needs me," he insisted and took a step forward, intending to move her from his path. The room pitched alarmingly and he tipped forward, falling helplessly against her. Together, they toppled to the floor. He managed, but only just, to shift his weight so that he did not land directly on her. His conscience was pocked enough without adding the crushing of some poor girl to his long list of many sins.

Still, she was trapped beneath him, their legs and arms entangled. Even in his present weakened state, the sensations were familiar enough to stir the more animalistic aspect of his nature.

Lady Vale squeaked in alarm. "Oh, dear. Let me help you up!"

It was his little fox who uttered in her ever sensible fashion, "He is far too heavy. Fetch the footmen to help or we'll only drop him and do further injury!"

"You're right, of course!" Lady Vale agreed. "I'll go fetch them straightaway!"

Benedict managed to shift his weight enough to make eye contact with Elizabeth just as Lady Vale exited into the corridor, shouting for help. "We seem to keep winding up in this position, Miss Masters. First, on the street and now here… if I didn't know better, I'd think you were trying to take advantage of me!"

She rolled her eyes heavenward. "Arrogant, egotistical and utterly impossible! I was attempting to save you from your own foolish pride! You have been shot, sir. I cannot imagine that even if you were to encounter whatever villain has made off with this woman you seek, if that has, in fact, happened, that you'd be properly capable of mounting a rescue!"

He started to respond, but then the room began to grow very dark. Without ceremony or warning, Benedict promptly slipped, once more, into unconsciousness, brought about solely by his own foolish pride.

Chapter Seven

L YING ON THE floor, nearly crushed beneath his weight, all the while feeling the warm rush of his breath against her neck, Elizabeth fumed. It wasn't anger at him, so much, though there was a goodly portion of it. She was angry at herself, angry at the reawakening of her true self.

She'd been convinced that she'd put her lustful ways behind her, that she would never again fall prey to her own desires. Yet, there she lay, consumed with lustful thoughts for a man who was practically at death's door. If ever she'd required proof that true wickedness lurked in her soul, it had certainly been amply provided.

Lady Vale entered, two of the stronger footmen rushing in her wake. They managed to lift Mr. Mason off her and place him back into the bed. She felt immediately bereft of his warmth and the press of his body against hers.

What on earth is wrong with me?

He was a stranger, a man she'd only just met. And yes, it was certainly true that he had very bravely placed himself in danger in order to save her, but that certainly did not warrant her throwing herself at him like some wanton hussy.

Lady Vale fussed over his covers, getting him tucked into bed much like she would if he was a small boy.

"He was always willful," she said. "Very determined."

"If he is your son… it is a very big if, my lady, and a remarkable coincidence, do you not find it strange that Madame Zula, a woman proved to be a charlatan before our very eyes, warned you that he was closer than you ever imagined only to run into this man right outside her home? It smacks of collusion between them at best!" It was one more attempt at reason and, while she knew it would fall on deaf ears, Elizabeth felt compelled to make it.

Lady Vale sighed heavily before turning to face her. She wore an ardent expression as she pleaded her case. "I grant you, Miss Masters, that it is all very strange. And naturally, your distrust of Madame Zula is well founded... but I would rather believe every young man I meet to by my Benedict returned to me than to become so jaded and cynical that I might actually meet him and disavow him one day. What would you do, Miss Masters, if you had a child that had been taken from you so cruelly?"

In the face of such an argument, Elizabeth could do nothing other than relent. "I concede, Lady Vale. I cannot begin to conceive of what you suffered. I only wish to spare you more pain and to protect you from those who would exploit what you have already suffered."

"Because you are well compensated to do so," Lady Vale pointed out.

There was an accusation buried within that statement that perhaps any expression of concern was motivated entirely by monetary compensation rather than any moral or ethical concerns. It was insulting, but it was also, given the history of individuals who had used the tragedy of Lady Vale's life to further their own ends, understandable.

Setting her hurt feelings and pride aside, Elizabeth explained, "It is what I have been appointed to do by Mr. Middlethorp, yes. But it is also the right thing to do... the moral and just thing to do. I am not attempting to be the villain of the piece, Lady Vale. Only to do what I have been asked—what you agreed to with Mr. Middlethorp as one of the conditions for allowing you to maintain a separate household! My purpose here is to protect your interests and to prevent others from taking advantage of you. I am sorry that you do not agree with my assessments of the dangers of this situation, but that doesn't change them."

Lady Vale was chastened, but far too proud to admit it. She rose to her feet with all the haughtiness of a queen. "I have some correspondence to attend to, Miss Masters. You will continue to oversee the care of our guest?"

"Certainly, Lady Vale. I will see to it," Elizabeth agreed.

Lady Vale exited the room and Elizabeth sank into the chair beside the bed. Her gaze drifted to the too-handsome man who, for all intents and purposes, appeared to be sleeping in quiet repose.

Reaching out, Elizabeth touched his brow with the back of her hand. His earlier antics had spiked his fever again. His skin burned beneath her and she feared that if it continued to grow worse they might never have answers.

Before she could pull her hand away, his came up. Large fingers clasped her wrist, circling it so firmly she could not break free. The hold wasn't painful, but it was quite forceful.

His eyes opened, but only slightly. "I have to find my Mary."

"Then let Lady Vale's investigators help you," she urged.

"But you want me gone from this house… far from your half-mad mistress who sees a ghost in every face she passes," he replied.

"I wish for you to discourage her belief that you are her son. Do not allow her to pin her hopes on such an unlikely outcome. Will you not help me dissuade her from this?"

He laughed, though the sound was more bitter than amused. "It has been my experience that a determined woman is never dissuaded… even when reason and evidence demand it."

"Then in lieu of discouragement, a lack of encouragement will suffice. Accept her help… I certainly can't imagine what any woman taken by those ruffians must be feeling. As frightened as I was by an attempted kidnapping, she must be terrified."

His frown deepened. "Mary is not unfamiliar with fear and even with brutality, sadly. Whatever is happening to her, she does not deserve it and I should have been more diligent in my duty to protect her. Regardless, she will persevere and prevail. That is what we do."

Elizabeth would have asked more questions. What he'd said

piqued both her curiosity and her sympathy for both her rescuer and the missing woman, whoever she was to him. But his hand slipped from her wrist and his eyes closed once more. Given the injuries he had sustained, it was unlikely he would wake again for some time.

As she sat there with him, the silence of the room was broken only by the soft cadence of his breathing, strangely peaceful. In a house where she had no friends, either because the servants distrusted someone who was not yet one of them and not yet a member of the upper class or because they disliked her allegiance to Mr. Middlethorp, she'd had no human contact, no intimate conversations, in her life for years. She found herself in a situation where she could pour out all the things she'd been holding inside with no one the wiser.

As he slept on, she found herself speaking in hushed tones of her life before—of the mistakes she'd made, of the regrets she had and the painful truth. "I wonder who this woman is to you. This Mary? Your lover or your betrothed? Perhaps she is a relative? Or even your wife— I will never marry… I'd have to confess all my past transgressions to a husband. It would only be right, after all. And what man wants to marry a woman who is—who behaved so recklessly and improperly when no promises had been made or understandings reached? Certainly, I believed that Fredrick loved me and that we would one day wed. Why would I not have?"

Anger bubbled inside her, anger and resentment. No, Freddy hadn't made promises. But she'd spoken of their future together, of getting married once the scandal surrounding her family's loss of fortune had passed. In all the times she'd talked so excitedly of that future, he'd never once corrected her, never once stated that what she wanted for them had become an impossibility. He hadn't lied to her, but he hadn't been truthful either. Instead, he'd permitted her to lie to herself because it had been convenient for him… until it had not been.

She could still feel the crushing weight of rejection when she'd heard the news that he'd announced his engagement to someone else. The humiliation she'd felt when people had whispered and stared while they sat in their respective pews on the opposite side of the small village church on Sunday mornings. All those humiliations could have been borne, but not the humiliation she'd felt when he'd made the assumption that their relationship would continue in spite of his newly betrothed status. He'd thought she would simply be his mistress, had truly believed that she would accept that status and be grateful for it. It was then that she'd recognized the truth. He'd never loved her, and her love for him had been naught but an illusion, a fantasy created by a young girl too gullible and naive to recognize him for what he was.

Elizabeth looked back at the man lying in the bed. He wasn't that sort. She didn't trust him. In truth, she did not trust any man. Yet, she believed with her whole heart that he was not the sort to simply lie without cause. But finding his Mary—for that cause there was nothing he would not do, and that meant she'd have to guard her heart and her more amorous feelings very well against him lest she fail in her duty to protect Lady Vale.

FENTON HARDWICK STOOD before the man he feared and loathed beyond anything in this world. He'd been summoned, brought by carriage with a hood pulled low over his face, same as it was every time he was brought before his master. His whole life had been spent in servitude to the monster before him. Dressed in fine clothes and moving through the highest levels of society didn't hide the evil in him. Fenton could see it. Had seen it plain as day the very first time he'd laid eyes on the man. It was a pocket he wished he'd never picked.

"Where is the girl?" the man asked. He paused in sipping brandy from a cut glass snifter to brush an imaginary speck of lint from his finely tailored coat. The words were uttered softly, but they were no less menacing for it.

"We didn't get her," Fenton admitted. He didn't question that the man already knew, that he'd known from the outset of sending for him. He had eyes and ears everywhere. If the bastard didn't know, he wouldn't have bothered having Fenton fetched like a misbehaving schoolboy.

Fenton had tried to run from him once, to escape it all. It had been a woman, of course, who prompted such hopefulness within him. It had been quashed easily enough and he'd learned, as he'd watched her walk away from him to become the mistress of a wealthy and powerful man his employer had sold her to, that loving anyone, caring for anyone while in his employee would only see them destroyed.

The man cocked his head to one side. He still wore the wigs that had been popular a generation before. The elaborately-coifed curls brushed against the gold embroidery that bedecked his frock coat. "But I paid you to get her, Hardwick. I pay you to get all of them. That is your job, is it not?" Despite his seemingly civil tone, there was a wealth of menace in his voice. Fenton had seen him kill men for less.

"There was a gentleman there… hiding, watching us, I think. He intervened. We had no choice but to abandon the whole operation before the watch came," Fenton explained. "We can still get her. But we'll need help from the mystic and her pretty boy."

An elegant hand slammed down on the top of the table, his ornate ring smacking against the wood with a sharp crack. "You will get her and you will not tell me how it is to be done! I know what is required. Have I not been issuing your orders for nigh on two decades? Was it not your own botched attempt to retrieve my property from Vale that spawned this entire scheme?"

Fenton ducked his head. "Yes, it was, sir."

A soft chuckle escaped him, the sound echoing in the library and sending a chill up Fenton's spine. It was like hearing the devil himself.

"Selling off that little towheaded brat was the most brilliant idea you've ever had in your life… you managed to show me just how profitable it could be to trade in human flesh," he reflected. "It's been, I daresay, as lucrative as blackmail ever was. Of course, it helps that if we sell to the right sort of individual, blackmail can still be a nice secondary income. Now can't it?"

And he would burn in hell for it. "Yes, sir."

"Where are your compatriots?"

"Albert is dead. I had to shoot him. Henry took off in another direction. We'll meet up soon enough and plan our next attack." He hoped Henry, for once in his life, had the sense to run and keep running. The big oaf had been roped into this mess the same as the rest of them, but Fenton knew it pressed more heavily on the soft-hearted giant of a man. It had always had.

"Meet up with Henry and get rid of him. He's a liability and always has been. Too much brawn and not nearly enough brain. Do nothing else until you hear from the Irishman. I will be paying him and my dear Zella a visit. They may be required to take a more active role in this. It is very rare, after all, that we are asked to obtain a specific female rather than simply a type. Blond, brunette, redhead. They're all the same in the dark, aren't they?"

"Yes, sir," Fenton agreed. His disgust was something he was long used to hiding. He agreed to save his own skin, because it was expected of him.

"I do like it when they have a bit of fight in them… not too much, but a little. Adds sport, doesn't it?" the man asked, sipping his drink once more. He chuckled softly as he lowered the glass again, clearly amused by his own humor.

"That it does, sir," Fenton agreed, the lie bitter on his tongue. He'd done a lot of things in his life that he wasn't proud of, things that he'd pay dearly for in the next world, but he'd never stooped to raping women or, God help him, children. But that didn't remove the stains from his soul, because he'd put many a woman and child into the hands of monsters who bought them for just that purpose. Might as well be guilty of it himself, he thought.

His employer picked up a letter opener from the desk. It was thin bladed with an ornate handle, a replica of a rapier. "It's a fine piece isn't it?"

"It is, sir," Fenton agreed. He wasn't oblivious to the only barely veiled threat of the man holding a wicked-looking blade in his hand. But acknowledging it or showing fear would only make matters worse for him. Despite his bravado, Fenton couldn't prevent a flinch as his employer stopped before him, blade in hand, and pressed the tip of it to his gut.

"If you fail again, I'll see you dead. Do you hear me? If you're not of use to me, there's no point in keeping you around… and given what you know, I can't exactly just release you from service, can I? It's hardly like pensioning off the butler! Remember that, Hardwick. You work for me and you work well or you die. The choice is yours. Dull as this blade may be, I'll gut you with it. Understood?"

"Yes, sir," Fenton agreed.

"Go back to your hovel, Hardwick… I'll send word when you are needed again."

Fenton bowed stiffly and moved toward the door. But as he touched the handle, the man called out again. Fenton stopped, turned back and faced him. "Yes, sir?"

"Your little light o'love… what was her name, again? Margaret?"

Gooseflesh raised on Fenton's skin, prickling against the rough fabric of his clothes. "It's been so long I can't remember," he lied.

His employer laughed. "I remember. I never forget. She's no longer with Cavendish… he grew tired of her I believe. Lost her in a card game to Buckley. I remember, Fenton. And pretend as you might, I know you still yearn for her. I know that you've also been writing to her for the last decade. It'd be a pity if, now that she's with a relatively kind man, her life were to abruptly end, now wouldn't it?"

"I'll do what you ask, as I've always done," Fenton agreed. "But leave her out of it. She's suffered enough for having had the misfortune to be tangled up with the likes of me."

His employer shrugged. "She's a tool, Hardwick. Something I can always use as a threat against your life to keep you in line. I'll use her as I see fit. Remember that. Now get out of my sight."

I could kill him, Fenton thought. He'd hang for it, but Margaret would be safe, or as safe as she could ever be. But even as the thought entered his mind, he shrugged it off. It required more courage than he possessed after years under the bastard's thumb. Instead, Fenton nodded again, and walked out the door.

Chapter Eight

AFTER HIS HUMILIATING collapse the day before, Benedict had been more cautious and circumspect. He'd sat up in bed first. After managing to remain upright for a significant amount of time, he had stood and walked to the window before retreating to the bed and tucking himself back in like the invalid he had been for the last day. All the while, Miss Masters had slept on, blissfully unaware as she curled up in her chair.

She'd talked through the night it seemed, but most of the time he'd been too exhausted and insensible to understand her or take in the details of what she was saying. But he heard something behind her words, something that he responded to on a deep and visceral level. Loneliness. It was something he understood all too well.

Having tested his strength and still finding it lacking, Benedict tamped down his frustration and impatience and returned to his bed. Walking the few paces from the bed to the window and back had left him breathless and exhausted.

A soft knock sounded at the door and then Lady Vale entered. She paused and glanced at Miss Masters' sleeping form. Then with a vindictive and petty gleam in her eye, she cleared her throat loudly.

Miss Masters let out a startled squeak and sat upright in her chair. "Forgive me, my lady, I must have dozed off."

It had been more than a doze. At one point, she'd snored. Uncertain of the underlying animosity between the two women and where it was coming from, Benedict wisely kept his thoughts to himself. At this point, he needed Lady Vale's assistance to locate Mary. Without it, all hope was lost. And Miss Masters... perhaps he didn't need her, but he did want her. That was an unforeseen complication.

It left him in the very uncomfortable position of swallowing his pride and asking for the help he'd dismissed so carelessly only the day before. "Lady Vale, I must apologize for my less than gracious response yesterday when you offered the assistance of your investigators. It has become clear that I am in no condition to seek Mary's return myself."

Lady Vale clasped her hands in front of her and looked down at the carpet. "Mr. Mason, I want you to understand that the fault does not lie with those in my employ, but with my late husband. I was not permitted to hire those investigators to search for you—for my son—while my husband lived. It was more than a decade after my son was taken that he died and I was able to do what was necessary to try to find him—to find you. By then, any leads had grown cold and while most of the villains responsible were identified, they had already been hanged for other crimes and it was too late to question them. That is not the case with your... forgive me, but who is it you seek?"

He'd been reluctant to explain earlier, uncertain of Miss Masters' curious response and worried that anything he said about how Mary had been brought into the Masons' care would only further support Lady Vale's belief about his identity. "My adoptive sister. She was brought into the same home where I was being raised by the Masons when she was a young child of no more than two... her name is Mary and she disappeared after visiting the same house your companion was nearly abducted in front of," he answered.

Lady Vale appeared taken aback by that. "It appears that we have stumbled into something very dark, indeed. My previous assertion that nothing ever happens in Bath seems both naive and foolish now." Her earlier animosity forgotten in the wake of such a revelation, she looked at her companion with concern in her gaze. "Miss Masters, you will not leave the house without at least two footmen to accompany you. Not even on your half-day!"

"Yes, my lady," Miss Masters agreed with a jerky nod. "I had not thought to leave the house for any reason at all, frankly. I find myself quite reluctant to face the dangers outside these walls."

THE RELIEF ELIZABETH felt at knowing the woman he searched for was a relative and not a lover or a wife was utterly preposterous. She had no claim on him, nor did she want one, Elizabeth told herself. She'd had her brush with scandal in the past and inappropriate gentlemen to boot. It was not a road she meant to travel again. Just because it was impossible to ignore how handsome he was, she reasoned, did not necessitate that she act upon it.

From the first moment her gaze had lit upon him, she'd been unable to deny the fact. But handsome was such a passive thing and, while he'd been unconscious, it had been not easy to ignore, but easier to dismiss. Awake, the fierceness of his personality, the intensity that was simply a part of him, took what had been handsome and now made it compelling, magnetic even. He was invading her thoughts and her senses, as evidenced by the strange fluttering of her pulse whenever he glanced at her. But she was no longer an ignorant girl to be led by such things. She knew precisely what sort of ruin awaited her should she give in to baser feelings. And then there was the other thing, that ephemeral and yet inescapable knowledge that he was not at all what he appeared.

His angelic countenance concealed a hidden darkness in him. She sensed it swirling and eddying under the surface. There was violence in him. She'd seen glimpses of it while he'd lain senseless in the bed from striking his head. Strangely, she did not feel unsafe near him. Quite the opposite.

It wasn't as if he'd threatened them. In fact, he'd been all that was noble and heroic if his actions were not orchestrated as part of some greater plot. A fact of which she remained unconvinced. Still, awake, aware and on alert, it was easy enough to recognize that he was a dangerous man. They'd brought the fox into the hen house, it seemed.

Lady Vale spoke again. "As for you, Mr. Mason, you cannot leave here... firstly, because you are in no condition to do so and, secondly, because I cannot let you leave without knowing the truth," Lady Vale said. "I will put all of my resources at your disposal. My investigators are yours to use as you will, at no cost. And I will have Madame Zula and her manservant brought here so that you may question them. Regardless of Miss Masters' skepticism, I cannot help but feel that Madame Zula was being quite honest when she professed that her skills were real even without the theatrical trappings."

Elizabeth balked. It was not possible that he just remain indefinitely. Lady Vale was practically giving him carte blanche. Mr. Middlethorp would be furious which would, no doubt, result in her being sacked. More to the point, she couldn't possibly remain under the same roof with him indefinitely. It was nothing short of a recipe for disaster. Every remaining hint of recklessness and wickedness that lurked within her responded to him in a fashion that was impossible to ignore.

"Lady Vale," she began, "we can hardly hold the man here against his will. Once he is well enough, I am certain that he would want to be directly involved with the search for his sister!"

Lady Vale nodded. "Of course. And when he's well enough, he will certainly do so. But how much better would it be to use my home as a base for your operation than to work out of some dingy inn?"

"I thank you, Lady Vale, but I—" he began, but Lady Vale immediately cut him off.

"Please do not reject my offer out of hand. I accept the possibility that you may not be the person I believe you to be," she admitted tearfully. "But until we've exhausted every option, allow me the peace and comfort of that hope. I beg you. Please!"

His expression firmed. The indecision that warred in his gaze did more to soften Elizabeth's stance on his character than anything else. It was clear that he did not wish to cause Lady Vale undue pain, but it was also just as clear that he was calculating how helpful her offer could be to him. Finally, he said, "I must say that I find the scenario of being your long lost son highly unlikely, but I will consent to remain here and operate my search for Mary from this home. The first course of action will be a meeting with Madame Zula and these investigators of yours. I hardly believe in mystics, but it cannot be coincidence that Mary went missing after having last been seen at that address and that Miss Masters was nearly abducted from the very same spot."

Lady Vale seated herself on the edge of his bed. It was a very familiar gesture, something that a mother might do with her son. It made Benedict distinctly uncomfortable. He didn't believe that she was his mother. If the truth were told, he couldn't allow himself to believe it. But there was also an aching familiarity in the gesture, one that sparked his battered memory and made him question whether or not, at any time in his life, someone had cared enough to sit on the side of his bed and offer him comfort.

"I would ask you questions about your childhood and your adoptive family, Mr. Mason. If you would permit it," she added softly.

"You may ask any questions you like, madame, but I cannot guarantee that I will answer them."

She dropped her gaze to her clasped hands resting in her lap. After a short pause as she considered his reply, she gave a jerky nod. "That is fair enough, Mr. Mason. Be truthful with me and if you feel you cannot answer for whatever reason, simply tell me that."

"Then ask your questions," he agreed. The reluctance in his voice was quite obvious and he'd already stated once before that he did not wish to discuss his family.

"Do you know about how old you were when they took you? What is your earliest memory of being with them?"

He appeared to be considering his answer very carefully. Finally, after a long while, he said, "I can recall a church where we stayed. We didn't have a home when we arrived in that village, wherever it was. There was no place to stay that we could afford and my adoptive father sought refuge there until he could find work and secure lodging for us. I remember the vicar guessing my age to be about five or six and asking me if I could read... I could, but only just. So he sat down with me and helped me practice my letters and read from a primer that he had."

"You could read, but only a little," Lady Vale answered, "when you were taken from me. You'd been tutored by Mr. Morris and would continue with him until you were old enough and would have moved on to Harrow. It was a tradition in your father's—in my husband's family," she explained. "It's very unlikely, don't you think, that the son of a transient or nomadic mason would have learned to read at all by the age of six?"

"It's unusual," he agreed. "But it's hardly proof that I'm the missing son and heir of a viscount."

Tears glistened in her eyes, "Of course, it isn't proof. It's been two decades. Proof is not something I can hope for, when time has changed us both so much. But there is reason enough with that kind of information, with your appearance which is so very similar to my own, with the fact that you are close in age to what my son would be, that you were adopted by a rather unlikely pair—it's the sum of these things, Benedict. Can't you see that?"

"It's not so unlikely. My mother adopted us so there would be someone else in the house for my sot of a father to take his anger out upon. The more children they acquired for him to beat, the fewer beatings she'd have to take herself."

Lady Vale's face went white. She lifted her hand and pressed it to her heart, almost as if he'd struck her there. Elizabeth had sat quietly during the interrogation to that point, but she couldn't allow it to continue. She rose to intercede but Lady Vale stopped her with a glance. The older woman looked up at her and held up her hand in a staying gesture.

"I understand your need to lash out, but the truth must be—"

Benedict cut her off quickly. "You do not want to know the truth about where I have been, what I have seen and what I have done. Even if, on some strange and slim chance that I could be your son, you're better off to go on believing me dead or missing. Can't you see that?"

She took a calming breath and dropped her hands, once more, to her lap, folded them primly together and offered him a sad smile. "What I can see is that you've had a great deal of pain in your life... pain that I would have had you spared whether you are my son or not. I am sorry for that. But it doesn't change anything for me. There is nothing in this world so painful as not knowing what has become of my child. And if you must lash out, then I will bear it, until the truth can be uncovered."

"Lady Vale," Miss Masters interjected, her tone both disapproving and concerned. "Perhaps it would be best to let Mr. Mason rest for a bit. He is quite tired, I'm sure, given his setback from yesterday. Perhaps, tomorrow he will be more amenable to continuing this vein of questioning?"

"I have only a few more questions... do you recall the name of this vicar?"

Benedict sighed. "It was Endicott, or at least I assume it was. The name had been inscribed inside that primer."

"That is a starting point, is it not? We can, perhaps, locate this vicar and the church records may tell us when your family was there," Lady Vale said with a curt nod. "If we narrow down the time, we can determine if that event happened before or after my own son was taken. Surely you cannot object to such a reasonable course of action?"

Elizabeth watched him closely, noted the clenching of his jaw and the firm set of his mouth. He was nearing the end of his patience.

"Let him rest, Lady Vale. No doubt, he'll be more agreeable about the wisdom of your actions tomorrow."

Lady Vale nodded reluctantly and rose from the bedside. "You are quite right, Miss Masters. I will go and send a note to Madame Zula now. I will have her here this evening. Please do not tire yourself out... and a meal will be delivered to you shortly. You must be utterly famished."

Before she left, she turned back to Elizabeth and added, "I will not have you telling the servants that I believe him to be my son so that they treat him like a confidence man and lock up the silver."

"Then how shall you explain his continued presence here?" Elizabeth demanded. "Do you not think that the servants would be suspicious of you simply inviting some total stranger to remain here indefinitely?"

"It is simple enough, is it not? He came to our rescue, aided us and prevented unimaginable horrors from being visited upon us. It is no less than our duty to assist him in locating his missing sister," Lady Vale answered, her tone clipped. "And you will not gainsay me on this, nor will you rush off to inform Branson of my current foible! I'm not mad! I am not a child having a tantrum! I'm not simply grasping at straws! I am exploring the possibility that this man, who bears a shocking resemblance to me and to all the members of my family and who has admitted that he has no knowledge of his own origins, might, in fact, be my son!"

In the face of Lady Vale's clear grasp of the situation, Elizabeth was forced to make a choice. It did not sit well with her most of the time that she was viewed as the tattletale of the house. And since Lady Vale was still admitting that there was a possibility that Mr. Mason was not her son, she had to relent. Elizabeth nodded her agreement, reluctantly. "I will consent to your terms, Lady Vale. But at the first sign that he is not who you believe him to be or that he could be part of a greater scheme to ingratiate himself to you, I will have no option but to inform Mr. Middlethorp."

Lady Vale nodded, "I will make the arrangements for the investigators to come here and meet with you." With that, she turned on her heel and left the room.

Elizabeth turned to him and uttered a warning with soft menace, "Do not think to use her grief to your own advantage. Whatever fate may have befallen your sister, I am not without sympathy. But that woman has suffered enough. Do not think to abuse her trust."

He stared back at her levelly, his expression inscrutable. "Tell me, Miss Masters, what have men done to you that you distrust them all so? Or is it just me?"

"I have found," she answered with just as much equanimity, "that the more handsome a man is, the more likely it is that he cannot be trusted."

"So you find me handsome?" he asked, his lips curving slightly with a hint of smugness.

Elizabeth's lips firmed into a thin, disapproving line as she surveyed him. "You know perfectly well what you look like. There's no need for me to expound upon it further and feed your conceit and arrogance. Just be aware that I am not fooled by your exterior. You will not charm me nor will you sway me to your cause. My duty, first and foremost, is to see to it that Lady Vale and her interests are protected."

"That's quite an undertaking for a woman. Will you shoot me? Put another pistol ball in me to go with the one that was landed by the men who would have succeeded in kidnapping you had I not intervened?" he asked. There was nothing soft about the menace in his voice. That history of violence she'd sensed in him seemed to be bubbling just beneath the surface like a cauldron ready to boil over. Just as quickly, he pulled it back, tamping it down and covering that crack in his charming façade with smooth disdain. "Think what might happen, Miss Masters, if I had not been present."

She drew herself up to her full height. "Are you threatening me?"

"Not in the least, Miss Masters. I'm merely pointing out that you cannot protect Lady Vale when it is quite obvious you are not even capable of protecting yourself," he answered. "However it might have happened, you have found yourself and, by virtue of proximity, your employer, in the midst of something that is far reaching and terrifying. You need an ally, one who isn't afraid to get his hands dirty if need be."

Elizabeth would have said more, but he had tossed the covers back and was rising from the bed. "What are you doing?"

"I've been in that bed for some time now. I'm disinclined to continue attending nature's call as an invalid would. If you've no wish to witness it, Miss Masters, I suggest you leave and quickly."

Realizing precisely what he meant, Elizabeth blushed furiously and made a hasty retreat. If the door slammed more firmly behind her than was necessary, so be it.

SHE BOTHERED HIM.

Watching her exit, listening to the slamming of the door behind her, Benedict could admit that to himself. While her suspicions of him were perfectly natural and even reasonable given the circumstances, they goaded him to no end. It was a puzzle because he'd long since stopped caring what most people, especially tightly-wound ladies, thought of him.

There was something about Miss Masters that appealed to him, however; and it was a dangerous predicament to find himself in. Injured, weak as he was, in the midst of his search for Mary, and she was, inconveniently enough, one of the most fascinating women he'd ever met. The more prickly she was, the more adamant she became in her less than glowing assessment of his character, the more he wanted to prove her wrong.

As for Lady Vale, he still believed she was completely mad. Kind, to be sure, but grief-stricken and chasing phantoms not so different from his own. He was not her son. He was completely certain of it, even if he had no memory of the time before he'd been given into the care of the Masons. The very idea that he might have been born a gentleman, much less a peer, given how hard he'd had to work to assimilate even remotely into the upper echelon of society that his gaming hell served was proof enough of that. Blood tells, he thought bitterly. And his blood, wherever it came from, had marked him for the gutter and little better.

After seeing to his immediate needs, Benedict struggled to make it back to the bed. When they'd said he was as weak as a kitten, the assessment had been humiliatingly accurate. The room swayed about him and it was all he could do to remain upright. Gripping the edges of the bed, he lowered himself once more onto it, but only to sit on the side of it. He would not lie down and give in to the weakness. There was too much to do. Benedict forced himself to consider all that he knew about Mary's disappearance, all the while denying himself the lure of sleep.

It wasn't very much, sadly. She'd come to Bath to visit an old friend who had married well, a cloth merchant by the name of Simms. Mary had reported that the union did not appear to be a happy one and she felt certain she would be cutting her visit short. She'd also told him of her appointment with a mystic, but she had not named them. He'd tracked Mary to Madame Zula's residence by speaking to several chair porters. Luckily, Mary's petite frame and almost-white blond hair was memorable enough that those who had transported her around the city recollected her easily enough. But it was the porter's memory of the large, hulking fellow in the rough clothes that had been the most telling. The porter had seen him about town a time or two, always trailing in the wake of some pretty young woman.

On that street, he'd spoken to a porter who recalled transporting Mary to Madame Zula's but never picking her up. None of the porters he'd spoken to had known anything about what went on at that address, only that they often delivered ladies to it. Now, knowing that it was a mystic telling fortunes and reading palms, that made infinitely more sense.

A helpful maid he might have flirted with had confirmed his worst fears. She'd told him about hearing a woman's scream and seeing a youngish woman with brown hair being carted away by three ruffians. That was the sum total of his knowledge.

He needed to speak with Madame Zula and he needed to confront the Simms'. Why had they not contacted him to let him know Mary was missing? Had they been involved in her disappearance in some way? He should have gone there first but, if he had, he would not have been in the position he had been to prevent a similar fate from befalling Miss Masters. He had to take heart that, perhaps, it was all coming out as it should.

A knock sounded at the door and a footman entered bearing

steaming water. Another followed in his wake with a tray of food. A smallish man trailed behind them with fresh clothes and a shaving kit.

"I am Tinsleigh," the man said, his voice pinched and a bit nasally. "I am the under butler here, but am a valet by trade. Lady Vale has asked me to attend you."

"I've no need of a valet," he answered immediately. He'd never had one in his life. It was pointless to start now. A man of his station hardly required that kind of attention. He could dress and groom himself well enough without any assistance.

The man sniffed, his overly-large nose flaring with disdain and what appeared to be indignation. "I see, sir. And shall I inform her ladyship that you intend to undo all the nursing and care that was provided by her and Miss Masters when you attempt to shave yourself? No doubt, such vigorous movement will only reopen your wounds and do further damage."

How a man who was a foot shorter than him managed to look down at him, Benedict couldn't quite fathom, yet he managed. More to the point, did he really want to have another run-in with Miss Masters' disapproval or Lady Vale's desperation? No. Not at all. "Very well," he relented. "I will consent to the temporary appointment of you as my valet, Tinsleigh."

The small man nodded and all the unpleasantness previously displayed simply vanished. He became all that was conciliatory and even toadying in that moment. "Certainly, sir. Shall I address you as Mr. Mason, sir?"

"You may," Benedict agreed.

"Very well, Mr. Mason. We shall not do a full bath in deference to your wound, but we shall endeavor to wash your hair and see you sponge bathed and dressed. I am told to expect Madame Zula this evening. Prior to her arrival, Lady Vale has arranged for you to speak to Mr. Adler, an investigator. He is expected to arrive just before tea time."

Benedict nodded. "She arranged all that very quickly," he commented. So quickly, he thought, it seemed to have been prearranged.

To what purpose?

"Indeed, sir," Tinsleigh said, setting up a chair and a basin in the connected dressing chamber. Benedict dutifully took his seat when indicated. "Lady Vale has kept Mr. Adler on retainer for some time. Any questions she has or any information that she thinks may be pertinent, he comes for straightaway."

"I see," Benedict stated for lack of anything better to interject. He did not see. If Lady Vale had hired investigators to look into her son's disappearance and in two decades they'd managed to unearth nothing, how skilled could they be? Then he remembered that she had told him she only had the investigators at her disposal after her husband died. But still, ten years without any progress made him wonder.

"She sent footmen around to deliver a message to Madame Zula, as well. I understand that the attack on poor Miss Masters occurred right outside her establishment, did it not?"

"It did," Benedict agreed. "You seem remarkably well informed, Tinsleigh."

The little man puffed up even more. "I do pride myself on it, sir! As for summoning Madame Zula," he continued, "I imagine that Miss Masters had a hand in that. She's little use for mystics and the occult... not that Lady Vale does! Simply that Lady Vale does want so badly to learn of her poor son's fate that she is willing to resort to unorthodox methods."

Benedict realized that he didn't have to question Tinsleigh at all. In fact, he could sit there stone silent and just let the man natter on and he'd get all the information about the household he required. "I see."

"Yes. Madame Zula is not the first mystic her ladyship has employed," Tinsleigh said, working a lather of sandalwood-scented soap into Benedict's hair. "She does come far more highly recommended than most. Even Lady Castlery herself has gone to see the woman!"

"But Miss Masters disapproves?" Benedict prompted.

Tinsleigh made a clucking sound much like a perturbed hen. "Indeed, sir! But Miss Masters is very disagreeable and disapproves of many things!"

"I could sense that about her," Benedict agreed. He wanted the little valet to continue. Servants' gossip was often the best source of information. When it came to extending credit at his gaming house, it was often his first choice beyond even the avowal of other patrons.

"Well, she is not the first companion that Mr. Middlethorp has engaged for Lady Vale," Tinsleigh offered in a conspiratorial whisper. "The first two were much worse. Unpleasant, unattractive and genuinely an utter bore to be around. They made everyone in the house quite miserable. Miss Masters is at least pleasant enough when she doesn't feel that Lady Vale is—well, Lady Vale is desperate to locate her lost son. Who would not be in her situation? It often makes for unwise decisions."

"Indeed, I can certainly understand her plight. How did Lady Vale learn of Madame Zula?"

"Quite by accident, I do believe," Tinsleigh said. "She was taking the waters and overheard two women discussing her."

"And was Lady Vale acquainted with these two women?" Benedict asked. It was an old trick, planting people in an audience to talk up the performance.

"Well, no, sir! I do not believe she had ever met them. She did have someone else introduce them that day so as to obtain Madame Zula's direction."

"I see," Benedict mumbled in reply.

The remainder of his toilette was akin to torture. Everything the valet did for him was a reminder that he himself was currently unable to attend even to his own most basic needs. From being bathed by another man, shaved, having his hair dressed, it was humiliating. That he was exhausted and trembling by the time all was said and done did little to improve his mood.

"You are looking quite pale, Mr. Mason! I do wish you could rest, but I'm afraid the investigator is set to arrive at any moment. Perhaps I can assist you downstairs?" Tinsleigh suggested.

Loath to admit the other man was right, Benedict agreed nonetheless. "Yes, Tinsleigh. Loath as I am to admit, I'd not make it by myself.

Thank you for your assistance."

A knock sounded at the door and Lady Vale entered immediately afterward. "Mr. Adler has arrived! I'm so anxious for you to meet with him, Benedict. He'll be able to help us get to the bottom of everything. I am certain of it!"

Chapter Nine

LADY VALE HAD gone on ahead as Benedict took the stairs slowly behind her. Tinsleigh hovered behind him as if he might somehow catch him if he were to take a tumble. The end result would undoubtedly be the both of them lying in a tangled, broken heap at the bottom. In light of his present weakness and the fact that the stairs and foyer beyond shimmered before his eyes, Benedict kept his hand firmly on the bannister. He resented the weakness, resented that his body would not function the way that he needed it to.

"The investigator is waiting for you in the drawing room, Mr. Mason," Tinsleigh said. "I do hope that he'll be able to help you with whatever it is you're searching for, sir. He'd surely have to be more help to you than he has been to poor Lady Vale."

"You seem to lack confidence in his abilities, Tinsleigh," Benedict commented.

The little man gasped, clearly horrified at having said something that would cast aspersions on his mistress' ability to hire competent men. "Not at all, Mr. Mason. Lady Vale would hire only the best—tis simply that the matter Lady Vale has him looking in to occurred some time ago! I'm sure since the events he'll be examining for you are much more recent, they are, therefore, much more likely to be solved!"

"Naturally," Benedict said. Thankfully, they reached the foot of the stairs without incident and both his neck and his dignity remained intact.

A footman stepped forward and opened the door to one of the

rooms right off the foyer. Voices were low and muffled from within as he approached. Stepping inside, he waited for the door to close behind him. When it had, he spoke softly, "If it's quite all right, I'd prefer to have the servants know as little of my reasons for being here as possible. Without knowing what has happened to Mary, I feel every precaution must be taken to preserve her safety but also her reputation."

Lady Vale nodded sympathetically. "Of course, Ben—Mr. Mason. We'll be as circumspect as you require... and you will tell my investigator, Mr. Adler, everything you remember about your adoptive parents and how you came to be in their care."

She was cagier than he'd expected—bartering with her offer of aid. Others saw her as fragile. He himself had viewed her as a madwoman, one who was all but demented by the loss of her child. But the truth was far more complex. Her desperation was both her weakness and her strength.

"I will tell him what I know about how I came to be with them," he agreed, offering nothing further. It was a dangerous thing for him, to poke into the past so. If the truth came out, it would only make matters worse.

"Very well," she conceded. "I will leave you to speak with Mr. Adler. Madame Zula will be arriving within the hour."

As the door closed behind her, Adler wasted no time. He turned to Benedict with a disgusted expression. "I have tried for a decade to make her accept the fact that her son is likely dead. And every time I think I have made progress, some charlatan like you shows up and sends her spiraling back into hysteria."

"For the record, I do not claim to be her son. I do not believe that I am her son and I do not wish for her to believe that I am her son... Miss Masters was attacked outside Madame Zula's and the intent appeared to be abduction. I intervened and was injured in the process," Benedict stated, his tone clipped and sharp. He was quickly growing tired of accusations. Hardly a heroic figure, he certainly wasn't the villain everyone portrayed him to be at the moment. "Now that we've established my lack of ulterior motives, shall we discuss my missing sister and how you mean to locate her?"

Adler eyed him cautiously for a moment. Then with a curt nod, he retrieved a small, leather-bound journal from his coat. "What can you tell me about when you last saw her?"

"I last saw her in London. She came to Bath to visit a friend of hers, a Mrs. Simms, whom she'd known as a child. Mrs. Simms had only recently married a merchant here in the city. She stayed with them for some days, though from Mary's letters, I sensed that things in the Simms' house were not as they should be."

"Do you have these letters?" Adler asked.

"In my bag at the inn… The Three Sisters on Broad Street," Benedict answered. "I brought them with me, along with a miniature of my sister."

Adler stopped making notes then. "Miniatures are a costly trinket. What sort of business is it that you are in, Mr. Mason, that affords you such luxuries?"

Benedict considered lying. Answering honestly could very well get him tossed out on his ear. But if Adler was any sort of investigator at all, it wouldn't take very much digging to uncover the truth about his current occupation. "I own a gaming hell in London… The Bronze Pair near Covent Garden."

"The Bronze Pair? That's an unusual name," Adler pointed out. "I believe that it was owned by a man by the name of Trenton."

Benedict was left with little choice but to acknowledge the unfortunate truth. "The hell came with it, the name that is. There are two matching statues in the foyer of generously-endowed women. As for Trenton, he wagered the establishment and lost."

"But it's a hell and not a brothel?" the investigator demanded, clearly skeptical.

"It is now," Benedict answered. "What it was in its past incarnations, I cannot say." He could, but he chose not to. As Mary had continued to live with him, that aspect of the business had been something that had to cease immediately. It was bad enough that she lived in an apartment above a gaming hell. He certainly wouldn't have allowed her to live in an establishment that was actively engaging in prostitution.

Other than a raised eyebrow, Adler had no response to that. He waved his hand, motioning for Benedict to continue.

"Both Mary and I were adopted by the Masons. And no, that was not their actual name. I've never known their true name. Our father took that name because it was his profession and they moved us around every year or so."

Adler held up a hand. "Where?"

"What do you mean, where? We moved so frequently we hardly bothered learning the names."

Adler stopped his scribbling, pushed his spectacles up the bridge of his nose and met Benedict's gaze directly. "What cities or villages can you recall living in? If your father was a mason, someone in one of those locations will surely remember the lot of you. Surely you remember one or two?"

"I remember a city... a large city, but I have no notion which one. Perhaps York, since I know we were far in the north. But I was very young then. The first village I recall was Halsham, in Yorkshire. Then Aberwick in Northumberland. Those were the places we stayed the longest, though no more than a year in any of them. There were others. But we rarely stayed long enough to develop any connections in the area," Benedict said. Of course, the last place they'd lived with their parents had been Berwick-on-Tweed but he would wisely keep that to himself. It was a risk to let Adler look into his past, but it was the price he was paying to have someone else search for his sister until he himself was able to do so.

"And how is that you knew you were adopted? You said yourself that you were very young. Did the Masons tell you this?" Adler asked the question almost casually, but there was an undercurrent in his tone, a hidden accusation there.

Benedict tensed, every muscle in his body coiled as the memories washed through him. He despised looking back, despised letting those feelings of fear and anger consume him, but it was the price he had to pay for obtaining their assistance in finding his sister. And since he was not in any condition to look for her himself, there was simply no other option. "They reminded us of it. At every meal, every time we were presented with someone else's castoffs to wear… we were reminded that no one had wanted us. That we'd been tossed away as infants like so much refuse and were it not for their *generosity,* if you could call it such, that we'd have long since died from neglect."

The other man was silent for a moment, letting that nugget of information hover between them. When at last he spoke, Adler asked a very pointed question. "Did it never strike you as odd that they would take on two children they did not have to be responsible for when they couldn't even put down roots in one area for long?"

The simple truth was that Benedict had not allowed himself to think about his childhood or his adoptive parents in years. As far as examining their motives, he had never wanted to know. The darkness of his past, of the endless torment they'd put both him and Mary through for all those years, had kept him from looking into the abyss of his memories.

"No. Most of my attention was focused on how to avoid the back of my father's hand or the heel of his boot on my backside," Benedict answered, keeping his voice intentionally light and devoid of any hint of anger and pain.

"He was a drunkard," Benedict continued after a pause to collect his thoughts and his courage. "He often wound up in brawls with villagers at whatever local inn or tavern served the cheapest ale. He'd leave a job unfinished or do shoddy work while recovering from a night of excess. There were always reasons for why we picked up and left, and they were rarely ever shared with two children who were seldom seen as anything more than extra mouths to feed."

"Fair enough," Adler answered. "But I'll check in those areas and see if anyone has seen or heard anything of them in the last few years. That's for Lady Vale's benefit. Now, on to your sister, tell me where she was last seen here in Bath."

"Outside Madame Zula's... Mary, in the last few years, has been obsessed with the idea of finding where we came from, who our real parents were. I can only assume that she thought Madame Zula would be able to help with that."

Adler made a sound that eloquently relayed his opinion of Madame Zula without actually saying a word.

"I'll question Madame Zula first," Adler said.

"You can ask the questions, but I plan to be there to hear her answers," Benedict replied sharply. "Mary is the only person in this world I give two bloody damns about and I'll not be an idle spectator in this."

Adler nodded his agreement. "Fair enough. And I have developed a certain amount of affection and respect for Lady Vale. I will not allow you to harm her, whatever your intent is. Keep that in mind as we go forward. I am looking into this at her request, but my first loyalty will always be with her."

There was no adequate response to that so Benedict remained quiet. He nodded his assent instead.

Adler then added, "Sit down before you fall down. You've less color in your face than some corpses I've seen. Madame Zula will be here soon enough."

❧

"MISS MASTERS, I find I am quite chilled. Would you be so kind as to go and fetch my wrap?"

Elizabeth looked up from the embroidery that she was doing. Typically, Lady Vale would have sent for her maid to take care of such a task. That she hadn't was suspect enough. But as Elizabeth absolutely despised embroidery and the threads she'd been working with were tangled into a Gordian knot, she was glad for any distraction.

"Of course, Lady Vale. Is there anything else you require?"

Lady Vale smiled. "As we've elected to keep my suspicions about Mr. Mason a secret, perhaps if any of the other servants are gathered outside the library, you might instruct them on other tasks they could be attending to now?"

So that was it, Elizabeth thought. She was being sent on an errand to disrupt those servants who would report back to Mr. Middlethorp, of which she was normally one. "Certainly, Lady Vale. Shall I tell them you've asked for changes to be made to the dinner menu?"

"Yes, that should do," Lady Vale replied, continuing with her embroidery as if they weren't carrying on like spies behind enemy lines.

Stepping out of the drawing room and into the hall, Elizabeth saw the group of servants poised outside the door to the library where Mr. Mason was currently speaking with Mr. Adler. She cleared her throat, and half a dozen heads swiveled in her direction, eyes wide and mouths agape. "I believe that Lady Vale has decided to make some last minute changes to the dinner menu. Perhaps one of you would be so good as to fetch Cook for her?"

They all straightened in unison and scattered in different directions like bugs. Before Elizabeth could ascend the stairs, the door to the library opened and Mr. Adler stepped out. "I need a word with you, Miss Masters, and Lady Vale also. It's about the men who attacked you."

"Certainly," Elizabeth replied. She had no sooner turned toward the drawing room door than Lady Vale emerged.

"I heard, Miss Masters. You needn't concern yourself with my wrap. The fire has been built up nicely in the library. No doubt we'll be warm enough," the older woman said. With all the grace of a queen, Lady Vale crossed the expanse of the hall and swept into the other room.

Elizabeth watched her for a moment, once again envious of the grace and ease with which she moved. Her own forays in society had been limited to the social gatherings in Hertfordshire. And while they hadn't been the very height of fashion, they'd been pleasant enough and there'd been many a social butterfly present who rivaled even her ladyship in grace and poise. Feeling dowdier than usual in her drab brown dress, she followed on Lady Vale's heels vowing to herself that it had nothing to do with the beautiful but untrustworthy man who had been thrust into their midst. She laid the blame for it at Mr. Mason's feet. That wild and reckless part of her, the vain girl who'd flirted and danced and behaved so foolishly, was slowly being resurrected in his presence.

It didn't matter, she reminded herself, that his profile was perfect enough to have been carved by the ancient Greeks, or that his blond hair gleamed like gold in the candlelight, or that his brilliant blue-green eyes sparkled in a way that made her heart flutter. He was a liar. What he was lying about, she could not be certain, but she'd learned from harsh experience to listen to her instincts when it came to trusting men. Regardless of his heroics on her behalf, he was not at all what he seemed.

"Forgive me, my lady, Miss Masters," Adler apologized. "But I need to question you about the attackers. Had you ever seen any of them before? Think very carefully... perhaps you passed them on the street while out shopping, or they delivered coal or some other item here to the house? Anything at all?"

Elizabeth started to deny it, but she paused. Perhaps it was nothing, she reasoned, but she did recall a large, hulking beast of a man hovering outside the Abbey after they'd left the Pump Room on the day of the attack. "I think I saw the larger man... but he didn't approach me." Relaying the memory, she added, "I cannot be absolutely certain it was him, but I'm not certain it wasn't either. I had crossed paths with Mr. Mason as well. In the square just outside the Pump Room. He was following the man, I think."

Adler looked back to Mr. Mason who nodded. "Yes. I'd followed him there and noted him watching Miss Masters rather intently... I'd received a description of him from a chair porter who had told me that he'd seen the man about several times when he'd transported my sister around the city."

Adler nodded. "That does add a new twist on things, doesn't it? Odds are, if you noticed him, others did, too. Mr. Mason found him on his own, no doubt he won't be too hard to locate. I have a colleague whose aid I would like to enlist, with your permission of course, Lady

Vale."

Lady Vale blinked in surprise, as if it hadn't occurred to her that anyone else would be required. "Certainly, Mr. Adler, you may enlist anyone you wish… is there some reason why you cannot attend all of this yourself? I only ask for the sake of discretion. My suspicions about Mr. Mason's origins aside, his sister—her reputation would be sullied beyond repair if it was to be discovered that she had been, that is to say, that she had been without proper chaperonage during her absence."

Adler nodded thoughtfully. "I understand your concerns, my lady, and if I didn't think it was absolutely necessary I would not suggest it. Unfortunately, we're investigating two different things now in two very distant regions… Mr. Mason's past and his sister's, as well, but also her current whereabouts. It requires traveling far north to look into one and remaining here in the city to look into the other. I could certainly see to both given enough time, but his sister's disappearance is, I believe, especially time sensitive. As you well know, the longer a person is missing, the more likely it is for them to remain missing." Adler looked pointedly at Mr. Mason as he uttered the last, silently communicating and confirming the awful speculation that they were all silently engaging in. Mary might never be found. It might, in fact, be too late already.

"Naturally, additional funds will be made available to cover any expenses you may incur during this process, Mr. Adler," Lady Vale answered just as the heavy brass knocker on the front door fell with a loud thump. "That will be Madame Zula. I'm sure Calvert will show her in momentarily."

Elizabeth felt her gaze drifting toward Mr. Mason. It was the first time he'd been out of bed since taking a pistol ball to his shoulder and laying senseless with fever for two days since. She reasoned that her concern was well-founded and would be the same degree of concern she would show for anyone. It had nothing to do with how devastatingly handsome he was, or how vexing he was, and the fact that their verbal sparring earlier in the day was the most alive she'd felt in years.

From the moment he'd entered her small and colorless world, she'd been more and more painfully aware of just how devoid of any excitement her life was.

She'd fallen into old habits it seemed, being unaccountably drawn to a gentleman who was, no doubt, ill-suited to her and likely would lead to her ruin. It was a character flaw, she reasoned, one she'd thought herself to have conquered. Apparently, that was not the case.

Taking stock of his appearance, her own unfortunate response to his nearness became secondary to the greater concern of his current wellbeing. His pallor was markedly wan and, while he appeared stronger than he had even earlier that day, she couldn't help but feel it was far too soon for him to be up and around. "I think, perhaps, Mr. Mason should rest. I know Madame Zula will be here shortly, but you are recovering, sir—"

"I'm not an invalid, Miss Masters," he snapped. "Though I daresay, given your general distrust of all men, you'd prefer it if I were. I'm perfectly fine to remain here while Madame Zula is questioned."

Her face flamed at his response, but she nodded her acquiescence. "Certainly, Mr. Mason. Forgive me for suggesting that being shot and suffering a debilitating head wound that could well have ended your life as reasons for taking extra precaution with your health." Her tone was all that was conciliatory, even if her words held a sting.

"I'm perfectly fine," he replied. "Thank you for your... *concern*."

"About the attackers, Miss Masters," Adler redirected, "can you recall anything about them? Height, weight, hair color, any scars or distinctive markings?"

"One of them smelled rather like fish," she answered. "I can only assume that, perhaps, he lives near a fish market or near the water."

"Or that he's a fisherman by day and a would-be criminal by night," Mr. Mason added. "I recall it as well now that you mention it. As for their appearance, the fog was too dense to make out much beyond their general shape and size. The only one I can describe is the larger fellow seen earlier in the day. His size alone should set him apart from everyone else. He was nearly a head taller than I am and had me in weight by at least three or four stone. What happened to the dead man?"

"Dead man?" Adler queried. "You killed one of the attackers?"

"No," Mr. Mason explained. "I struck him and he was left unconscious. The leader of this little band of miscreants then shot him rather than carry him away. I imagine it was the most expedient method of ensuring he wouldn't be able to offer up information that would identify them or their employer."

"This employer," Adler queried, "what precisely was said about him or her?"

"Nothing of any note," Mason replied. "I overheard them speaking. One of the men, the man who was killed in fact, struck Miss Masters and the man who eventually shot him responded that they would not be paid as well if she were to be marked in any way. The largest of the men, the one who knocked me on my... who knocked me senseless, stated that he didn't know who their employer was. He said that he didn't know where the women were taken, that 'he never tells us where he takes them'. I'm assuming by that he meant their de facto leader, but it could have been their actual employer he referred to. I simply don't know. Of course, it also highlights the disturbing reality that my sister is not their only victim."

Adler made more notes in his little journal. He paused, tapped his pencil on the book thoughtfully for a moment, scribbled more and then, as if remembering he wasn't alone, looked up. "I'll speak to the watch and see what, if anything, they know of the dead man. If they found him, perhaps they've identified him and we can use that information to track his known accomplices." Before he could say anything further, a knock sounded at the library door.

The butler entered, his nose high and his back straight. "There is a Madame Zula to see you, Lady Vale. She informed me that she is expected."

Elizabeth noted the censure in Calvert's voice. No doubt, this would all be delivered in a letter, posthaste, to Mr. Middlethorp.

"Thank you, Calvert," Lady Vale said, her voice never giving away her distaste for the man. "Madame Zula is here to be questioned regarding the attack on Miss Masters two nights ago in which dear Mr. Mason was injured. Please show her in and then have tea served here in the library. That will be all."

Elizabeth looked once more in Mr. Mason's direction. At that precise moment, he was also looking at her. Their gazes locked and something flashed between them beyond simply their shared belief that Madame Zula was a fraud. There was an awareness, a frisson of, if she had to put a name to it, attraction. It was, in short, the exact moment of her downfall.

Chapter Ten

MADAME ZULA ENTERED the library with the same degree of theatricality she utilized in the salons hosted in her home. Draped from head to toe in rich wine-colored satin, a matching turban perched upon her head, she looked like an exotic bird. She was not as young as she appeared at first glance. As she stepped into the room, the light from the window shone directly on her face and revealed faint lines that marked her far closer to Lady Vale's age than to Miss Masters'. She paused as she neared Benedict, lifted one hand to her head as if she felt faint or weak, and turned toward Lady Vale. "It's as I said it would be. He is returned to you."

Benedict didn't roll his eyes, but the urge to do so was quite intense. "I am not returned anywhere, madame. I am here to recuperate and then continue the search for my sister. We have questions that pertain very much to the here and now rather than whatever metaphysical realm you are currently inhabiting."

Madame Zula laughed then. "My dear sir, Mr. Mason, I believe your name is… you and Miss Masters are quite peas in the pod it would seem. Neither of you is at all shy in expressing your somewhat ill-informed and certainly premature opinions of my abilities."

Benedict said nothing more on the matter, but waited for her to take her seat and finish the grand production that was her entrance. Given her age, it was likely that she was a retired actress. As most actresses supplemented their income by taking protectors, he had no doubt that she had learned the value of information over the years. She was simply acquiring it in a different fashion now. "My sister came to see you," he began, after she finally took a seat, perching on the edge of the settee like she was royalty. "I want to know what was said to her and I want to know where she intended to go after leaving your establishment."

"As Mr. Mason is asking pertinent questions, I'll ask you to go ahead and answer them," Adler followed up. "But I've a few of my own when he's done."

Madame Zula inclined her head in a regal manner. "Your sister, Mr. Mason, came to me to ask about her family… her true family, those to whom she was born and not those cruel individuals who reared her. But you are well aware of that, already, are you not?"

Benedict nodded his response. She was cagey and far too clever. Anything he said would be twisted by her or used to supplement what she was telling them already.

"You have grown taciturn rather suddenly, haven't you?" Madame Zula asked. "But I understand your reluctance to speak… when you fear that I will twist and use your words to my own advantage. And I may. I'll not deny that part of my gift is knowing how to read people, how to take what they've told me both with their words and their gestures. The body speaks, you know? It tells the truth even when our lips do not. For example, Miss Masters is quite concerned for you right now. But you are somewhat of an enigma to her. She keeps her face averted from you, but her eyes seek you constantly, and her body is turned toward you, perhaps because she fears you may require assistance?"

"You're changing the subject, Madame Zula," Adler pointed out. "Miss Masters is not the subject of conversation at this time. Miss Mason is. You will answer the questions about Mr. Mason's sister, if you please. What was the date when she came to see you?"

The woman waved her gloved hand. Immediately, the manservant who had accompanied her bustled forward, retrieving a leather-bound book from inside his waistcoat. As he passed the book to her, their hands brushed in a manner that was not at all like servant and employer. Benedict glanced at Adler to see if he had noted it and was pleased to see that he had. The investigator was watching the pair with a speculative gleam in his narrowed eyes.

"What day was it when we saw Miss Mason, Dylan?" Her tone was cool, completely unruffled.

"It was precisely one week ago today, Madame Zula," the servant answered.

Madame Zula then opened the book and flipped back the pre-scribed number of days to her notes. "She had booked a private appointment at eight in the evening on the fourteenth. She stayed for three quarters of an hour and then left promptly at a quarter till… and it appears, as she was leaving, I had a vision about her."

"Yes, madame," the manservant, Dylan, said. "You sent me out after her. It was too late, however. When I opened the door, the street was empty and there was no sign of her save for a ribbon that had fallen at the base of the steps."

Madame Zula opened her hand, and the man immediately pro-duced a small pouch from the other side of his waistcoat. He did not touch the contents, but opened it and allowed the length of violet ribbon to fall into the woman's outstretched hand.

Benedict said nothing, but the sight of that ribbon broke his heart. He'd given it to her because the color perfectly matched her eyes. He'd promised to have a new gown made for her to match as soon as she returned from Bath. As he looked on, Madame Zula made a great show of removing her glove and placing the ribbon on her bare skin. Immediately, her eyes closed and when she spoke, her voice had dropped so that it sounded as if coming from a great distance away.

"She is in a dark place, your sister. The walls are cold and damp. There is a man with her… he has not harmed her. Not yet. For now, he is simply a voice in the darkness, one that taunts and teases cruelly. They are saving her for something later, for a grand ritual it would seem."

"If you've finished your little jaunt into the spirit world," Adler commented, unmoved by Madame Zula's performance, "I'll thank you to address the questions we've asked. How many times did Miss

Mason come to your home in total?"

Madame Zula drew herself up, shoulders back and chin tilted at a haughty angle. "She came to my establishment on only two separate occasions. The first was to schedule her appointment and the second was the night she disappeared."

"I see," Adler nodded. "And how was it that Miss Mason came to be aware of you and your questionable talents?"

Madame Zula blinked at him for a moment. Then a smile spread across her face. "Well, I couldn't possibly say, sir."

"Is that typical? You have no concerns about how a client might have been referred to you? You don't want to thank your existing clients for the recommendation or be certain that the person coming into your abode is not a thief or, worse perhaps, someone intent upon exposing you as a charlatan? I find that curious, Madame Zula," Adler replied. "I have never taken on a client without at least posing the question of how they came to have my name."

Madame Zula waved her hand dismissively. "I am not limited by such pedestrian methods of garnering knowledge of the character and intentions of a person, Mr. Adler. I had a sense immediately that Miss Mason was most sincere in her quest for information through unorthodox means."

"Is that why you found it so inconvenient when I scheduled an appointment for myself that was, in fact, for Lady Vale?" Miss Masters interjected. "It clearly caught you by surprise."

Madame Zula's smile tightened, taking on a hostile and almost feral appearance. "Miss Masters, I cannot be attuned to everything. It would be utterly exhausting. I'd like to point out that I have been all that is cooperative and helpful. If you wish to interrogate me as you would a criminal then by all means bring charges and have me arrested… oh, but you have no reason to, do you? You have nothing but ugly suspicions and conjecture."

"How many women have gone missing from outside your home, Madame Zula?" Adler inserted himself into the conversation again, drawing her ire in his direction instead. "Two abductions, one successful and one foiled, inside of a week... those are poor odds, Madame Zula. I'm sure it will take very little effort on my part to uncover the truth. It might be best if you simply tell us now."

Madame Zula did not answer the investigator but, instead, turned to Benedict with beseeching eyes, as if she were truly invested in the welfare and safe return of Mary. "If you want to find your sister before it is too late, before her life has been wrecked beyond repair, you will heed me!" Madame Zula snapped. "She is being held against her will. She was taken... as other girls have been. The others were younger, not of quality, but if you ask you will be able to find who they were easily enough. Maids, governesses, companions... they go missing and people make assumptions that they've run off with beaus or eloped with an unsuitable man. But your sister had no reason to run off. She never intends to marry and you are perfectly aware of why!"

Those words cut Benedict to the bone, reminding him of his failures, reminding him of the things Mary had suffered that he had been spared. "You are a fraud!" The words were hollow, lacking his earlier conviction.

"She is alive and if you heed me, you will find her. All of this is connected—all of it—to the night you disappeared, the night you were taken from Lady Vale as a small boy." She turned toward Lady Vale then, her expression and speech imploring, "If you find the book, Lady Vale, you will find the man who has his sister. There is one villain behind it all."

"This is utter foolishness," Adler insisted, tossing his hands up.

"I concur," Benedict said. "If you've nothing constructive to offer, Madame—"

Lady Vale had sunk onto the settee beside Elizabeth at the mention of the book. Her face was pale and she appeared quite shaken. "The book?" She looked up, her gaze falling upon Benedict imploringly.

"Yes," Madame Zula said. "The one his abductors were looking for the night they came and stole your Benedict away. They wanted your husband's book... the one where he kept all of the secrets he bartered.

The information you need to identify the villain in both crimes, his abduction and now the abductions of these poor girls, it's hidden there. I promise you."

"You are being intentionally provocative in an attempt to sway her to your side," Benedict accused. "I've no doubt that an endorsement from someone of Lady Vale's social cache would cement your position in society here quite well, Madame Zula."

"I've no need of her social support, Mr. Mason. People will always require answers that cannot be found through traditional methods… I speak nothing but the truth here, whether you choose to accept it or not," Madame Zula insisted. "I can see things… and those things haunt me. Yes, I've learned how to support myself by using this ability that is both gift and curse. But I'd like to point out, Mr. Mason, that you used your own somewhat unorthodox skills in order to support yourself and your sister. Yes, I know about the gaming hell you run, I know that you won it in a card game and I know that there were many who questioned whether or not the game was won honestly!"

Benedict's eyes narrowed in quiet fury. "I won that game honestly. I'll be happy to meet anyone who says differently on the field of honor."

"But you're not a gentleman and so no one who is a peer or gentry would ever deign to challenge you," Miss Masters said. "They would consider it beneath them."

That stopped him cold—in part, because it was true and, in part, because he needed to know if that was her opinion of him. "Is that how you see me, Miss Masters? Beneath your exalted status as a companion?"

She blanched. "Not at all. I was merely pointing out that the rules of society, as they are, would make it unlikely for any gentleman to acknowledge you that way, not that they were justified in doing so! There is nothing exalted about my current station, Mr. Mason, as you well know."

Benedict turned back to Madame Zula. "Tell me something now that you could not have gleaned from gossip or that is more than just conjecture."

Madame Zula held out her hand to him. He accepted the challenge and placed his hand in hers. She turned it over, pressed her palm to his and closed her eyes. Her head dropped back and she sighed deeply. After a moment of low moans and whispered words that were completely unintelligible, she lifted her head again and gazed directly at him. "I know why you left the north."

"There are still traces of my upbringing in my speech. It would be easy enough for you to guess," he dismissed.

"Berwick. I know why you left Berwick, Mr. Mason. I know what you did," she whispered, her voice too soft for anyone but him to hear.

Benedict felt the blood drain from his face. The room swayed. Rather than see himself sprawled on the floor, he reached backward and found a chair. Lowering himself into it, he stared at her with dawning horror. He didn't know if she was telling the truth. What he did know was that regardless of how she'd garnered the information, he'd called her bluff and lost. She had the power to destroy him entirely.

ELIZABETH WATCHED HIM and knew the exact moment that Madame Zula uttered some truth that altered his stance regarding her. Whether he believed in her abilities or not, she had clearly said something that irrevocably altered the dynamic between them. Whatever else he was hiding from them, his response to the mystic was completely genuine. Gone were the confidence and the hint of swagger that, even near death, he could not keep at bay. "Madame Zula, what is this book and where can we find it?"

Madame Zula sat back, all hints of mysticism gone, and her accent once again taking on the curious hint of Cornwall. "I believe, Miss Masters, that you will find it in London… but not in the home that Lord Vale once occupied. I imagine it would be at a place where he felt equally comfortable."

"The home he kept for his mistresses," Lady Vale surmised. "He was there far more frequently. It would make sense. I will write to Branson and have him go there. Perhaps he can locate it."

Elizabeth frowned. "The house is unoccupied then?"

"Branson is a single man with no attachments and no wife to question him. He's no need to utilize that house." Lady Vale's reply was clipped and while her tone wasn't sharp, precisely, it clearly indicated that she found the subject matter distasteful. "It has been unoccupied since before my husband's death. His last mistress was a woman with a home of her own... or her husband's, I suppose I should say. They did not bother attempting discretion throughout the course of their affair, even at its disgraceful end."

Elizabeth sighed. "So what should we do now?"

Adler rose. "I'll go and speak to some members of the watch. If the body was discovered, we may have some information to work with. If they came back and removed it, and if they were smart, they would have, then we're very much back to our starting point. I'll bid you good day, Miss Masters, Mr. Mason, and you Lady Vale."

Elizabeth watched Mr. Adler leave and noted how cool he'd been to Mr. Mason. Whether it was because he had little belief in Lady Vale's assertion that Mr. Mason was her long lost son or because he was simply erring on the side of caution, she could not say. Regardless, she found herself unaccountably curious as to what it was that Madame Zula had whispered to him. Clearly, whatever she'd said had set him back on his heels. She would find out, Elizabeth vowed, even if it meant bearding the lion in his den so to speak.

A soft knock at the door interrupted them and a footman entered with the tea tray.

"I am too overset, Miss Masters. Will you pour?" Lady Vale asked.

Taking a deep breath to steady her own nerves, Elizabeth replied, "Certainly, my lady." Once the tea was poured, the pot and cups bobbled only once or twice, Elizabeth seated herself once more and surveyed Madame Zula cautiously.

"You said other young women had gone missing. Were these

other young women also abducted or vanished outside your home?"

Madame Zula arched one eyebrow. "Are you accusing me of something, Miss Masters?"

"No, Madame Zula. But your stock in trade is knowing what others cannot. It would stand to reason that you would know, then, what is going on right outside your front door," Elizabeth pointed out. She kept her tone intentionally light and non-accusatory despite the inflammatory nature of her words.

"I deal primarily with the dead, Miss Masters, not the missing. If someone from the other side wishes to guide me or offer insight, I gladly take it," the woman answered flatly. "I see many things. It is often difficult to understand their significance until it is too late to do anything about them. I have been all that is cooperative in assisting you here, and I shall continue to be. But I will not be accused of anything so villainous as having a hand in the abduction of young women."

Elizabeth inclined her head in both acknowledgement and a less than sincere apology. "Certainly, Madame Zula. I meant no offense. I was only seeking clarification of your earlier statements. How many women total have vanished?"

"I am sure I don't know," the woman said. "So many things are hidden, Miss Masters, even from one who sees with more than just the eyes."

"You were forewarned by those spirits you mentioned about Miss Mason's abduction... but too late to intervene on her behalf. And when those men attempted to abduct me, did you receive a similar warning?" Elizabeth continued.

"This interrogation has grown wearisome, Miss Masters." Madame Zula rose. "I must return home. I have an appointment this evening that I must prepare for. Remember what I told you the other night, Miss Masters. It is up to you to find the courage to change your fate and seize the future that is yours by right of destiny. Do not let fear and the censure of others sway you from it."

Madame Zula left and Lady Vale shook her head. "What a curious woman. I still do not quite know what to make of her. I want so desperately to believe that she speaks the truth and, yet, I find myself growing more and more doubtful. Did she upset you very much, Benedict dear?"

"Not at all, Lady Vale," he said, and stood up from his chair. His face was still unaccountably pale and he appeared quite shaken. "But I find myself quite tired. With your permission, I will retire."

"Certainly, my dear. This has been too much for you so soon after your injury! Miss Masters, please get the footmen to escort him to his chamber. Those stairs are treacherous in your current state," Lady Vale said worriedly.

"I will escort him myself, Lady Vale," Elizabeth offered. It was the perfect opportunity to question him further, she decided.

With an arched look, Mr. Mason replied, "Your concern is both welcome and surprising, Miss Masters. I'll be glad of your company."

Placing her tea cup on the tray once more, Elizabeth rose. "Come along then. Let's see you to your room that you might rest and further recuperate."

As they passed through the doorway to the library and moved on toward the stairs, Elizabeth noted Calvert watching them from the foyer. His disapproving glance was unsurprising. He would make trouble for Lady Vale and that, in turn, would make trouble for her.

"Tell me, Mr. Mason," she said as they neared his chamber door. "What did Madame Zula say to upset you so?"

"Other than her nonsense about my sister being held in a dark place by an unseen man?" he fired back.

Elizabeth smiled at his attempt to deflect her. "I have the distinct feeling that what Madame Zula said to you was not about your sister at all. It was rather personal and pointed. She cannot be trusted."

"On that point, Miss Masters," he said, "we are in total agreement."

ZELLA PATTED THE seat beside her and Dylan, her young and beautiful lover, immediately crossed the rocking expanse of the carriage to sit next to her. "We must vacate the city, Dylan. It is too dangerous to remain here. He'll be angry, but he'll be even angrier if we remain here and endanger the entire operation."

He frowned. "You said yourself that our obligation to him has not been fulfilled... even with the tavern girl I took to Fenton, it will not be enough!"

"We will fulfill our obligation... but not from Bath. The failed attempt to abduct Miss Masters has created an unfortunate series of difficulties that there is simply no recovering from," she insisted. "We will head to Liverpool next, I think. It's far enough away to avoid Lady Vale and her dogged investigator, but near enough that we'll still be able to deliver all he requires."

Dylan kissed her then, passionately and with all the ardor and devotion he felt for her. It mattered little that she was twenty years his senior and that to the outer world he would never be viewed as anything more than either her servant or accomplice. He adored her and had since he had been little more than a boy. There were those who would say she had used him, exploited his youth and naivety. They would be correct, but that did not alter the fact that her love for him was quite genuine. She touched his face, marveling at the silken texture of his still smooth skin. How could she not love someone as beautiful as her Black Irish boy? There was nothing he wouldn't do for her.

"I shall make the arrangements at once," he offered. "We'll move under cover of darkness and they will never be the wiser. What did you see when you held his hand, my love?"

Madame Zula's eyes shuttered. "I saw nothing, Dylan. How dear you are to still believe in my gift when it has failed me so miserably in these last years!" She'd sacrificed it, she thought, offered it up like those poor young women were. Oh, there was the occasional flash of insight, the skills of reading palms and cards remained, but the clarity of vision she'd enjoyed in her youth was missing.

"All of that information was gleaned from what Miss Mason uttered in confidence during her session. When she spoke of her adoptive brother, I should have paid more heed. He is a dangerous man, Dylan. One who will not hesitate to do whatever is necessary to protect his sister. I wish I had seen that when reading Mary Mason's palm. I was too blinded by her desperation to find the family she lost to see the dangers presented by the family she currently has. We've overstayed our welcome in Bath. The sooner we depart the safer we'll be... I can only hope by setting them on the path of that damnable book he was after all those years ago, we can have the distraction we need to get away from the city safely."

Chapter Eleven

B ENEDICT CLIMBED THE stairs slowly, Miss Masters at his side. He was acutely aware of her, of her suspicions and her utter lack of trust in him. But it was her scent that teased and tormented him the most in that moment. She smelled faintly of lilies. It was her soap, he supposed, as he doubted she'd be one to indulge in such fripperies as perfume. As he had no notion of what the going rate was for a companion's salary, he couldn't even say that she might have afforded to indulge such a whim even had she been inclined. That sparked a moment of sympathy along with the urge to offer her all the things she could not afford for herself. It would be a disaster and such an offer would likely be tossed back in his face, regardless.

"You are quite fiercely protective of Lady Vale and yet I feel she is not so fond of you as you are of her," he observed. It was simply a way of breaking the silence between them, and also of stirring the antagonism that existed between them. He had no wish to indulge tender or sympathetic feelings toward her and stirring that particular hornet's nest would, no doubt, see them well at odds.

Miss Masters halted and faced him. "Lady Vale is sometimes resentful of the fact that her brother-in-law, as a condition of allowing her to maintain a separate household, requires her to have a companion of his choosing. I have tried to make my presence here of as little discomfort to Lady Vale as possible. But in these situations—"

He leaned against the doorframe and crossed his arms over his chest. "You mean situations where she brings some stranger into her home and identifies him as her long lost son? You must admit, Miss

Masters, your loyalty aside, that it's quite mad."

He'd said it precisely to get a rise from her and it worked. She prickled instantly—shoulders squared, chin inched upward, eyes narrowed. Oh, yes. He'd succeeded admirably in setting her off. If he'd wanted to ensure that they remain at odds, he'd done so admirably.

"Mr. Mason, you will not speak of Lady Vale in that manner. Neither of us can possibly imagine what she has suffered and for you to make light of it—"

"I make light of nothing," he corrected her. "At this moment, the only person in this world I give two damns about is missing... and if that odd bird in her bright plumage is to be believed, she's in grave danger." Benedict had just enough space between himself and the whispered words of Madame Zula to once again find his footing. It wasn't second sight that had told her that. He didn't believe that for a minute. No doubt, Mary had said something to her when meeting with the woman. The only information she'd truly offered had been the name of the village. Everything else had been vague and shrouded in carefully articulated mystery.

"Mr. Mason," Miss Masters began, "I will thank you to tread carefully. Lady Vale is—"

"Mad," he insisted. The woman was chasing ghosts. "She's utterly mad. I am not her son... we both know it. And in her heart, I've no doubt she does as well!"

"How dare you speak of her so!" Miss Masters hissed. "She has been all that is kind to you... she brought you into this house, obtained the best of doctors for you, and is offering every resource at her disposal to help you locate your sister! And you thank her by offering such uncharitable conjecture about her mental status?"

"I dare because the truth needs to be stated, Miss Masters—Elizabeth!"

She drew herself up in a fit of righteous indignation. Unfortunately for him, her sharply indrawn breath and stiffened shoulders only managed to thrust her rather impressive bosom forward and draw his eye.

"You do not have leave to use my given name, *Mr. Mason!*" she snapped. "We are not friends or compatriots. You are here because I owe you a debt. But if there is even a hint that you mean to use Lady Vale's grief against her in some way—"

He'd wanted distance. He'd wanted to put them at odds. He had not accounted for her ability to get under his skin as much as he got under hers. Benedict cursed himself for a fool even as he grasped her wrist and pulled her to him. Her breasts were crushed against his chest and their mouths were scant inches apart. Her eyes widened, her cheeks flamed, and their eyes met. It was all sparks and shooting flames, like the fireworks he'd witnessed as a boy in a distant memory. But even as she looked at him, her cheeks pink with anger, her breasts heaving with short angry breaths, she did not pull away.

"Aren't you tired of being indignant all the time?" he queried. "Can't you envision a better use for your lovely lips than dressing me down yet again?"

"I don't know what you... that is... unhand me, Mr. Mason. This very instant!" she stammered. But as her hands came up to push against his chest, for a moment, she didn't push him back. Instead, her fingers sank into the firmness of his flesh, seeking and hungry.

"I will... when I'm ready," he said. "And I'm not ready quite yet."

The kiss had been intended to teach her a lesson, to put her in her place. The moment their lips touched and he felt the softness of her lips beneath his—tasted the essence that was simply her—all thoughts of anything but the kiss itself fled. It took on a life of its own. His mouth moved over hers and, heaven help him, her lips moved in kind. Pressing against him, testing the contours and firmness of one another's flesh. It was not a deep kiss, merely a touching of lips. It was no less carnal for it. That simple touch incited his lust like nothing else ever had. That she had responded so readily, so fully, and had kissed him in return with the same degree of ardor was telling. Whoever Miss Masters had been in her previous life, she was not the untutored innocent that some might suspect. When at last the kiss broke, he drew back from her and met her gaze.

There was no fear in her. There wasn't even any anger or maidenly offense. And she wasn't shocked. What Benedict saw in her gaze was awareness and anticipation of what would come next. It only confirmed his belief that she had known a man's touch before. There was a wanton inside her, a creature of passion and unmatched desires, regardless of whatever drab mask she put on.

"I'd ask if I offended your maidenly sensibilities," he said. "But much to my great pleasure, it appears you have none."

THOSE WORDS STRUCK her as surely as a physical blow would have. How many years had she struggled to put her hedonistic ways behind her? And all for naught. With nothing more than a touch, he'd reawakened that part of her she'd battled in dormancy.

Elizabeth stepped back. He let her go easily, without protest or reservation. If his fingertips lingered too long, if the soft movement of them over her skin as she retreated hinted at reluctance, he did not show it in any other way.

It had been ages since any man had kissed her. Certainly, it had been ages since any man had truly looked at her beyond the shabby disguise of her plain dresses and hair. That he saw through all of it, that he saw her, did not aid her in remaining unmoved by him. But it was the kiss that was her undoing. Every shred of passion that she'd tamped down, all the yearning and regret that filled her seemed to have come to a head in that one moment.

She wanted nothing more than to throw herself at him, to beg him to touch her again, to kiss her again, to make her feel whole again. But she did none of those things. Instead, she smoothed her skirts and her hair as she struggled to regain her composure.

"If you were seeking to cool my ardor, Mr. Mason, making such wild speculations about my lack of virtue is certainly one way to do so," she said softly.

"It was not intended as an insult, Miss Masters," he said. While his tone was not at all apologetic, it was still markedly sincere. "On the contrary… it may surprise you to know that I hold shockingly egalitarian views on carnal relations. If a man has the right to take his pleasure, why should a woman not as well?"

She laughed at that, but it was not a sound of humor or amusement. It was bitter and cold, and far more telling than she would have liked. "Then you are, indeed, a rare man, Mr. Mason. Nonetheless, you have effectively reminded me that my behavior is not as it should be… I will strive to rectify that by taking my leave of you now."

"Don't go," he said. "Not like this."

"And why should I stay? You, sir, are in no condition to engage in whatever it is you believe was about to happen between us."

"I had thought to kiss you again, and to talk with you," he said. "We do not have to be enemies. I have no designs on the title or your mistress' fortune. I only want her help to find Mary and then I will be gone."

"And that, Mr. Mason," Elizabeth said firmly, "is all the reason I need to keep my distance. I won't be any man's diversion… not again."

He started to speak, to urge her to change her mind. It was clearly written in his expression. In a rare stroke of luck, a door opened further down the corridor and a wide-eyed maid emerged, gaping at them both as though they were pugilists ready to do battle.

Taking her cue from the maid's behavior, Elizabeth perpetuated the charade that they were ready to tear out one another's throats rather than simply rip away one another's clothes. "This has been a trying day, Mr. Mason. We've allowed our tempers to get the better of us. Excuse me, please. I am quite tired and think I will retire for a bit before dinner." If her voice trembled and her words came out slightly breathlessly, well, it was hardly worth noting, she reasoned. The maid disappeared down the hall, scurrying away like a scared rat.

"I kissed you for all the wrong reasons," he said. "The next time I kiss you, it will be for the right ones."

"There will not be a next time, Mr. Mason," she vowed.

He smiled. "Of course there will. We both know that. Good evening, Miss Masters. I'll take my supper in my rooms so you can take comfort in the lies you'll be telling yourself about that… at least for a little while."

Elizabeth was not foolish enough to argue the point. She understood the importance of a strategic retreat. Turning on her heel, she didn't exactly flee, but her steps were much quicker than she would have liked. She wasn't running from him, but from her own reckless nature, the very one she'd been fighting against since coming to Bath.

BRANSON MIDDLETHORP POURED himself a snifter of brandy from the decanter on his desk. He was bone tired and wearier than he'd been in ages. It wasn't physical exhaustion, but ennui. He had little in his life to provide respite, to provide any semblance of joy.

The house was empty save for servants. With no wife and no children of his own, the void in his life was becoming more and more acute. But he'd had his reasons for refusing to marry. Those reasons stood, even twenty some years on. He'd vowed that there was only one woman who could tempt him to the altar. Sarah had been the love of his life, always unrequited and always from afar. He'd never had the courage to confess his feelings for her. After what his worthless brother had put her through and after all that she had suffered at the hands of his family, any hope in that direction was futile.

Reaching for the stack of correspondence balanced on the edge of the desk, he skimmed through them. His secretary could have done it the following day, but as he had little else to occupy his mind, there was no point in delaying it. Halfway through the stack he paused. One of the letters was marked Bath. For a moment, he let himself entertain the notion that it might be from her, but then he dismissed it. He knew her hand as well as his own and the scrawled letters on the parchment were nothing like the elegant script she favored. It had been twenty-nine years since he'd first laid eyes upon her, twenty-nine years since he'd fallen hopelessly in love with the woman who was betrothed to his own brother. And still, he could not entirely give up on hope. Who would have thought that underneath his gruff exterior, that lurking behind the mask he showed to the world and the horrible things he had done in the name of king and country, beat the heart of a romantic?

Shaking his head, Middlethorp exorcised those thoughts. They were a pointless waste of his time. Besides, he'd already heard from her once in the past week. Short, stilted and filled with thinly veiled hostility, it highlighted that nothing between them had changed and reinforced his belief that it likely never would.

The brief note that had arrived from her only the day before would likely be the last he would hear from her for months. Her simple missive to inform him of the attack on Miss Masters and their subsequent hospitality to her injured rescuer had been curt to the point of rudeness. She despised him because she believed he was cut from the same cloth as his brother had been. Knowing just how cruel his brother could be, he could only imagine what she had suffered at his hands during their marriage.

Forcing himself to put such disturbing thoughts far from his mind, Branson looked back at the piece of parchment and sighed. Calvert, he thought. It would be one of his many spies, as she called them. He'd long since given up taking offense to the sentiment. There was truth in it, after all. He did set spies on her, but it was only for her own protection because her pain and desperation at the loss of her son made her vulnerable. Protecting Sarah, Lady Vale, the widow of his late brother, had been his sworn duty since the day his brother passed, even if she disliked his methods.

The Honorable Mr. Branson Middlethorp, Esquire

Mr. Middlethorp,

Forgive me for writing in such a hurried manner, but I felt it impera-tive that I inform you at once of her ladyship's latest escapade. She and her companion have brought home some gentleman—and I as-

sure you, sir, that I fear he is anything but—whom they claim rescued them from footpads outside the establishment of a mystic whom her ladyship chose to visit against my advice.

The gentleman has been shot and has been treated by her ladyship's personal physicians. On the surface, it would appear to be nothing more than charity and perhaps a sense of obligation, as he was injured while protecting them. But the gentleman is of an age and of a certain physical description, possessing both light-colored eyes and blond hair, that lends me to believe her ladyship may harbor suspicions about the young man's identity that would be harmful to her.

Your loyal servant,
Calvert

Branson read through the missive once more before cursing and tossing the balled up piece of paper toward the hearth. It was difficult to fault Sarah for her obsession with her lost son. He had no inkling of what she must feel. It had been supremely painful for him to have lost the boy, as he'd doted on his only nephew. But it was hardly the same thing. Still, it did leave her vulnerable to any number of schemes and confidence games. Grief made one an easy target. There was nothing he would not do to protect her and spare her more pain and agony— even if it further cemented her hostility toward him. That had been his primary reason for insisting that she have a companion who reported to him about her continued search for Benedict.

Miss Masters' primary responsibility in her current position was to keep Sarah from bringing home any stray who claimed to be Benedict. But under the circumstances, if they truly had been set upon by common thieves and the man injured while protecting them, they could hardly have left him to bleed to death in the street.

Rising to his feet, he rang for the butler. When Toombs entered, he looked at the man levelly and, without any hint of the excitement he felt at the prospect of seeing her, he said, "Inform my valet to pack a bag for me and the driver to have the coach readied at dawn. I leave for Bath at the break of day."

"Certainly, sir," Toombs said with aplomb before sketching a bow and backing from the room.

He would get to the bottom of this and see to it that she was safe. If it meant he would get to bask in her presence for a few days, that was no one's business but his own.

Chapter Twelve

M ARY HAD DONE everything she could think of to pass the time. She'd recited passages of Shakespeare in her mind, she'd sang songs to fill the vast emptiness of her current cell, she'd paced, counting the steps to calculate the size of her enclosure. All the while, she'd been planning.

It had been days since she'd been brought there. There had been another room before, smaller and dingy in the dim light, but no doubt still far superior to her current accommodations. But her memory of it was fuzzy and indistinct. No doubt, she decided, she had been heavily drugged while being held there.

She'd been giving it a great deal of thought and could only surmise that, in the first instance, they'd been in a city where there were neighbors or someone to overhear if she were to shout for help. Now, isolated and no doubt far into the countryside, her captors no longer felt the need to take such measures. The countryside posed greater risk. There would be fewer people to offer aid even if she did manage to get away. There were wolves still in the woods and wild dogs. If she wandered onto an estate, it was possible she'd be mistaken for a poacher and shot, or fall into a poacher's trap. Even as she enumerated the dangers in her mind, she steeled her resolve.

She would take those risks gladly rather than wait for whatever fate others held in store for her. Staying there—well, she refused to think of what might become of her if she did.

Was Benedict searching for her? He would be, of course. She didn't know what day it was but it stood to reason that it was well beyond the date she had told him that she would return to town. He had always protected her, always taken care of her. But in the last year, he'd also allowed her an inordinate amount of freedom, much more than most females of her acquaintance were blessed with. It was that freedom that had allowed her to begin her search for their true families. Benedict professed not to care, claiming that she was his only family and all that he required. But that wasn't true. She knew of his nightmares and knew that not all of them originated with the callousness and brutality of their adoptive parents.

Would that change when she returned? *If she returned.* Perhaps, she reasoned. He would blame himself, would, as always, take on the responsibility for events that had occurred solely as a result of her own actions. She did not blame herself for the actions of her abductors, but if she'd hired a companion, or taken it upon herself to hire a carriage and not gone off entirely by herself, she might not have been such an easy target.

Memories stirred, flitting through her mind, of the strange conversation with Madame Zula's manservant. He'd been quite insistent that she come alone. Perhaps the entire thing had been planned from the start? Perhaps Madame Zula was the mastermind of the entire thing? A procuress or abbess posing as a mystic would certainly have her pick of foolish young women coming and going from her house.

It hadn't been Madame Zula who had interested her though. She'd gone in because of the other man, the one she saw frequenting the house. He never entered by the front door but always descended the narrow steps to the servants' entrance. After encountering Lady Vale in a shop in London months earlier, she'd immediately noted the shocking similarity to Benedict. It hadn't taken very much digging to uncover the truth about the beautiful but tragic woman. The loss of her son, the posters and rewards still offered for information on the kidnappers. And one of those posters had depicted the very man she'd seen coming and going from the servants' entrance of Madame Zula's home.

A noise in the corridor alerted her. It was the distant opening of a creaking door. Her guard was arriving with the slop that posed as an evening meal.

With only her own mind for company, she'd concocted a plan. He always demanded that she answer him when he called out from the other side of the door so that he could determine her position in the room.

"Where are you, little mouse?" he called out from just beyond the door. She could hear the clinking and shuffling as he balanced the tray of food.

"Please, help me!" she called out, letting her voice quake. It wasn't fear or pain, but anticipation and a healthy dose of nerves. "I was bitten by a rat."

"There are no rats in here," he barked.

There were. She'd heard them. It was where the idea had come from. "There are! I was sleeping and one bit my ankle! It was after you brought breakfast... I can't stand now. The wound is festering."

He cursed and she knew she had him. Another clink had him placing the tray on the floor. The locking mechanism on the door groaned as he turned the key, begging to be oiled.

Sitting on her small cot with its straw ticking, Mary clutched the single weapon that she'd been able to procure. The same loose stone she'd nearly tripped over that morning would perhaps be her salvation.

Light, dim and yellow, from lanterns hanging in the corridor filtered in behind him. He wasn't overly large, no more than average in height. If his silhouette was anything to judge by, he was softer in the middle, likely having a taste for ale and pies.

"Come over here into the light so that I can see," he demanded.

Mary rose, affecting a limp, as she made a great show of struggling toward him. She even allowed herself to fall once and cried out as she picked herself back up. He made no response to her suffering and she imagined that he was a man quite like her adoptive father, that he took joy in the suffering of others.

When she did reach him, she leaned heavily against the wall, panting as much for show as from the exertions she'd taken in her performance.

"Lift your skirts," he demanded.

Intentionally misinterpreting his statement to keep him from guessing her true purpose, Mary feigned indignation. "I am injured, sir! Ill! Surely you would not think to take advantage—"

"So I can see this bloody rat bite, you cabbage brain!" he shouted.

Mary sobbed in mock relief and carefully lifted her skirt to just above her ankle. She'd smeared a great deal of dirt on it earlier to mask the fact that there was no blood or obvious injury. When he stooped in front of her to examine the "wound", she clutched the rock still held in her hand and raised her arm high above her head. She brought the stone crashing down on the back of his head with all the force she could muster. He staggered but did not fall, so she hit him again, this time across his face. She saw blood. Rather than being horrified, she felt a moment of satisfaction. She wanted him to bleed, to suffer.

Lifting her leg, she pressed her foot against his chest and shoved him backwards, far enough to be clear of the door. She rushed through it, but he was not out just yet. He scrambled after her, slower and clumsy. He managed to insert one hand through the door, preventing her from closing it completely. Knowing that he had to be behind it, Mary used it as a weapon, shoving it open with all the strength she had. It connected with a heavy thump and he tumbled backwards. When she closed the door again, there was no impediment. The key was still in the lock so she turned it with a satisfying click and then pocketed it.

She was free. Somehow, her plan, foolhardy and fraught with peril as it had been, had worked.

"Now what?" she muttered aloud in the dim corridor.

IT WAS NEARING midnight when the last of Madame Zula's clients had left for the evening. Removing the turban from her head, she removed the pins from her hair and let the still dark mass tumble over her shoulders. It was like taking off a mask. Madame Zula was no more. She was simply Zella Hopkins, a one-time actress, some-time whore, and a woman who wanted nothing more than to retreat to the countryside of her youth. Or America, she thought. Perhaps across the vast ocean in a land of rebels, she would finally find freedom.

"I'm going up to bed, Dylan. Will you lock up down here and put everything away?" she asked as she rose from her seat at the table. George, the tiny man who remained hidden under the table for most of their sessions had already gone, slipping out the back of the house so as to avoid being seen.

"Of course, my love. I'll take care of everything. Don't I always?" he asked, offering her the same winsome smile that had won her heart.

"That you do, my darling. That you do," she agreed as she made her way toward the stairs. Each one was taken more slowly than the last and by the time she reached the top, she wanted nothing more than to fall into her bed with exhaustion. It wasn't the work, or even her ever advancing age that had worn her down. It was worry. Fear pressed in on her—fear of discovery, fear of the man who held their lives in his hands, the fear that ultimately she would have to pay for all of her many sins.

Entering her chamber, she paused. Even in the darkness, she knew she wasn't alone.

"How did you get in?" She didn't bother to ask who was there. There was only one possible option.

"Oh, my dear Zella, there is nowhere that I cannot go if I desire it. You know that! You've disappointed me greatly," he said, his voice low yet shockingly civil. It was nonetheless menacing for it.

With hands that trembled, Zella moved toward the small table beside her bed and fumbled in the darkness for the tinder box. Once the candles were lit, the dim glow bathed the room and dispersed all but the deepest of shadows. She was reluctant to turn and face him, but it was even more dangerous to keep her back to him. It was a lesson she had learned the hard way.

"It was an oversight. When Miss Masters booked her appointment, we truly thought it was only for her and not for Lady Vale. Had we known she would not be coming alone we would have made other arrangements. I am very sorry. The other girl—"

"The little, low-born, tavern wench? She's fine for a diversion, but my client wants Miss Masters. He asked for her specifically by name. As for Sarah, Lady Vale, that woman has been naught but a nuisance in my life for far too long. You will get Miss Masters. I will not be made a fool of here!"

Zella sank onto the bed. "We will get her. It may take us some time."

"You have until the end of the week," he barked. He then paused and took a breath, so that when he continued, his tone was the same modulated and well-controlled one that allowed him to move through society with no one ever guessing just what a monster he was. "That is when I promised delivery... and I need to make that delivery. I will not disappoint my client! That is unacceptable."

"We made one attempt already! If another attempt to abduct her is carried out, do you not think it will look suspicious?" Zella demanded.

"You are foolish if you think I care. If you go to the noose for it, so be it!"

"I will not go alone," she warned.

It was the wrong thing to say. She recognized it instantly as he sprang from his chair and closed his hand about her throat. "I made a vow to you once, Zella, that I would squeeze your neck until I watched the life fade from your eyes. I can do that tonight and not lose a second's sleep for it... but then what becomes of your pretty Irishman?"

"Leave Dylan out of this!" Zella gasped.

"He left his home country under a bit of scandal I believe... something about a fire?"

She'd known that, of course. He'd been little more than a child then and had made a foolish mistake. It was still an offense that would see him executed if ever brought to trial. "What do you want me to do?"

He smiled coolly at her. "My dear, your pretty Irishman has all the skills necessary. If you want to flush the fox out of the den, then you use smoke… get the whole household outside in the dark of night and it will be easy enough for someone to grab Miss Masters and drag her into an appropriately speedy carriage."

"We'd be identified," she protested.

"As you were planning to leave Bath anyway, it doesn't much matter, does it? What name will you use in your next city… Madame Zoey? Madame Zara? You're running out of alliterations, my dear."

"How did you know we meant to run?"

He chuckled then, a soft but cruel sound. "I can smell your fear. I always could. That's how I knew you had betrayed me, and that's how I keep you in line now. Get her for me, and then go on to Liverpool or wherever else you mean to start procuring other girls for my very demanding clients. But don't think you can hide. There is nowhere you can go that I will not find you."

The bedchamber door opened then and Dylan entered, pistol at the ready. "Unhand her. Now."

"Don't be foolish, boy! You shoot me and it'll be the end of you both," he said, but he let go of her just the same and stepped back. "Besides, my old friend Zella and I have come to an agreement. Haven't we, love?"

Zella nodded her head in agreement. "It's fine, Dylan. Everything is fine, I promise. Put down the gun."

Dylan lowered it to his side, but kept it in hand. "If she says it's fine, then fine it is. But I'll thank you to be taking your leave now. And if you ever again want to speak to her, you can do so in the parlor or the drawing room. You'll not be in her bedchamber ever again."

He laughed. "What a gallant lad you are! Just so you don't forget where everyone ranks in this particular situation, I was in her bed before you were even born. What were you, darling? Fifteen, I believe, or younger still? I will say, you are aging remarkably well… but what a sight you were then. The firmest, lushest breasts I've ever taken to my mouth."

Dylan raised the gun again, but Zella rushed forward. She understood how he worked, how he loved to torment and manipulate the emotions of everyone around him. "Don't let him taunt you this way! Don't. If you shoot him, we both hang. He's only goading you to get to me."

Her young lover looked past her, his gaze flat and hard as it fell on the man who was slowly ruining their lives. "Get out," Dylan said. "I'll not ask you again."

He left then, chuckling all the way down the stairs. When the door closed behind him, Zella sagged against Dylan's chest. "I can't lose you. Please don't ever be so reckless again!"

"He was your lover, wasn't he?" Dylan asked softly.

It had always been an issue between them, that she had been experienced in carnal matters, had, in fact, introduced him to the joys of lovemaking. He often felt insecure in his ability to please her, though the truth was she'd never known pleasure with anyone such as she did with him. She had given him far more than just her body. He was the only man, in all of her life, to whom she'd given her heart.

Zella sank onto the bed. "No," she denied softly. And it was true. He'd had her, he'd taken her, but it had never been anything tender or sensual. It had been about power and control, about the infliction of pain on someone who simply did not have the freedom to fight back.

"He was never that," she continued, telling a story that she despised. "I never wanted him and I certainly never loved him. He bought me, you see... the same way he now sells the girls we provide him with. My own father sold me to him, for enough money to buy some gin. That is what will send me to hell... that I know precisely what awaits those poor women and I do it anyway. I sell them the same way my father sold me."

"You have never willingly partaken of it. We both know that. I've never understood why. What is it that gives him such power over you?" Dylan demanded.

"I was foolish enough to betray him to the late Lord Vale. The man was a blackmailer you see. He kept track of everything in a book." Her breath shuddered out of her, as she let the memories of it all wash through her. "I told him everything I knew about my so-called protector, hoping to buy my freedom. But it didn't work. He knew just as much about Lord Vale's wrongdoings as Lord Vale did about his."

She laughed bitterly. "It was a sad and desperate attempt and it failed fantastically. He knew that I betrayed him—and because of that, he owned me. He said that I would never be free of him and that, for the rest of my life, I would either serve in his bed or help him to obtain other young women to do so. This is my punishment for defying him. To be enslaved to him forever. And now, with all that I've done, the abductions, and even more things I don't dare even tell you for fear you will turn your back on me for good... I would be hanged at Tyburn before the ink on the sentence was dry if he were to but whisper in the right ears."

Dylan stepped forward, but he didn't sit on the bed with her. He dropped to his knees in front of her and clasped her hands in his, pulling them to his chest. "Then let us kill him and be done with it. I can put a pistol ball between his eyes and free us both," Dylan urged.

"It would never work. There are records, Dylan. He's kept a detailed account over the years. If something were to happen to him, that account would be made public. We are stuck, my darling, well and truly. Or at least I am. You could be free of it all... you have but to walk away right now. I would understand. It would not change my feelings for you." It nearly broke her to offer him his freedom that way, to imagine the endless loneliness that would be her constant companion if he were to take that suggestion. She didn't know that she would be able to live without him, but she also knew that she could not condemn him to continue on the same dark and unholy path that was her destiny.

"I'm not leaving you, Zella. Not till the good Lord or the Devil himself sees fit to part us," he vowed. "I'll do what he wants done... I heard him talk about the fire. I'll get Fenton and, in the wee hours, tomorrow night, when everyone will be asleep, we'll do it. They'll all come rushing out to safety. Once the smoke sends them all into the street, he can take Miss Masters and we will be long gone from here."

"Where we could we possibly go?" she cried.

"By the dawn two days hence, my love, you and I will be on the road to Liverpool. But we're not stopping there. Take everything that we can, all the money, and anything we can sell or pawn. We're taking the first ship to America and that bloody toff be damned."

"Do you really think we could outrun him? He has eyes everywhere!" she protested. "He's a man of wealth and power, with an unholy obsession to avenge himself on anyone he thinks has betrayed or wronged him. He would follow us to the ends of the earth."

"Let him then," Dylan stated passionately. How she loved the fire in him!

"America is a different country," he continued.

"There, we are not bound by English law. It's a wild place, filled with wild men and there are places there where the only law that exists is the one you make and enforce with your own guns or your own fists. Let him come."

Zella closed her eyes then and, for the first time in decades, she prayed to a God she'd all but forgotten.

Chapter Thirteen

ELIZABETH ENTERED THE breakfast room the following morning and found herself face to face with Mr. Mason. He was clearly feeling much improved.

"I see you are much recovered," she said coolly.

He inclined his head in greeting and rose to sketch a slight bow. "I am recovered enough to take a meal at a table rather than in my bed like a sickly old man. Is this the normal way of things? For a companion to eat with the family?"

"It is not in most houses," she answered as she took a plate from the sideboard and began to fill it. "But Lady Vale always breakfasts in bed and I am unwelcome in the servants' quarters. They find it unnerving to have one of their 'betters' dining in the kitchen with them. They'd find it equally unnerving to have to serve my meal on a tray in my room as if I were a guest. So a breakfast is laid out, I eat, and whatever is left is taken to the kitchen and garden staff."

His response was not flippant or cold, but thoughtful and clearly heartfelt. "It is difficult for you... living between two worlds. Raised in a genteel manner but working in a position that is still not quite a servant, but far below what your upbringing prepared you for—I am sorry, Elizabeth."

"Miss Masters," she corrected.

"No," he replied. "I will not pretend we are strangers. Not when you have cared for me, not when we have kissed."

Elizabeth gasped and glanced around the room. Thankfully, the footmen were all out in the corridor and no other servants appeared to be lingering at the moment. "Will you kindly not say those things? What if someone heard you?"

"What if they did?" He placed his fork on his plate with enough force that it clattered. "You are a young, unmarried woman and I am a young, unmarried man. People would be more shocked if we're not engaged in a flirtation than if we were!"

"What you are suggesting goes beyond flirtation," she replied. "And I am not that sort. Not anymore."

He frowned at her. "What did he do to you? Did he break your heart, Elizabeth? Did he hurt you physically?"

"He lied. He lied about everything," she answered hotly. "And when he betrothed himself to another woman, he assumed that I'd be happy to exchange my expectations of matrimony for the reality of being his mistress. I declined."

"There is more to it than that," he insisted.

Elizabeth had seated herself at the table but, with the topic of conversation, her appetite had left her entirely. Pushing her plate away, she then threw her hands up. "Fine. If you must know, Freddy was most displeased at what he saw as my rejection of him... he told everyone. The gossip followed me from Hertfordshire to London and back again. It followed me into my first position as a companion and again in my work as a governess. It wasn't until I came to work for Lady Vale who disdains society completely that I have managed to free myself from it."

He settled back in the chair. "He deserved a thrashing if not more."

"Well, he won't get it. He's a lord and my father was not. He was simply a local landowner who made the grave mistake of not holding on to his wealth. Being poor left me with few marital prospects, being foolish left with me even fewer."

"And your family? Did none of them stand for you when this all came to light?" he asked. There was no pity in his tone and a kindness that she had only seen in him that day in the Square.

Elizabeth shrugged. "Why should they have? All that they taught me, every lesson about decorum and morality that they attempted to instill in me, I had tossed away for nothing. My father insisted I leave and, luckily, one of my aunts was kind enough to help me find a position. I haven't spoken with any of my family since."

"Do they not even write you?"

It was a painful admission, made all the more painful by the fact that only a few days earlier her last letter to them had been returned, unopened and refused. "No. They do not. They have made it quite clear that they wish nothing more to do with me. The least that I can do is attempt now to be the dutiful daughter I should have been all along and respect their wishes."

BENEDICT STUDIED HER expression, looking for any crack in the veil she wore. There was none. She believed it, he realized. She was utterly convinced of her own wickedness and the fact that her family was right in disowning her.

"Judgmental prigs," he said.

Her eyes widened at his coarse language. "Mr. Mason!"

"They are," he insisted. "I told you once before, I only look like a gentleman. I learned to speak as one, dress as one, and comport myself as one because it's good for business. It afforded me opportunities to support myself and my sister in a way that would allow us to be comfortable and to have options. But I thank God that I do not now and will never think like them. The lot of them are fools!"

"You only say that because you don't understand—"

He shushed her. "I operate a gaming hell. I assure you, I do understand them. I see them when they come in betting money they don't have, losing land, losing family heirlooms, writing markers for more than all their properties together will earn in a year. They drink, they game, they whore. And then they turn around and do it all again regardless of whatever consequence they've had to face because of it."

She clammed up then, unable to refute what he was saying.

"But you," he continued, "by virtue of being a woman, are allowed not even one mistake… not even one ill thought out and impulsive affair because you believed yourself in love. Am I correct?"

She continued to stare at him wide eyed. "You're only saying things you think I wish to hear. You may describe yourself as egalitarian if you choose, but I cannot believe that anyone is truly that accepting!"

"Then I am very sad for you, indeed, Miss Masters, because it appears that no one has shown you any mercy or understanding in your life. And that is an utter shame."

"I find I am no longer in the mood for breakfast. Excuse me, Mr. Mason. There is some correspondence for Lady Vale that I must see to," she said stiffly as she rose from her chair.

"Don't," he said.

"Don't what?"

"Do not run away from me… do not assume that I am like the people you knew before. There is a connection between us, Miss Masters. It was there from the moment you first barreled into me in the Square. Tell me you do not feel it… I dare you."

"It is nothing more than a simple attraction," she denied. "And whether you are who you claim to be or who Lady Vale believes you to be, there is reason enough on both counts not to indulge in it."

"Because I'm not a gentleman?" Was she as small-minded about such things as the people who pushed her into her currently lowered status?

"No. Because we are barely acquainted and such forward conversations do not serve either of us well. And also because it is quite apparent to me that you are not a man with marriage on his mind, and I am not a woman who can afford to entangle herself with any man who wants less than that," she insisted. "Excuse me, Mr. Mason."

There was a finality in her voice as she said it then, a tone that brooked no argument. Her head was high and her back was completely straight as she walked out of the room. She was right, of course. He did not have marriage on his mind. It was something that he assumed he would do one day as all men did, but he had not yet in his life met a woman who had immediately brought the topic to mind. *Until her.*

He'd heard Mary waxing poetic about love at first sight. The idea that a man and woman might be destined for one another, two halves that would make a whole in anything more than a physical sense, had always seemed silly to him. He found himself less certain of that now. In the face of his immediate connection to her, her ability to alternately arouse and infuriate him, the fact that he seemed to have a nearly identical effect on her—all of that supported the notion that whatever existed between them was something significant, something larger than they themselves were and something that was simply meant to be.

He'd come to Bath to find Mary. It seems all he'd found were other women to vex and drive him mad. Between Lady Vale's delusions, Miss Masters' prickly nature and Mary's foolishness in placing herself in harm's way, he was at his wits' end.

Benedict pushed his own plate back, his appetite gone. He rose slowly, still moving with far less speed than he was accustomed to. His shoulder ached, but the throbbing of the wound that marked it as fevered had finally abated. Within a matter of days, he would be able to once more search for Mary himself. Until that time, he would simply have to remain dependent upon Lady Vale's hired investigators.

Leaving the breakfast room, he prayed fervently for Adler to find something that would lead him to his sister's whereabouts. Until that time, he would just make peace with the current Bedlam he found himself in.

Chapter Fourteen

E LIZABETH HAD STAYED with Lady Vale in the woman's chambers for most of the morning, writing letters and seeing to her normal daily tasks as if their world had not been turned upside down. Lady Vale had taken her daily sojourn to the baths afterward and Elizabeth had pleaded a headache to avoid going.

She didn't want to admit it, but fear played a large part in her reluctance. The events that had occurred outside of Madame Zula's had left her shaken and had reminded her of just how vulnerable she was. Lady Vale had studied her for a moment, concern etching her features, and had then nodded her agreement with an expression of both pity and understanding in her eyes.

Of course, retiring to her room for the afternoon had other benefits, as well. She could continue her intentional avoidance of Mr. Mason. Their charged exchange at breakfast had left her shaken. His very presence was enough to rattle her. When he began espousing ideas that were contrary to everything she'd ever learned about the world and her own place in society—well, it was a bit much to take in.

A soft knock on her door brought Elizabeth out of her reverie. Lady Vale could not have returned so quickly. She had been gone from the house for less than a half-hour which was hardly time enough to get to the Pump Room.

Opening the door, she met the suspicious gaze of Calvert.

"Forgive me, Miss Masters, but I thought perhaps, given Lady Vale's absence from the house at this time, that you should be informed of Mr. Adler's arrival. I have shown him into the library."

The butler was stiff and cold as always, more than just a hint of his disapproval showing in his sour facial expression.

"I see. Has Mr. Mason been informed?" she asked.

Calvert sniffed in disdain. "Not yet, miss. I thought to inform you first. Should I not have?"

"No, Calvert. That is quite all right. I will attend to Mr. Adler immediately. But please do have Mr. Mason fetched to the library. I've no doubt that Mr. Adler has some information that will be of use to him," she said.

"Very well, miss. I will see to it."

As Calvert turned on his heel and disappeared down the hall, Elizabeth took a deep and fortifying breath. She was not prepared for another encounter with Mr. Mason, but she was also very keen to discover what Adler may have found. Had he located Miss Mason? Had he determined what Mr. Mason's origins might be?

Taking just a moment to tidy her hair and brush the creases from her gown, not that it did anything to improve its degree of attractiveness, she left her room and headed for the stairs. Mr. Mason, *Benedict,* was waiting for her at the top.

"It's difficult to be nosy and intrusive while still avoiding me, isn't it?" he asked slyly.

"Must you always be so provoking?" Elizabeth fired back.

"I wouldn't have to provoke if you only stopped repressing your true nature," he replied evenly. "What could be more natural than to be a passionate woman with an inquisitive nature?"

Elizabeth glared at him. "Stop. Stop acting as if there can be something between us when we both know it's impossible!" With that, she turned and marched down the stairs.

"Improbable, I will grant you. But not impossible," he corrected, descending behind her.

Nothing more was said between them as they entered the library to find Mr. Adler awaiting them. He had what appeared to be a valise with him.

Elizabeth noted that Benedict's demeanor changed instantly. "That belongs to my sister."

Adler nodded. "I found the woman she'd been staying with… where her letters had been posted from. What did she tell you brought her to Bath again?"

Benedict's gaze remained locked on the bag as it was clearly a tangible reminder of the fact that his sister was missing. "She stated she wished to visit a friend of hers from school, a woman by the name of Mrs. Simms. She was recently married to a merchant here in Bath."

Adler nodded. "Mrs. Simms was not a friend of your sister's from whatever school you had enrolled her in. There was no Mr. Simms who was a cloth merchant. Rather, Mrs. Simms is a widow who lets rooms to young women that are in the city seeking employment… of which your sister professed to be one," Adler explained.

"How did you find this out?" Benedict asked.

"The posting on the letters. I found the shop near Trim Street where the letters had been posted from. They directed me to Mrs. Simms' house. It's not uncommon for them to see young women of varying degrees of impoverished gentility there, posting letters and asking after positions in local homes as either governesses or companions. Your sister stood out in their memory because she never once asked about a position… only about whether or not Lady Vale was much in society in Bath," Adler explained.

An ugly suspicion was birthed in Elizabeth's mind then. Was Mary Mason even missing? Was this all some elaborate scheme to get Benedict close enough to Lady Vale for them to attempt to carry out their grand confidence game of passing him off as a missing heir? "How on earth would Miss Mason even know who Lady Vale is? More to the point, why would she even care?" Elizabeth asked.

"I'm rather curious about that myself, Mr. Adler," Benedict answered. "My sister and I live comfortably off my income but we do not move in such exalted circles. Even if we did, Mary would have no reason to interact with Lady Vale at all."

Adler opened the valise and removed a simple, leather-bound volume from it. "Your sister's diary… apparently she did not meet

Lady Vale, but had seen her. They were frequenting the same bookshop in London only one month ago when Lady Vale was last there."

Elizabeth recalled that shopping trip. She also recalled that they'd encountered a pretty young woman with blond hair in that shop. She'd taken one look at Lady Vale, her eyes had widened and she'd dropped every item clutched in her hands. That girl, near her own age, had looked at Lady Vale as if seeing a ghost.

Benedict sank down onto one of the nearby chairs. He appeared perplexed and incredibly worried. "It was about that time that Mary's curiosity, I'd even go so far as to say obsession, with finding out where we'd come from—who our true families were—had begun. But, there is still no good reason for her to have lied. I would not have prohibited her from coming to Bath even if that was her motivation."

Adler cocked his head to the side. "You really don't understand how keen the resemblance is between the two of you, do you?"

"No. I honestly do not see it," Benedict said. "Though to be fair, I spend very little time looking at my own face. Beyond my morning shave, I see little point to it. When did Mary seek out Madame Zula? Had she arranged that before leaving London? I don't trust what they said here."

Adler held up his hand. "She wasn't coming here to meet with Madame Zula. I think that was, perhaps, something she did impulsively. She came to Bath solely to gain more information and to observe Lady Vale." Adler passed the small book to him.

"She became obsessed with the notion that you could be the missing heir to the Vale line. She believed it wholeheartedly based on what I read," Adler insisted. "It was that which brought her to Bath."

Guilt flooded him. "It's my fault," he said. "She's been taken and it's because of me that she was put in danger."

"She's in danger because somehow she garnered the attention of a kidnapper," Adler said. "I spoke to some of the neighbors and to Mrs. Simms. They'd all seen that big bloke hanging about there, watching her. No one put any real stock to it until she went missing. Mrs. Simms was on the verge of selling her things to a ragpicker to cover the rent on her room. Lucky I got there when I did."

"Is there anything else that you've discovered, Mr. Adler?" Elizabeth asked. The grim reminder of just how many days his sister had been missing appeared to have taken a toll on Mr. Mason. His expression was dark, his brow furrowed with worry.

"Not much else, miss. But I do have questions for you, Miss Masters—when did you go to Madame Zula's to schedule the appointment?"

"It was on Tuesday," she replied.

Adler nodded. "You scheduled your appointment the same day Miss Mason did. Given that she was watching Lady Vale, I'd have to wonder if she didn't follow you there."

"Oh heavens," Elizabeth breathed out. "I hadn't even considered that!"

"If they were watching the house on the Tuesday when the appointments were made, and then watching it again the nights when Mary was taken and when they attempted to abduct Miss Masters," Benedict mused, "there is no chance at all that the mystic is not involved in some way in these disappearances herself. She would have to be."

Adler nodded. "That is the truth of it. And that's why the remainder of my investigation will be spent focusing on her and whoever comes and goes with any frequency from her home."

AFTER ADLER LEFT, Benedict opened the simple diary and began to read the most recent entries. It didn't feel right to violate Mary's privacy so, but given what they were up against, he had no other options. Every entry since coming to Bath involved all the ways she'd tried to insert herself into Lady Vale's path. Going to the Pump Room, shopping at the same stores and merchants, frequenting a tea room near the Abbey to watch the comings and goings on days when she could not get into the Pump Room herself.

There were notations about Lady Vale's companion, remarks about the large man who watched them from a distance. At one point, Mary even suspected that the man had been hired to protect them. How wrong she had been, Benedict thought.

"I am very sorry."

The softly murmured apology drew his gaze to the very woman he'd been reading about. "What are you sorry for?" he asked.

"I cannot help but feel, since these men have been following Lady Vale and me for so long that, perhaps, your sister has been put in harm's way because of us," Elizabeth answered.

"As Adler said, the only people responsible are those who took her. What put her into their path is not anyone's fault and it certainly isn't adequate reason for her to be in danger. When I find these men, Miss Masters, and I will, there will be a reckoning," he warned.

"You are very close to your sister," she commented.

"Aren't most siblings close?" he asked. Based on their earlier conversation he would have to imagine that her answer would be no. She'd never indicated one way or another if she even had brothers or sisters but, if she did, they had turned their backs on her.

"No, they most certainly are not," Elizabeth answered. "You know that my past is less than proper. My own sister, who is much older and very advantageously married, gave me the cut direct in London not so very long ago."

Benedict said nothing to that. There was nothing he could say. For the entirety of his life that he could recall, he'd always had Mary there to defend him and he her. The idea that he might never see her again was beyond painful, the idea that something might occur between them that would result in his willfully refusing to even acknowledge her was completely foreign to him.

Miss Masters crossed the room to the window, putting distance between them but, more than anything, he realized, giving herself the opportunity to shore up her weakening defenses. A sad smile curved her lips as she looked back at him, "She's lucky in that regard, as are you, to have someone who cares so deeply."

"And who cares for you, Miss Masters?" he asked pointedly. There was a deep loneliness within her. In moments such as this, with her guard lowered, he could see it. He recognized it because it mirrored his own. Yes, he had his sister, but there was a gaping hole in him. Where did he come from, where did he belong? For him, it was question after question. For Miss Masters, she had been given those answers. She belonged nowhere. No one mourned or searched for her. Her family had cast her off while his own remained a mystery.

"No one," she answered. There was no self-pity in that statement. It was made matter of factly but with firm conviction.

"On that score, I would have to beg your pardon as I disagree in a most impassioned manner. You are cared for."

"Mr. Mason—"

"Miss Masters," he stopped her. "Do not think to tell me what I do and do not feel. I have made no professions of undying love. I have not sworn my unyielding fidelity to you. You have made your feelings on such promises from men quite clear. But mark my words on this account, if I tell you that I care, I do. And I will. Forever."

Rising to his feet, Benedict kept the journal tucked into his hand. He advanced in her direction, his movements slow and deliberate. When he reached her, he placed one hand beneath her chin and tilted her face upward.

He had told her that he would kiss her again and for the right reasons. In that moment, as his lips descended on hers, it had nothing to do with inciting passion or initiating seduction. It was something much more tender and with far deeper meaning. The gesture, simple as it was, had been intended to bring comfort to both of them. And while it succeeded, it also complicated things infinitely more. With that kiss, the soft melding of their lips for only the space of a few seconds, neither one could continue to claim that what existed between them was only a simple attraction without deeper feelings involved.

Stepping back, Benedict felt the breath shudder from him as he accepted the undeniable truth. Miss Elizabeth Masters, for better or worse, was his. She might not know it yet, she might not be willing to admit it, but come what may, he would have her and he would keep her. "I'm going upstairs for a bit. I plan to read every single entry in this book, regardless of how uncomfortable some of them might be for me, and try to determine if there is anything else of use in it. I will see you at tea time."

Chapter Fifteen

E LIZABETH LAY IN her bed, staring up at the ceiling in the darkness. She was exhausted but unable to sleep. Memories of his kiss plagued her. The fiery and passionate man from the night before, the sweet and tender man who had comforted them both that afternoon. Was it possible that both of those were simply facets of the same person? He accused her of not trusting men, and that was true to a degree. But more so, she no longer trusted her own judgment.

How long had it been since someone had touched her with such tenderness and caring? In truth, never. Her own family had been cold at best. She had not suffered as cruelly as Benedict and his sister had at the hands of their abusive, adoptive family, but she hadn't been loved and cared for either. And while that kiss and the wealth of feeling she'd thought she read in his gaze had made her heart leap and inspired the girlish dreams of a grand love to once more spring to life, it was the other kiss that kept her awake. She was tormented by her own response to it—to him.

She had thought herself beyond such temptations, that perhaps she had managed to subdue that weakness within herself… after the last time. It had been years since she had felt a man's touch, much less a kiss. Even then, she had been a girl and her lover had been little more than a boy. Benedict, however, was a man grown, with a man's needs and far more skill than anything she had experienced in the past.

Turning onto her side, her eyes were drawn to the pale sliver of light that filtered in between the curtains. Her skin felt too sensitive, even the weight of her night rail against her flesh was more than she could bear. It wasn't just the lingering desire ignited by his kiss, by the hard press of his body against hers, but also the disquiet of her own thoughts.

Being forced to acknowledge and to accept that she was not as far removed from the woman she had once been as she had thought was difficult to come to terms with.

"Damn," she whispered. It felt so good to utter that curse into the darkness, to let some small bit of the wickedness inside her out into the world.

Unable to sleep, unwilling to continue lying in her bed and letting the frustration eat away at her, she shoved back the bed clothes and sat up. With her feet planted firmly on the floor, she rose and tugged her wrapper on, tying the sash with jerky and agitated movements.

There was brandy in the library. She would get a book and a little dram of it to help settle her nerves and, hopefully, lull herself to sleep.

Easing her door open, she stepped into the hall and peered carefully about her. She did not want to bump into Benedict—Mr. Mason, she corrected herself—in the dark. He was dangerous enough to her even in the bright light of day.

With the corridor deserted, Elizabeth made her way quietly down the stairs. Perhaps it was instinct, perhaps after the attempted kidnapping she was more attuned to her surroundings. Regardless, halfway down the stairs, she stopped. With one hand clutching the railing and the other gripping the sides of her wrapper together, Elizabeth was overwhelmed by the sensation of not being alone.

"Hello?" she whispered. Part of her desperately wanted someone to answer while another part of her was terrified that they might.

"I won't bite you."

The response came from the bottom of the stairs, an acerbic tone to a voice that was becoming dangerously familiar to her. She'd left her bed to avoid memories of Mr. Mason and had, instead, run directly into the man himself.

"What are you doing down there?" she demanded. *As if she had the right!* It was not her place to question him.

"I couldn't sleep," he admitted. "I thought brandy might help. Dare I say that you seem to be suffering a similar predicament?"

"I heard a noise," she lied.

His grin was evident in his voice. "How very brave you are, Miss Masters, to investigate it all by yourself. Brave enough that you deserve a reward... if you come down, I will share my brandy with you."

The idea of being alone with him in the darkness, of letting him steal another kiss, was far more intoxicating than any brandy ever could be. Against all reason and defiance of everything she knew she ought to do, Elizabeth found herself descending those stairs to where he waited in the shadows below. It was far too late to retreat now. Her pride wouldn't allow it.

When she reached the small pool of light that poured from the library, she hesitated again. He stood just inside the door, a second snifter of brandy in his hand and a speculative gleam in his eye.

"I won't accost you in the library... Elizabeth," he promised.

His tone was low and alarmingly seductive. The way his lips positively caressed her name rang every warning bell that she possessed. But once a hedonistic and willful hellion, she thought, always a hedonistic and willful hellion. Try as she might to deny and crush that part of herself, it was still there, lurking beneath her prim, drab clothes and her stiff demeanor.

"I still have not given you leave to use my name," she reminded him as she took the glass from his hand.

"I've tasted your lips, *Miss Masters*. Twice, as a matter of fact. It seems the worst kind of hypocrisy to retain such formal address when the intimacy of our acquaintance has already surpassed such nonsense," he replied smoothly. "Tell me, what disturbing thoughts dragged you from the comfort of your bed this evening?"

"You, *Mr. Mason*." It was not an admission of the nature of her thoughts, only that he occupied them. "I cannot help but wonder at your true identity and your true purpose here... at what manner of man you actually are. You appear to have a very changeable nature."

"That again," he nodded. "It is a conundrum, Elizabeth. I can assure you that I did not intentionally allow someone to shoot me just to gain entrance to this house. I have no designs upon a title that is most obviously not mine. Regardless of what you may think of me, financially I have no need of anything that belongs to Lady Vale. There are more than enough reckless young bucks willing to throw the family fortune upon any table in my establishment. More often than not, they leave a healthy chunk of it behind."

"You do not aspire to her wealth... you do not aspire to her title and position. So what are your aspirations, Mr. Mason? What precisely, other than your conveniently timed heroics, has brought you into our midsts?" She wanted to anger him, to offend his honor in such a way that he would have no choice but to leave and she could at least attempt to put him from her mind and continue on with her peacefully boring existence. It was better that way, to force him out before she, once again, felt the bitter pain of disappointment.

He stepped forward, close enough that their bodies nearly touched. As he loomed over her, she had to tilt her head back to meet his steely gaze and to measure the tension of the ticking muscle at his jaw. She wanted alternately to step back and give herself space to breathe but also to provoke him, to tease the fire of his anger to the point that both of them would lose all sense. It wasn't simply that she wanted to lose control, but to cast it off like an offending garment and embrace her inner wickedness.

When he spoke, his voice was perfectly modulated, his tone completely civil, and nothing in it indicated the cold fury she saw banked in his eyes. "To find my sister and nothing more. I could not sleep because every time I close my eyes, Miss Masters, I cannot help but envision all the horrors that could be visited upon her... the same horrors that might have been visited upon you had I not intervened. And I wonder, Miss Masters, what will become of you if I leave here as you are surely trying to encourage me to do."

Despite the well-modulated and civil tone, there was a note in his voice, a hint that perhaps he had witnessed those kinds of horrors firsthand, that perhaps his sister had, as well. What did they know of him really? He admitted that his adoptive parents had been cruel people but, beyond that, they did not know anything of the couple. In truth, they knew nothing of him. And while her first instinct was to trust him, her instincts had been wrong in the past and she had paid dearly for it.

"Then why have you not left to find her, Mr. Mason? You are not being held against your will." That wasn't entirely true, of course. If he attempted to leave before Lady Vale was satisfied that he was not her missing son, she might very well attempt it.

He didn't answer immediately, but took a sip of his brandy instead. "Because I have to admit that I am not able to do so. Right now, if I were put in a situation where I had to fight for Mary and for myself, I would fail. Also, Lady Vale has resources at the ready, and as I am currently unable to adequately pursue her captors myself, I am dependent upon her assistance. Despite my initial misgivings, Mr. Adler is proving to be more than competent. That is all. I tolerated your accusations earlier because you had no knowledge of who I am or what I'm about. I find that I'm less inclined to tolerate it politely any longer."

Elizabeth laughed at that. "Tolerate it politely! Ha! You are not a gentleman, Mr. Mason. Do not pretend to be."

"And you are not a lady. I'll drop all of my pretenses if you drop yours," he challenged.

The accusation stung, primarily because there was more than a small kernel of truth in it. "How dare you!"

"I dare because you constantly accuse me of being untruthful, Elizabeth, when the only person lying is you. You lie to yourself and to the world at large every time you don one of your drab, ugly gowns and pretend to be meek and obedient. That isn't who you are! Be true to yourself and what your cold-hearted and soulless relatives think of you will matter less and less every day!"

She drew her hand back as if to strike him. It was an instinctive response, a need to make him stop saying the things that echoed the traitorous whispers in her own mind. Before her hand could touch his cheek, he caught it, his long fingers wrapping about her wrist in a hold that was gentle but unbreakable.

"Do not test me, Elizabeth," he warned softly. "You will find that I dare many things."

"I am not afraid of you and I will not be cowed by you! You do not know me and you have no right to dictate to me how I should be living my life!" Her words were whispered, hissed out between clenched teeth as she glared at him. Because it felt good to be angry, because it released some of the misery she'd been carrying around inside her for so long, she continued, "You are not Lord Vale! You are not her vanished son returned to her! For the sake of her already broken heart, can you not at least attempt to make her see reason?"

He let go of her abruptly and scrubbed his hands over his face and let his fingers comb through his golden hair, sending the locks into disarray. "I have told her, Elizabeth. Every time I have been in her presence, I have told her. Short of being unnecessarily cruel to a woman who is already beyond fragile, what would you have me do?"

"Lie," Elizabeth said. "Tell her you remember your true parents. Just tell her anything that will keep her from clinging to this false hope."

"And if it isn't?" he retorted. "What bothers you the most, Elizabeth? That right now I'm the completely disreputable owner of a gaming hell you shouldn't even speak to much less kiss? Or is that I might be the lost lord... and too far above your own lowly station?"

It was both. She hadn't allowed herself to actually put it into words, not even in her own mind, but there was no denying the truth once he uttered it. In his current position, to entertain any sort of romantic entanglement with him was to toss away any remaining vestige of respectability that she possessed. But if he was, in fact, the missing Lord Vale, she would never be anything to him other than a mistress, too far beneath his station for anything more concrete.

Perhaps she wasn't as hedonistic as she'd once believed herself to be. Even in her brief affair with Fredrick, she'd believed, somewhat naively, that she would one day be his wife. She no longer possessed the ability to lie to herself to that extent. There was no future with Benedict Mason, regardless of how attractive she found him or how much she was drawn to him. Not that he had expressed any interest in the future. Everything he appeared to want was in their very immediate present.

"Is it wrong that I know my place in this world, Mr. Mason? That I understand the standards of behavior I must adhere to in order to maintain my position? I have no aspirations to climb any higher, but I refuse to fall any further than I have!" she snapped.

⚜

BENEDICT WASN'T ENTIRELY sure what it was that infuriated him so in her heated response. Perhaps it was simply that everything she said made perfect sense, and sense was not what he wanted in that moment. He wanted recklessness and heat—he wanted to feel her come undone beneath him and, for once, to have her look at him without suspicion and caution. She stirred something in him that was beyond simple attraction and desire. It maddened him. Crossing to the desk again, he refilled his glass and took a healthy swallow of the amber liquid.

"To hell with your place in the world and to hell with mine! If I'd listened to everyone who told me where my place was, I'd still be stacking rocks in the north country, stooped over with an aching back and hands too rough to even touch you with," he said. "Make your own place, Elizabeth. Decide what you want and then do whatever it takes to get it."

"Is that what you did?" she asked. The heat in her voice had subsided, leaving in its stead a wistfulness that pricked at his more tender feelings. The nightmarish visions that had plagued him had left him feeling raw and eager to lash out at anyone who might strike his ire. But those feelings faded in her presence, faded as they both carefully lowered their guards and met one another on even ground.

"It's what I mean to do now," he vowed.

Placing his glass once more on the wooden surface of the desk, he took two steps toward her until he could grasp her wrist. A simple tug was all it took as he pulled her to him, because there was no resistance in her. It was clear from the way she leaned into him, from the soft sigh that escaped her lips as their bodies touched, that it was what she wanted, as well.

"Why do I crave you?" he asked. "It is glaringly apparent that no two people have ever been more ill-suited to one another... and yet, from the moment I first spied you in that square, all shy and proper, then later hissing and clawing like a feral cat in that alleyway, I could not get you out of my mind."

"I wish I knew the answer to that. We should not continue this," she said. But even as she uttered that small token protest, she made no move to break free of his embrace. Instead, she pressed her face into his chest, resting her head against his shoulder.

Dipping his head, Benedict inhaled the soft scent of lemon verbena that clung to her hair. It was a scent that would haunt him for the remainder of his days. "If I kiss you again, Elizabeth, it will not be enough."

"You kissed me twice and it hasn't been enough," she murmured.

Chapter Sixteen

B ENEDICT PLACED HIS fingertips beneath her chin and tipped her face up until he could settle his lips on hers once more. From that moment in the corridor earlier, the need to taste her again had tormented him. He'd enjoyed women in his life—their softness, their often quixotic nature, the way they could, by turns, be shyly demure and wildly passionate. But he'd never known a woman that, for lack of a better description, crawled beneath his skin and invaded his being. He wanted her in the same way that he wanted his next breath—fierce, primal, willing to fight hook and claw for it.

It was not as it had been before. During their first kiss, she had been hesitant, kissing him back reluctantly. This time, whether it was their verbal sparring or simply acknowledging the inevitability of all that lay between them, she welcomed his touch immediately and responded with the full force of her passion.

It was both staggering and humbling to know that her desire equaled his own, to know that she longed for him just as he longed for her. He was not a man given to romantic notions or flights of fancy, but there seemed to be something between them that was simply fated. She called to parts of him that he'd thought long buried, inciting a swell of tenderness inside him that would have shocked her.

Benedict pulled her closer, holding her tighter to him. The tie of her wrapper shifted and the garment parted, revealing the white lawn of her night rail beneath. The knowledge that she wore only that, without the restrictive stays or numerous petticoats beneath added another even greater intimacy to the encounter and greater temptation, as well. It was no longer simply a kiss, but a prelude to something far more carnal and earthy. Benedict slipped his hands beneath the heavy wool of her wrapper, bringing them to rest on her hips. She swayed slightly, leaning into him, resting the weight of her body fully against his.

It was the sweetest of surrenders. It would have been sweeter were he able to simply lift her in his arms, bear her to the small settee and bring her to pleasure again and again. But he wasn't foolish enough to think himself fully up to the task. Instead, he walked them backward, keeping her in his embrace, kissing her senseless the whole time. When the backs of his knees bumped the settee, he eased himself down and pulled her with him.

Sprawled on his lap, her body pressed to him and her tongue tangling delicately with his own, there was no question that was knew what was about to occur.

He broke the kiss for a one moment, met her heavy-lidded gaze, and said, "You have to be certain."

"There are no certainties in life, Benedict... only moments. And whether it comes with a lifetime of regret or not, I mean to seize this one."

There was no need to ask for further elaboration on the point. She lifted her hands from his shoulders and dropped them to the simply tied sash of her wrapper. Her fingers worked the knot until it slipped free and fabric parted to reveal the simple night rail beneath. Even in the dim light of the fireplace, he could see the shadows of her body beneath it, dips and curves that hinted at the glory of her figure.

Benedict placed one hand on her thigh, let it slide upward and beneath the hem of her night rail. Gliding over silken skin until he found the curve of her waist, he used it to guide her, to move her until she was straddling his thighs. Unable to resist the sweet allure of her breasts beneath the crisp lawn, he kissed first one and then the other before parting the fabric and revealing the darker circles of her perfect nipples.

"You are so beautiful," he whispered.

"I'm not. Passably pretty, at best, and even then not when I tie my hair back so tightly and wear hideous, brown dresses," she admitted shyly.

He smiled at her sudden reticence. "Well, you aren't wearing a hideous brown dress now," he said. Reaching up, he tugged at the ribbon that fastened her braid. It slipped free and the used his fingers to loosen the plait of her hair until the rich brown tresses cascaded over her shoulders. "And never deny your beauty… if you could see yourself as I do in this moment—"

"Kiss me again," she urged. "Before I lose my nerve or we start to argue over how pretty I am or am not."

He might have laughed at that, both because it was true and because of her slightly petulant expression as she uttered it. But she rose onto her knees, planted her lips on his and took charge of the kiss. It was the kiss of a woman who knew what she wanted and was not afraid to ask for it, of a woman who understood passion and pleasure. There might have been some part of him that was jealous of the fact that another man, an unworthy man, had introduced her to such things. But there was another part of him that was grateful. He did not have to curb his desires. He did not have to worry that she would be shocked or frightened.

Benedict let his hands roam her body, testing every curve, learning each contour as the kiss grew. It consumed them, left them both breathless and aching. They would pause long enough to draw a breath and return as if ravenous for one another. When his hands closed over her breasts, his fingers circling the pebbled peaks, her gasp and cry was lost in that kiss.

When she reached between them, her fingers tugging at the fall of his breeches, he didn't caution her to slow down. He was at war within himself, alternately wanting to savor each second and to simply sink into the heat of her and lose himself in it. Delving one hand between her thighs, finding her wet and eager for him, need won out.

After managing to free the buttons of his breeches, her hand closed over him as he nipped at her bottom lip. She rose onto her knees again and he closed his hand over hers, gripping his shaft, and guided himself to her entrance as she sank down once more.

That moment of contact, when he was fully inside her, their bodies joined, was perfection. They both stilled, their breaths coming in sharp pants as their gazes locked. His hands settled on her hips, urging her on, guiding her as they began to move together. Neither made a sound, each one aware of the cost of discovery. But as her head fell back, her lips parted on a silent cry, he leaned forward and kissed the arched column of her throat, scraping his teeth lightly over that sensitive flesh.

She bit her lips as a muffled cry escaped between them. He lifted his hips, driving deeper into her as he felt her shudder about him. And when she clamped tightly around him, lost in the violence of her own passion, he followed her over that precipice, pouring himself into her.

In all, it was over quickly. So quickly he might have been ashamed had she not still been trembling from her own release. He could feel the quivering of her thighs against him, the spasms that still rocked her core as he softened within her.

"I won't say it was a mistake," she whispered, resting her head against his uninjured shoulder.

"But you will think it. Over and over again," he surmised with a sad smile.

"No. I don't think I will. But I will remind myself daily why it would be foolish to repeat it. Neither of us wants the consequences that may arise from it," she stated firmly.

"A child, you mean? Would it be so terrible then?"

She raised her head. "I suppose that would depend on whether you are simply a man who owns a gaming hell or the lost heir to the Vale Viscountcy. There are too many things unknown at this juncture for us to even think about what our future might hold... much less to consider bringing an innocent child into it."

That was not a statement he could refute. The wisdom of it was undeniable. Before he could formulate a reply, the sound of breaking glass echoed through the lower floor. Their brief interlude ended immediately. Elizabeth freed herself from their entangled embrace and rose to her feet. She stepped back, eyes wide with fear as she righted her clothes. "Did you hear that?"

"I did," he said grimly, getting to his feet and repairing his own garments. "Wait here!"

"No! I'm going with you," she insisted.

"If it's a housebreaker—"

"Then leaving me alone to fend them off by myself is certainly not the best course of action!" she stated firmly.

He grimaced. "Fine, but stay behind me."

Together, they left the library and followed the sound. It had come from the front of the house. Opening the heavy pocket doors of the drawing room, Benedict felt the cool night air from the broken window and cursed.

The room was obviously empty. Stepping deeper into it, he saw the heavy stone lying on the carpet. There was no note attached to it. It was not a warning sign or a threat, as such things often were.

"Benedict!" Elizabeth screamed.

He looked up just in time to see the flaming bottle sail through the now empty frame of the destroyed window. Ducking to one side, he rolled away from the collision point, even as it burst into flames. The curtains caught and flames immediately leapt up them, going nearly to the ceiling.

"Go upstairs! Wake everyone and get the women outside. We need all the men down here to fight the blaze!" he shouted, even as he grabbed the fireplace poker and began tearing down the curtains and forcing the flaming mass into the dampness of the night beyond.

He turned back to see Elizabeth standing there, eyes wide with terror, watching the flames as if in a trance. Closing the space between them, he grasped her arms and forced her to face him. "Elizabeth!" There was no response. "Elizabeth!" he shouted again. Finally, she blinked at him.

"Go upstairs. Now. Get everyone out of the house that isn't able to help fight this fire!"

She nodded and turned on her heel, heading up the stairs into the darkness. Facing the flames once more, he struggled simply to contain them. With his hands and arms singed from the flames, he did all in his power to keep the carpet from igniting further. He pulled furniture away from the origin point of the blaze. The stitches at his shoulder tore and blood seeped from the wound. Benedict ignored it.

By the time a bevy of footmen entered the room, he was exhausted. Each carried buckets of sand and water. Directed by Calvert, the butler, they worked much like a well-oiled machine.

It didn't take long before the smaller offshoots of the original fire had begun to die down or were extinguish entirely. Coughing from inhaling so much smoke, it was Calvert who gave him his marching orders.

"Mr. Mason, sir, you have breathed in too much of this foul air. You must go outside at once. We can manage the rest!" Calvert insisted.

"Are all the women of the household accounted for?" he demanded.

"Yes, Mr. Mason. They are all huddled together outside and you must go huddle with them. Now, please," Calvert insisted again.

Benedict didn't argue the point. He was beyond tired. His shoulder ached like the bloody dickens and all he wanted was to fill his lungs completely with air.

Chapter Seventeen

ELIZABETH WAS QUAKING with fear as she stood in a circle of women comprised primarily of kitchen maids. Lady Vale stood to the left, watching through the window. There was little doubt that her concern was more for the man fighting the fire than for anything in the house itself.

Forcing herself to be calm, to ignore the rushing of her blood and trembling of her knees, Elizabeth left the gaggle of female servants and approached her mistress. "I'm certain he will be well, Lady Vale. Calvert undoubtedly has things well in hand."

Lady Vale cocked her head and arched one eyebrow imperiously. "I'm certain that he does... the question remains, Miss Masters, what were you doing alone, in the darkest hours of night, with my son?"

"I went downstairs for a bit of brandy to help me sleep. Apparently, Mr. Mason was suffering insomnia, as well," Elizabeth replied smoothly. There was no need to divulge anything else. It wasn't a mistake, but it was not something she intended to repeat either, therefore, she reasoned, there was nothing to divulge. *Except that she had given up all pretense of being a well-bred and upstanding young woman and let him take her right there on the library furniture.* And might have done again had the fire not been started. In that one regard, perhaps it was a blessing.

"Do you think me foolish, Miss Masters? With all my mystics and soothsayers, undoubtedly I do give that impression to some," Lady Vale mused.

"I do not think you foolish, Lady Vale. Not in the least."

"Then mark me, Elizabeth Masters… my brother-in-law may be your employer, but if you are behaving inappropriately with my son—"

"He may not be your son. I know you want him to be. I'll even grant that there is enough of a resemblance to make one question it. But Lady Vale, what if he is not?" Elizabeth asked. It was a subject that needed to be addressed, but it was also a desperately needed change of topic that Elizabeth seized upon to save her own hide.

"Then he is a man who runs a gaming hell… and while I find no fault with his manners, it cannot be ignored that it is not a respectable occupation. If he is my son, you are reaching far too high, and if he is not, then you are digging your way directly to the bottom, my girl!" Lady Vale snapped.

Effectively put in her place, Elizabeth took a deep breath. "I am doing neither of those things, Lady Vale. While I was getting a drink, I heard breaking glass, as did Mr. Mason. We went to investigate it and someone threw a flaming bottle through the window! There are greater issues at stake right now, Lady Vale, than whether or not you would find me a suitable prospect for a man who may or may not be your son! Someone tried to commit murder this night… whether the intended victim was you, me, or Mr. Mason, remains unknown!"

Benedict emerged from the house then. He was coughing furiously and his shirt was stained with soot and what appeared to be blood. His wound had reopened. They would need to have someone fetch the doctor.

Stepping away from Lady Vale, Elizabeth meant to tell one of the maids to see to it. But the sound of hoofbeats and the clattering of carriage wheels halted her. A feeling of foreboding washed through her and she glanced over her shoulder in the direction of the noise. A wagon pulled by two horses was barreling down on them, heading straight for the crowd.

At the same time, the maids and other sundry servants seemed to realize it. With shrieks of alarm they scattered like birds, leaving Elizabeth alone there, an easy and well isolated target.

The heavy figure of a man was leaning from the back of the wagon, arms outstretched as he neared her. Panic had frozen her, but not so much that she did not recognize him. It was one of the men who had attempted to abduct her outside Madame Zula's.

"Elizabeth!"

Benedict's shout of alarm pulled her from her trance. She stepped back, trying to get out of reach of the villain, but it was too late. His hands snagged in her hair, pulling her off her feet and onto the small bench at the back of the vehicle with him.

She struggled, fighting him for all that she was worth. Her nails raked his cheek, leaving bloody tracks in their wake. He cursed under his breath as he tried to subdue her.

Without warning, another man rose from within the small cart and reached for her. He grasped her roughly, pulling her completely into the foul smelling confines of the small vehicle. She could hear Lady Vale screaming even over the sound of the horses' hooves clattering over the cobbled street. Landing with a heavy thud on the coarse wooden floor, she felt splinters puncture her palms and the rough jolt of the wheels beneath her.

The man who had grabbed her was large and beefy, but not the same man as before. That man had frightened her simply because she felt his gaze upon her, because he had watched her until she became aware of his presence. This man frightened her for very different reasons. Even in the dim light, she could see the speculation glittering in his gaze as it raked over her. Even in her night rail and heavy wrapper, she might as well have been naked for all the good it did. She felt exposed and violated by him when he had yet to even touch her.

The other man, the one who had been in charge the night they tried to take her from outside Madame Zula's, was climbing over the gate of the wagon, but he hadn't missed his cohort's hungry expression. "She's not for the likes of you. We'll turn her over unharmed, collect our payment and then you can hire every whore in Bath if you want."

"I don't want no whore, now do I? I likes 'em fresh."

The leader opened his mouth to speak, but a loud crack rent the night air. The sound of gunfire echoed through what were normally peaceful streets. The man let out a pained gasp as he clutched at the side of the wagon. The light color of his shirt grew dark with a spreading stain, his left arm hanging limp at his side. She could see the panic in his gaze as he lost his grip and tumbled to the street below.

Elizabeth struggled to sit up, to reach the edge of the wagon. She'd rather take her chances of being trampled beneath the wheels than with the disgusting man who eyed her so boldly. Within seconds, he'd grabbed her and hauled her back, holding her tight against him. She could smell gin and sweat, the foulness of his breath and the stench of a body too-long unwashed.

"I can't take you the way I want… but nothing to say I can't have a little feel, now is there?" he asked, as his hand cupped her breast roughly.

She slapped at him, pushing at his arms in a vain attempt to free herself. It was his laughter that made her stop. She realized immediately that he enjoyed her struggles.

"Every stolen touch will cost you… I will tell whoever it is that has asked for me that you violated their orders and took liberties. These are ruthless men, are they not? Men who are not above killing any who go against their wishes?"

He grumbled against her ear and shoved her away from him. She landed in the opposite corner of the wagon, her head connecting painfully with the wooden side.

"Go on then. Tell 'em, what you like. You'll be spreading your thighs for someone 'fore the night is through. We'll see how high and might you are then!"

⚜

BENEDICT RACED AFTER the wagon. In spite of his aching chest and the smoke that had left him gasping for breath, he pushed on. But he was only a man. With every passing second, the back of that wagon grew smaller and smaller until it eventually disappeared from his sight entirely.

Stopping, dropping his hands onto his knees and gasping for breath, he coughed as he tried to inhale great quantities of air. His lungs had seized entirely, whether from panic or exertion he could not say.

Turning back, the crushing weight of disappointment, of fear and failure, pressed in on him as he moved toward the servants that were once more gathered around Lady Vale. By the time he reached them, they were no longer shocked into silence, but were whispering so loudly it was like a swarm of bees about him.

A carriage had stopped down the street. It had been traveling in the opposite direction from the wagon that had taken Elizabeth, coming into town instead of leaving it. With no room to turn the vehicle, pursuit was not an option. The door opened and a man emerged. Tall, well dressed, his dark brown hair sprinkled with enough gray that even in the dim light of the moon it was visible, he strode purposefully toward them.

"What the devil is happening here?"

"A fire," Lady Vale said. "I very much fear that it was set as a lure in order to get us outside and put poor Miss Masters once more in harm's way! Oh, Branson! We must save her!"

Branson, a name Benedict didn't know but that still felt strangely familiar to him, appeared to be well known to Lady Vale. He reached out as if to touch her, then abruptly drew back, hands at his side, bearing as erect as any military man could hope for.

"You wanted rid of her, didn't you?"

Lady Vale looked up at him, her shock and utter appall written clearly upon her face. "Not this way! I resented having a keeper, Branson, but I would never wish for that kind of evil and misery to be visited upon anyone! She's only a girl... she's barely older than I was when I was forced to marry your worthless brother!"

It all clicked into place for him then. Branson Middlethorp, Esquire. He was Lady Vale's brother-in-law and Elizabeth's employer. She'd been naught but a bone between two fighting dogs, he thought.

Both Lady Vale and Middlethorp saw her as only a servant, something expendable.

"Sir, if I may have the use of your carriage, I will travel in pursuit of them. It shouldn't take long with such a fine team to overtake a simple wagon," he said.

"You're the hero," Middlethorp surmised. "The dashing young buck who rushed in to save her before… well, you can't. The team is worn out from the journey from London. We will go after her, but we'll need fresh horses to do it. In the meantime, we're going to interrogate that fellow I just shot and see what we can get out of him."

Middlethorp gestured to two footmen who were standing on the steps, dazed and clearly frightened by what had unfolded. "You there, get him up, get him in the house… and send someone for a doctor. I won't have him dying on us before he tells us what we need to know!"

Lady Vale moved closer to Benedict. "Oh, my dear, I know this must be very difficult for you. You've grown very close to Miss Masters during your stay with us."

"I have. And when I leave here, I intend to ask her to accompany me… I will not lose her. Whatever the cost, I will get both Elizabeth and my sister back," he vowed.

Lady Vale blinked at that. "But you are most likely Lord Vale, Benedict. You cannot think to marry so low when you are the presumed heir to a viscountcy!"

"I'm not an heir to anything yet. Nothing has been proven. And if it means I can't live my life of my own choosing instead of being bound by archaic class rules, then I've no wish to be Viscount anything," he answered hotly as the two footmen moved past him with the unconscious man carried between them. He turned on his heel to follow them.

He was done with Lady Vale's games, with her bargains and ultimatums. While he was appreciative of her help, it had only allowed him to determine that Mary had lied to him and that she'd been just as obsessed with this foolish theory surrounding his origins as Lady Vale herself was. He was done with the lot of it. Miss Masters and Mary would be rescued and they would both return to London with him,

THE VANISHING OF LORD VALE

one more willingly than the other, perhaps, but he was not taking no for an answer.

Branson watched the young man walk away, disappearing into the house. The resemblance, even in the dim light, had been uncanny. For once, he found himself questioning whether or not his own accepted version of events, that Benedict, Viscount Vale, was dead, was, in fact, accurate.

To Lady Vale, he said, "Well, Sarah, whether that boy is your blood or not, he certainly matches you in temperament!"

"This is not a time for jests, Branson! That boy, as you called him, is most likely my missing son, and the woman you hired to keep me from finding him may very well succeed in taking him away from me after all!"

"Not if you stop impeding what is very clearly a love match," Brandon said. "If he is your son, would you really be so blinded by the rules of society that you would force him to marry without love as you once did?"

She gasped, almost as if he'd struck her and stepped back. "It is not at all the same! James was cruel and vicious. I would never ask him to marry someone who would be so wicked!"

"No, but you would ask him to give up any chance at happiness and break his heart along with hers in the process. Do not repeat past mistakes, my dear," he warned softly. "Now, let us go upstairs and see what information we can glean from this worthless individual who is bleeding all over the good linens, shall we?"

He didn't wait to see if she followed, but swept into the house ahead of her. Sarah had been the love of his life. He'd watched her with envy and longing as she'd wed his elder brother. He'd watched her with pity and righteous indignation as she'd endured James' cruelty. He'd watched her nearly drive herself mad with the need to find her son when all evidence pointed to his no longer being amongst the living. But he would not watch her turn into the thing he most despised… a society matron like her own mother had been—a woman who would rob even her own child of happiness in order to meet the expectations of others.

Chapter Eighteen

B ENEDICT WAS STANDING at the foot of a bed in one of the guest rooms, looking down at an unconscious man and wanting nothing more than to plant his fist in the man's face. But that would not hasten his wakefulness and would not allow him to find Elizabeth. Instead, he clenched his fists at his sides and waited.

Someone fell in to place beside him and a glass of brandy appeared before him. It was Middlethorp, of course.

"Thank you, sir," Benedict managed. It was gruff, but nonetheless sincere. The spirits would hopefully calm the rage that bubbled inside him.

"We have not been introduced," the man said softly as if they were meeting at a social gathering rather than over the sickbed of a villain. "I am Branson Middlethorp… brother to the late Lord Vale and trustee of his estate."

Damn. It was another complication in an already convoluted mess. "I am Benedict Mason, Mr. Middlethorp."

"I know," Middlethorp answered. "The question remains, are you Lord Vale returned to us?"

"That is not a question for me," Benedict replied, stepping away from him and around the bed. He cocked his head, examining the man who lay there and appeared strangely familiar to him. He'd had the same thought when he'd seen him outside Madame Zula's on that first night. To Middlethorp, he continued, "I cannot tell you where I was born or who I was born to, but I strongly doubt it was Lord and Lady Vale."

Middlethorp eyed him speculatively. "You do not think you are Sarah's long lost son?"

There was something in the way that Middlethorp said her name that alerted Benedict. The man had feelings for her, deep feelings. "I do not believe so, no. I find it quite unlikely that a sort such as me could ever have been descended from noble blood."

Middlethorp made a noncommittal sound. "What sort is that?"

Benedict shrugged. "Low. Cagey. Lacking in honor… according to those that claim such a trait as their right. Little more than a thief some might say, but only if they lost heavily in my establishment."

Middlethorp snorted. "My brother would hardly have been considered noble. He was a bounder through and through. If you were his son, I'd say you did better for lack of his influence… not to mention a man who chases a carriage beyond the length of the Circus in an attempt to rescue a woman who can best be described as plain—"

"She is not plain," he protested. "It is perfectly reasonable for any attractive woman to take any necessary steps to make her appear less so while in service. Sometimes, it is their only defense against unscrupulous men!"

Middlethorp smiled. "I stand corrected. Miss Masters is not plain then, but a master of disguise. But about your upbringing, Mr. Mason, how old were you when you were adopted?"

"I can't say… old enough to know my name was Benedict and insist on being called that. I never liked Benny or any other nickname. Beyond that, I can't say."

Middlethorp's face paled a bit. As he raised his glass to his lips, it trembled slightly. "And with every word from your naysaying lips, you damn yourself more… I begin to think you are Lord Vale, regardless of what your desires may be."

Benedict had no response to that. "We need to question the kidnapper and find out precisely what he knows. They have Mary and now Elizabeth. There's no more time for chatter."

Middlethorp nodded and then unceremoniously tossed the remaining contents of his glass into the face of the unconscious man. He came up sputtering. To Benedict, Middlethorp said, "I shall assist you, if you don't mind? I'm less than pleased with a man attempting to burn down a house occupied by those I—who are under my protection."

"How did you know that would wake him up?" Benedict asked.

Middlethorp shrugged. "He's been awake for the last two minutes... playing possum as I've heard it called by some of the Americans I met during my time in the colonies. I could tell by his breathing."

Benedict had questions. He also had things that required saying that made him infinitely uncomfortable, but it was best to get them over with. "Thank you... for taking that shot. She's got a better chance against two than three, though the odds still aren't in her favor."

Middlethorp nodded, but his eyes never left the man who lay on the bed, clutching his wounded arm and watching them in return. "Calvert wrote to me that my dear sister-in-law had brought another imposter into the home... that is why Miss Masters was here after all, to keep her from giving away the entire estate to whatever young man looks enough like her lost boy to sway her too-soft heart."

"So Miss Masters will be sacked for failing in her duties, then," he surmised, "assuming that she can be found? At least that will help me sway her into joining me in London."

"No. You are not claiming to be Lord Vale. I cannot fault you for what Sarah believes. And given that you saved Miss Masters, I could hardly expect her to leave you bleeding in the street," Middlethorp replied reasonably. "At this juncture, I'm here to simply oversee this situation and ensure that everyone comes out of it as they should. However, if your intent is to marry the girl and not simply set her up as your mistress until you've grown tired of her, I'm not opposed to a few lies to ease the path of true love. If your intentions are not honorable, then I vow it will not go well for you."

The threat in his words was pointed and menacing, more in his tone than in what he said. Whoever Branson Middlethorp was, Benedict acknowledged, in that moment, that he was a dangerous man. "My intentions are as honorable as Miss Masters will allow them to be," he answered cryptically.

Middlethorp digested that response slowly before grinning. "You are cagey, after all. On to this fellow… there's a doctor on his way here now. He will dig that pistol ball out of your shoulder, but only on my orders. Also on my orders is the administration of laudanum before that task is undertaken. It can be as painful as you make it or as painless as you allow it to be."

"I've got nothing to say to you. Best to let this pistol ball kill me than to give up the one I work for," the man said.

"Your name, sir," Middlethorp continued, unfazed by the man's resistance. "I can do worse things to you than withhold medication for your pain. And whatever you fear from your employer, he is not here now. But I am."

Before Benedict could question what it was that Middlethorp meant to do, he rounded the bed, grasped the man's wounded arm and dug his thumb into the rent flesh where the ball had entered. The man howled in pain, flailing about and trying to dislodge the man who, only on the surface, appeared to be a gentleman. To say that he was surprised at the casual brutality of one he had deemed upon first meeting to be above such things was to put it mildly.

"Fenton! Fenton Hardwick!" The injured man finally squalled out the answer. In response, Mr. Middlethorp let him go abruptly and Hardwick fell back onto the bed, gasping and pale.

"Why were you looking for Miss Masters?" Benedict countered quickly, thinking it best to pounce on the man while he was still reeling from pain and likely to be more cooperative.

They were interrupted by the arrival of Lady Vale. She stepped into the room, her eyes lit upon the bed and a soft cry escaped her. Had Benedict not been watching the man on the bed he would have missed his response. Hardwick's eyes widened momentarily and then a look, fleeting as it was, that could only be described as regret crossed his features.

Middlethorp was assisting Lady Vale to her feet, but once she recovered them, she shrugged his hands away and dove toward the bed. She grasped the man by the grungy lapels of his coat. "Where did you take him that night? Where did you take my son? Tell me!"

Middlethorp pulled her back. "Sarah! Sarah! You must calm yourself!"

"I will not calm myself! That is the man who took my child from me... he pulled him right from my arms and ordered his henchman to leave me gagged and bound to the foot of my own bed," she whispered brokenly. "I know his face, Branson! I see it every night in memories that are far more cruel than a nightmare ever could be!"

He stared at her for a long moment, and then opened his mouth as if to placate her.

"I saw him, Branson!" Lady Vale snapped. "I know you think me mad, but I am not. He is the man who ripped my sweet Benedict from my arms all those years ago. I am unlikely to forget his face!"

Middlethorp sighed. "Sarah, we've had this discussion in the past. I know you want to find out what happened to your son, but you have been chasing ghosts for so many years that you see them even when they are not present!"

"Do not insult my intelligence! I am perfectly well aware of what others think of me," she snapped. "I've seen their pitying looks, the very same looks I've seen from you. I've heard their whispers as I walk past. *Mad Lady Vale. Poor dear, Lady Vale. Such a tragic woman—did you hear her husband died in his lover's arms?*"

Branson held up his hands in supplication. "I do not mean to offend, Sarah, and I do not in any way mean to belittle what has happened to you. I only want you to consider the possibility that your desire to find those responsible could be coloring your vision. Just consider it."

Benedict turned to Middlethorp. "Lady Vale is right. I cannot account for it in any other way. When this man laid eyes on her, I saw recognition in his gaze. Whatever strange set of circumstances have brought them into this space together, she is speaking the truth."

Middlethorp arched one eyebrow in response. "And would this have anything to do with it furthering your own cause?"

"If by cause you mean the safe return of my sister and Elizabeth—Miss Masters, then yes. That is my *only* cause!" Benedict snapped.

Middlethorp nodded. "Fine then. Let us get back to it. Did you abduct Lady Vale's son?" he demanded of Hardwick.

"I did. Maybe I recall it because it's the last thing in my life I did that I felt regret for… after that, didn't seem like anything else mattered. I'd already damned myself." Hardwick stared down at the counterpane, not meeting Lady Vale's gaze. "I never wanted to do it. But we needed something to make Lord Vale do what was asked of him. We never thought he'd say no."

Middlethorp launched himself at the man, grasped him by the throat. "Explain yourself!"

"Lord Vale knew we had the boy… we sent word to him that we had him. Told him we'd kill his son if he didn't give up the book back to its rightful owner. He sent word back to go ahead. Said he'd get himself a new wife and a new brat," Hardwick said. "I couldn't kill the child. He was just a boy. I've done a lot of things in my life to be ashamed of but I didn't do that."

Benedict felt his knees growing weak. He sank onto the nearest chair. "What did you do with this boy?"

Hardwick was teary-eyed when he confessed, "I gave him to a couple. The man was a drunk. The woman was hard, I suppose, but her man said it was because she'd lost too many children and couldn't have any more of her own. So, they paid me a shilling to take the boy and raise him as their own!"

Benedict couldn't ask any more questions. He couldn't speak past the lump in his throat. Lady Vale collapsed onto the floor, sobbing with a mixture of relief and hysteria. It was Middlethorp who continued the interrogation, who dug for the truth from a man none of them could trust. "And their names?"

"Didn't have one, as far as I know. The man was a stone mason… first name was Jasper," he said. "That's all I know. They took the boy and headed north and I never seen or heard from 'em again."

"Where are Miss Masters and Mr. Mason's sister?" Middlethorp continued. He was relentless, leaning over the man, the threat of more violence ever present in his menacing stance.

Hardwick grew suddenly taciturn, looking away and refusing to answer. Middlethorp pulled a small pistol, the kind ladies typically kept in their reticules, from inside his coat. He grasped the wrist of Hardwick's good arm and placed the barrel of the gun directly against his hand. "I can ruin you right now. If you go back to your employer with one ruined arm and a hand you can't even move then you're as good as dead."

The wounded man struggled, but it was to no avail. Middlethorp's hold on him was unbreakable. "You're as bad as he is, you bastard!" Hardwick shouted. "The lot of you using your money and your power to bring others to heel!"

At the end of his patience, Middlethorp said, "Talk. Tell us what we need to know and, much as it pains me, I'll do what I can to see you get transported rather than hanged."

Hardwick turned his suspicious gaze up to Middlethorp's face. "Why would you do that?"

"Because, right now, it's more important to find Mary and Elizabeth than to worry about what becomes of you," Benedict answered for the man who was most likely his uncle. "Why did you target Miss Masters for abduction?"

Hardwick's confession was spat out bitterly. "I was hired to take her. So I did."

"And Mary?" he demanded.

"Don't know her."

Fury washed through him, but Benedict tamped it down, forced it back as he'd done all those years during the brutality of his childhood. He needed to focus and to use his head, not his fists. "You took her from the street in front of Madame Zula's just over a week ago. Tell me why and tell me where to find her!"

The man screamed in pain. "I don't know... I don't know where he takes them! It's the truth!"

Benedict ran his hands through his hair in frustration. They were

THE VANISHING OF LORD VALE

talking in circles and the more time that was wasted with it, the farther away Elizabeth became. "Who? Where who takes them?"

The man looked up at him with pure hatred burning in his gaze. "He's a gentleman, but we don't know his name. It's always dark. If we're taken to him then we have to wear hoods to and from."

"You've been to his home? Seen the inside of it, then?" Middlethorp interjected.

"Yes," the man agreed, but offered nothing further.

Benedict eyed him coldly. "We've shown you that we're not above causing you a great deal of discomfort to get answers. But time is of the essence. He may agree to having you transported, but if I don't find those two women, it won't be the hangman who sees you dead. Understand?"

Hardwick nodded. "I'll tell you what I can, but I don't know if it'll be enough to save them."

"For your sake, it had better be," Benedict answered evenly.

Hardwick dropped his head to his chest but his voice was clear. "I've seen inside it. It's fancier than this house, bigger. Out in the countryside, but no more than a couple hours from the city," the man said.

Middlethorp muttered an oath under his breath. "How far did you travel to get to this man's estate?" he demanded of Fenton.

"It's about an hour… maybe more. Assuming they didn't drive us in circles," he answered.

"And this Madame Zula? What is her role in this?" Middlethorp queried. His tone was brusque and it was becoming more clear with each passing moment that he was at the end of his patience.

"She helped find the girls we were to take. Sometimes they'd ask for specific types of girls and we'd hire people to talk about Madame Zula in front of them, knowing most would be intrigued enough to visit her."

Benedict glanced at him. "Who asked for a girl like my sister… and for Miss Masters?"

Fenton clammed up then, refusing to say more. Benedict rose and moved toward the bed, ready to inflict any pain necessary to make the man speak, but Lady Vale stepped forward instead.

"I can only imagine that as unscrupulous as your employer is, you continue to work for him for more than simply financial gain. You fear him, don't you?" She posed the question softly, speaking conversationally to him as if he hadn't ruined her life, the life of her child and two young women that were connections of hers.

"We're all afraid of him," Fenton replied. "Everyone who works for him does so because they don't have a choice. He doesn't give you one. If you were smart, you'd be afraid of him, too!"

"We are, Mr. Hardwick," Lady Vale stated. "We just won't continue to live in fear. Please, tell us what we need to know to stop him. If you do, it frees us all!"

"It might free you... the only place I'm going is to the gallows!" Fenton barked at her.

If Benedict had thought her a forgiving sort, if he'd imagined in any way that she might be inclined to soften her heart toward the man in light of his fear, her next words disabused him of that notion.

"Mr. Fenton, if those young women die, or worse, remain lost for decades as my son did, you are going to the gallows regardless." Lady Vale's tone was firm and her expression completely unmoved. "Saving your life will not be an option, but cleansing your soul still is. Tell us what we need to locate Mary and Miss Masters. Help us to stop him from taking any more young women away from their families!"

Hardwick's gaze snapped to her, shocked but grudgingly respectful. "I don't have a soul to save. Not anymore."

"Are you a betting man, Mr. Hardwick? If so, I'd hedge my bets if I were you," Middlethorp interjected.

"Fine," Fenton agreed. "I'll tell you all I know, on one condition."

"And what condition is that?" Benedict queried, knowing the man would make a play to save his own skin.

Hardwick met his gaze squarely, unflinchingly. "You offered up transportation. I can't help where those girls are now and what's happening to 'em. But I'm doing everything you ask to help you save them right now. I don't go to the gallows. Have me transported like you offered. I'll go wherever I'm sent, and never darken English soil again... but I don't want to hang. It's not a fit way to die."

"I'll do what I can," Middlethorp conceded, adding the caveat, "but if those girls are dead, it will not be up to me. But you have my word to assist as much as possible. And if it comes to it, I'll find a better way for you than hanging from someone else's rope."

They both knew what that meant. Dying by one's own hand might have scared some, but only those who hadn't watched people dangle at the end of a rope as they struggled and gasped. Suicide wasn't pretty, but it was a better option. "Fair enough," Hardwick accepted. "When we were to go to his estate, we had to set out on the London Road and were to wait at the crossing there where the road heads off to Brighton. A black coach, no markings on it, would arrive. We'd all be given hoods to put on and driven to the estate. I can't swear to it, but I believe we headed west. It's a big estate, grand... lots of gilded furniture inside and marble floors covered in rugs worth more than I'd ever see in my life."

Middlethorp frowned. "There are only two men I know of who have 'grand' estates in that direction. One, I frankly can't conceive of him being involved in any scheme such as this... the other—"

Lady Vale made a sound of distress. "It's Harrelson, isn't it? All of this misery, from the taking of Benedict to the abductions of these poor young women can be traced back to my late husband, can't it?"

Middlethorp looked even more grim, if possible. "So it would appear, Sarah. I wish it were not so."

Lady Vale looked at him. "You could not have prevented it. James was a law unto himself... he followed no one's rules but his own. But are you satisfied now that Mr. Mason is, in fact, my son?"

"I am not dissuaded against it," Middlethorp granted. "That is all I can offer until we have this settled. We need your investigator... Adler?"

"He's been sent for," Benedict answered. "He should arrive short-ly... we still need answers about who targeted Miss Masters and

Mary."

"What does she look like, this Mary?" Hardwick asked.

Benedict sighed as he relayed the information. "Very petite, blond hair. It would have been just over a week ago that she was taken."

"I can't say who asked for her," Fenton answered. "But for her, we just nabbed the one what fit the description we'd been given. They wanted a small, blond woman... one who wasn't a child but could pass for one. I don't ask why. Better not to know with some, I think." He paused, then drew a deep breath and continued. "With Miss Masters, it was different. We were given specific instructions to take her and only her. That was why we hired those women to talk about Madame Zula at the baths, so they'd be overheard by Miss Masters and Lady Vale. I never made the connection who she was... not till later. It's been a long time. So I didn't think those biddies talking about a mystic would appeal to a woman of her age... it's usually younger women, single, desperate for love and romance that want to be told their fortunes. We were to take them to that same crossroads and hand them over to others. Sometimes it was the Irishman what worked for Madame Zula, and sometimes it was another man who was always with my employer. But we never knew who it would be."

"Someone wanted her specifically? You're certain?" Middlethorp asked.

"Yes. We were told in no uncertain terms that it had to be her. No substitutions would be accepted," Fenton answered. "I don't know what enemies that young woman could have made in her life but, whoever they are, they're quite determined to see her pay for whatever it was they think she's done."

Benedict turned his attention from Fenton to Middlethorp. The man knew something but he wasn't sharing it in front of Lady Vale. He knew Elizabeth had secrets and he knew that one of them was her former lover. There was a scandal there, and while it was unlikely that such a thing would be the root of all this, it was also the only straw left for him to grasp at.

"You said you didn't make the connection until later," Middlethorp countered. "What happened when you did?"

"I told my employer. He still wants the book... the one we were after all those years ago. I don't know what's in it, but he means to have it. You're still not safe from him. Not now. Not ever," Fenton answered.

Middlethorp frowned. "We need to see Madame Zula," he said, addressing Benedict. "I have a feeling that I know who is seeking Miss Masters. There was a scandal in her past, but it was something that I elected to overlook when hiring her. Her appearance was so far removed from the wild tale I'd heard that I assumed it had been greatly exaggerated or perhaps distorted to make the man involved appear less the villain for it."

Lady Vale gasped. "You hired her as my companion knowing this?"

"I know she has a past," Benedict said. "I only have a care for it because it might lead us to her now. It changes nothing of my feelings or my intentions toward her, regardless. Heaven knows I'm not without sin myself."

Middlethorp nodded. "Madame Zula first. Then we head on to Harrelson's and beard the lion in his den."

Benedict nodded his agreement. "Do you think she can be of use to us?"

"I think she can confirm for us where the women are taken to... at this point, we can't be certain they are on his estate. Without confirmation, approaching him may very well sign their death warrants."

Benedict knew that was the truth of it, but the delay worried him more. The sense of urgency was riding him hard and he felt that every second not in pursuit was wasted, whatever the wisdom behind it.

"There's still time," Hardwick said. "We weren't supposed to make the trade until tomorrow night. They'll hold her somewhere in town till then. Won't move her again till it's dark out."

"And can your companions be trusted not to harm her in the meantime?" Benedict snapped.

Hardwick looked away. "We don't get paid if we don't deliver them in one piece. I'd hope that was enough to keep her safe, but I can't make promises."

Chapter Nineteen

FEAR CONSUMED HER. Elizabeth had remained silent, curled on the floor of the wagon and feigning unconsciousness as they traversed the city in the darkness. But the first light of dawn was beginning to break, filtering through the fog and settling a soft glow over the city. The wagon had finally stopped.

She could smell the river. But as she couldn't hear the rushing water of the weir, she knew they were far removed from the more fashionable areas of the city.

A pair of strong but none too clean arms grasped her and she screamed. The hand that clamped down over her mouth and nose was just as foul smelling as the rest of him. But the lack of air made her panic and she pushed at him.

"Stop strugglin' and keep quiet. You ken?"

The menacing whisper against her ear prompted a jerky nod from her. Abruptly, the hand fell away and she was all but dragged from the back of the wagon. Stumbling on the uneven ground in her slippers, she was half-running as she tried to keep up with the man's longer stride. They were in an area of the city she'd never seen, filled with shabby-looking buildings and warehouses.

She had no notion of whether they were north or south of the Circus.

"You try to get away, you make me chase you," the man said again, his voice just as menacing before, "and I'll make you pay for it. I don't much care whether we get any money for you or not. You understand me, girl? Some things are worth more to a man than gold... I've never had me a lady before."

He leaned in and sniffed her hair, making a sound that made Elizabeth's skin crawl. "I doubt very seriously your employer would only withhold payment. He is apparently a very ruthless man and would not take well to being crossed."

"I don't take well to it neither," he said and shoved her toward the building nearest them.

Elizabeth listened to every sound. Just as they were about to enter, she heard the pealing of bells from the Abbey marking the hour. The sound was north of her and helped her to get her bearings. If she could escape, she at least knew in which direction to travel.

Stepping into the dirty and grim interior of the warehouse, she was escorted past stacks of crates and barrels and taken to a rickety staircase. Climbing upward, gripping the railing with fear as the steps creaked and groaned beneath their collective weight, they reached the upper level and she was shoved into a small, dark room. There was a single window, but it was so high she'd never be able to reach it. Just enough of the gray light of dawn filtered in to illuminate a dirty mattress on the floor. Turning to look at the door which closed and locked behind her, her eyes were drawn to marks on the back of it.

Closing the distance, she placed her hand against the door, curving her fingers until her nails fit into the grooves left behind in the wood by someone else who had tried to claw their way out.

"What on earth is to become of me now?" She whispered the question into the empty room, but knew that no answer was forthcoming. No rescue would be either. How would they find her? How would anyone even know where to look for her? It was impossible.

Tears threatened. Hopelessness pressed in on her, weighing her down. Elizabeth sank down onto the floor, but she did not give in to the urge to simply sob helplessly. Instead, she examined the lock, the hinges on the door, how securely every board was attached to the one next to it. Whatever it took, she vowed, she would not just give in to whatever fate they had in store for her.

THE CARRIAGE THUNDERED over the road, traveling at a speed that was impossibly reckless. Inside, Zella gripped the seat and hung on with all her might as every bump threatened to send her sprawling onto the floor of the hired vehicle. They had not dared take her own coach as she could not be certain which of her servants could be trusted. In the hired vehicle, the curtains drawn tight against the rising sun, they were making a desperate attempt to escape.

Their only hope was to get away undetected. If he knew they were making a run for it, he would move heaven and earth to stop them. Glancing across the darkened expanse of the carriage, her gaze locked with Dylan's. Even in the pale moonlight that filtered in through the carriage windows, she could read the tension in his posture. It was evident in the tightly-clenched jaw and the squared straight set of his shoulders.

"Whatever happens, know that I love you," she said. "You have given me the one thing I have never had in this life. You have given me hope."

She felt Dylan's gaze settle upon her and, even there in the dim light, she could see the glint of his beautiful smile. From the first moment she had met him, he had been the most beautiful person she had ever seen. In their years together, that had not changed.

"We will get out from under him," Dylan vowed. "Whatever it takes, my love, I will set us both free of his grasp."

Zella clenched her hands tightly onto the seat as they hit a particularly deep rut in the road. He was making promises that he would not be able to keep. He did not fully understand the power that Harrelson had. Dylan, despite his troubled upbringing, truly could not fathom the kind of evil that her former protector possessed. His inability to appreciate and to understand that kind of darkness of soul was one of the many reasons she loved him.

There was a part of her that believed they did not deserve happiness. They did not deserve to escape his grasp and start a new life of their own, free of his black influence, not when they had been complicit in robbing so many others of their freedom. She could not allow herself to hope. She could not allow herself to believe, even for a single moment, that they would truly ever get away. If she let herself believe it, and it failed to come to fruition, the pain of that was more than she could contemplate.

Abruptly, the coach slowed, so much so that she slid from the seat and onto the floor. Her hip connected painfully with the hard wooden trim.

Dylan rose from his seat and rapped his fist against the ceiling of carriage. "What's happening?" he demanded of the driver. "Why have we stopped?"

The driver didn't answer. From outside, there was nothing but the deafening sound of silence.

A sinking feeling settled over Zella. She had thought they would at least make it to Brighton, that they might even make it aboard a ship before he'd pull them back into his web. It appeared she was wrong.

"It's over. He's found us, Dylan. There is no escape from him… ever." She whispered the words into the darkened carriage but the weight of them and of the knowledge that prompted them was overwhelming. The offense would not be easily forgiven, if at all. They would pay dearly and the only thing she valued in the world was the man across from her. She served a purpose and Dylan did not, which meant that Dylan would die.

"It's probably a lame horse or a damaged wheel," Dylan said as he rose to exit the carriage. "He is not all-powerful. The driver is all but deaf. Likely, he didn't hear the question."

She grabbed his hand. "Don't go out there. Please, Dylan. Whatever you think is happening, I promise you it is more sinister than that. Stay in here. Please. I'm begging you!"

"Zella—"

"He wants me… I am of use to him, but you are not. If you go out there, he'll kill you to punish me. But if I go willingly with him, if I continue to play this macabre game of his, then perhaps he'll let you go free. I'd rather walk away from you now, though it breaks my heart, than to know I brought about your death," Zella implored him. "I can't be Zella Hopkins. He won't allow it. For the remainder of my days, I will be Madame Zula and he will use me as his procuress. But I will know you are alive. I will know that you are still in this world. I couldn't bear it otherwise."

"I'm not letting you go out there in the dark alone," he said.

"I won't be alone. I'll never be alone. And as long as he has use of me, I'll be safe. Let me go, Dylan. For both our sakes," she begged him. "Besides... I did something before I left the city. It won't save me, but it may stop him."

"What have you done?" he asked, fear strengthening the Irish lilt in his voice.

"He's not the only one who can keep records... and I can't imagine that the intrepid Mr. Mason will not discover our absence. When he investigates our former home, he'll find what he needs," she explained, whispering the words close to his ear as she kissed his cheek. "Take care, my darling boy. Find some young pretty thing and have beautiful Irish babies. Please?"

Zella rose and stepped from the carriage, leaving him staring after her. Just as she'd suspected, another carriage awaited her. Lanterns blazed from it and the coachman wore a heavy, dark cloak that concealed him entirely. As she approached, he nodded at her in acknowledgement. The carriage door opened and the steps lowered. Lifting her skirts, she stepped up and took her seat across from the man who had ruined most of her life.

"Zella, what a trial you have been of late," he said.

"Lord Harrelson," she acknowledged. "You have been nothing but a source of pain to me from the moment I first laid eyes upon you."

He smiled. "So I have. But that's why we understand one another, Zella. That is why we've worked so well together for so many years. Supplying young women, and occasionally children, as well, to discerning men such as myself has been a lucrative enterprise for us both, has it not?"

"Much more so for you than for the likes of me," she corrected. "I've never done any of this for the money. I did it to save my skin. I know what happens to those who defy you."

He drummed his fingers softly on the wooden trim of the window, tapping out a rhythm that set her teeth on edge.

"You do know, Zella... and that is why I am so very puzzled by this little rebellion of yours. It must be the influence of your young Irishman. They are an unruly lot, after all. It must be corrected," he mused. "Which begs the question... what to do now?"

Zella knew what he wanted. It was what he always wanted—to have her crawl before him. For him, everything came down to power, to knowing that he was in complete control and everyone else was simply a pawn in his game. "I'll continue to help you procure them. I'll never offer you a moment's trouble ever again... if you let him go."

He chuckled. "You are a bold one, Zella, to make demands. But I've always admired that about you, along with your penchant for the theatrical. If you hadn't played such a profitable role in my little organization, I'd be less inclined to be forgiving. So, I have a counter offer. I'll let your little Irishman go, but you'll never see him, speak to him, or question me about his fate ever again. You will resume your residence in Bath, though not for long. Recent events have made that location somewhat dodgy for us."

"Very well," she conceded. "Where will we go next?"

"Wherever I tell you to," he fired back, and the anger crept in then. He might be offering the guise of forgiveness, but it was evident from that little slip, she would pay for her transgressions against him for a very long time.

"You have my word," she replied.

"As if it's worth anything," he scoffed. Lifting his walking stick, an item that was more than purely decorative as it concealed a wicked-looking blade, he tapped on the ceiling and the carriage lurched forward. "My men will follow him... wherever he goes. If you think to betray me again, he will die for it. Is that understood, Zella?"

She didn't speak, couldn't get any words past the lump in her throat. Instead, she gave him a jerky nod and dipped her chin to her chest in order to hide her tears. He'd only enjoy them, and they were not for him. They were for her and her beautiful man and the future they'd almost had.

As the carriage rolled into the darkness, she left Dylan and any thoughts of either freedom or happiness in her wake.

⟡

THE CARRIAGE MOVED at a snail's pace, the wheels rumbling quietly over the cobbled streets as they approached Madame Zula's house. The day was breaking across the town. The bustling of day servants from their homes to their places of employment had just begun. But given the hour, the upper floors of most houses were still silent, the upper classes lying abed as they recovered from parties and balls from the night before.

The townhouse that had housed Madame Zula was quiet, however, with every window dark and shuttered. It was obvious that it was empty even from the outside. Houses that were uninhabited had a look and a feel to them.

"They've gone," Middlethorp stated matter of factly. There was a hint of frustration in his voice, but only that. The man had a masterful ability to conceal his feelings.

"It isn't a surprise. I still say we go in. There may be something they've left behind that will provide more information about their scheme and, perhaps, even a direction of where Mary might be. Fenton was the muscle, Madame Zula the lure... but I can't help but think she's a more integral part of the operation than he is. After all, anyone can do what he does," Benedict mused.

"True enough," Middlethorp agreed. "I take it you have experience as a housebreaker, then?"

"No. But I'm fairly certain you do," Benedict countered as he headed down the stairs to the servants' entrance. It was more shielded from view and their attempts to gain entrance would be less likely to garner attention.

The other man smiled as he followed Benedict down while he retrieved a small case from inside his waistcoat. The slim, leather sheath opened to reveal a series of tools. "I might have gone where not invited a time or two."

Benedict watched him open the lock with surprising speed and ease, seriously putting to question the number of times Middlethorp had reported. "Clearly. What, pray tell, are we looking for here if it's glaringly apparent that Madame Zula has made off like a thief in the night?"

"Answers," the older man replied cryptically as the door swung inward. "How she might be connected to Harrelson, how they select their victims, where they take them afterward… how they communicate with one another."

Following him into the darkened hall, Benedict surveyed the surroundings that were discernible in the dim light that filtered through the curtains. It wasn't much, just the impression of dark furnishings and heavy fabrics. Whether it was more or less depressing in daylight, he could not guess, but he supposed it was effective in setting the tone for Madame Zula's work.

"You check down here," Middlethorp suggested. "I'll go upstairs."

Benedict nodded his agreement and began searching each room methodically. The drawing room held nothing but an assortment of macabre decor. What had once been a dining room was obviously used for larger mystical gatherings based upon the heavy cloth draping the table and the continued array of terrifying objects d'art. Jars full of macabre and strange items shared space with crumbling texts and bone carvings that made him wish to be anywhere else.

The small study that was just off the transformed dining room was another matter entirely. There was a large and heavy desk, littered with papers. On the corner of it, were a candelabra and a tinder box. Striking one, the soft glow that fell over the room showed how dire the state of disarray was. But placed neatly in the center of the desk, wrapped in a pretty bow, was a ledger and a sealed letter atop it.

Benedict didn't open the letter immediately, saving that to be shared with everyone. Instead, he flipped open the ledger. There were a series of dates and addresses. Occasionally, they were accompanied by a name or a single word or short description. Blond, brunette, short, no more than fourteen—the descriptors painted a terrifying picture of precisely what he was looking it. Flipping to one of the last marked pages, he found the date of the first attempt to abduct Elizabeth. The initials "E.M." had been scrawled next to the date.

"Good God," he whispered. There had to be hundreds.

"You look as if you're ready to cast up your accounts."

Benedict looked up to see Middlethorp standing casually in the doorway. "I very well may. Did you discover anything upstairs?"

Middlethorp shrugged. "Half-empty drawers, discarded gowns. All the jewelry is gone which is a sure sign she doesn't mean to return. I take it you've found something more interesting here?"

Benedict held up the ledger. "If this book represents what I believe it to, the breadth of this evil is beyond anything I've ever seen. There are hundreds of dates, locations and descriptions in here. There is one that corresponds to Mary's disappearance and one that corresponds to the attempted abduction of Miss Masters. How could so many go missing without raising a hue and cry?"

Middlethorp shrugged. "Because he chose women that were alone in the world... widows, orphans, those who had no one to miss them when they were gone. I'd be curious to know what your sister said to them when she came here for her 'appointment'."

Benedict found himself curious about the same. "There is a letter, as well, but I haven't opened it yet." Passing the letter to Middlethorp, he watched as the other man broke the wax seal.

"If you've found this letter then I have fled. I do not expect to escape him unscathed and this evidence I've left behind is yours to do with as you please. I'd rather swing at Tyburn for my crimes than to continue in his service any longer, though I doubt it will ever come to that."
Middlethorp paused in the reading for a moment, letting that ominous statement resonate.

"If you haven't managed to identify him yet, then please allow me to illuminate you. His name is Lord Wendell Harrelson and he has been responsible for every bit of misery that has befallen Lady Vale. I was a young girl when I was sold to him by my own father. I was his unwilling mistress when he orchestrated the invasion of Lady Vale's home in search of the book where he kept all his evidence of others' crimes.

He had used blackmail to restore the fortune of his family and continued to use it to supplement the income from his estates and support his lavish lifestyle. Lord Vale took that book from him and left him with nothing. When his attempt to retrieve it went awry, rash decisions were made that would alter all of our lives irrevocably. Fenton Hardwick decided to get rid of the boy in what he saw as a more humane fashion and sold him. But the sale of Lord Vale's son to a wandering couple inspired Harrelson to a new stream of revenue— the peddling of flesh. Whether it is providing children for couples who cannot have their own or providing women and girls to men who would abuse them, he is without scruples.

He has Mary Mason and will no doubt be turning her over to her purchaser very soon. As for Miss Masters, that is a different matter. I am given to understand that Miss Masters was asked for by name, by someone from her past. The women are typically held in a warehouse near the Kennett and Avon canal… if not there, look on Harrelson's estate. There is an abandoned salt mine on the property that he has had converted into a series of cells. I cannot be certain in which of those places Miss Mason is held, but you will find her in one of them.

You need not worry about seeking justice for Harrelson or for me. I will see an end to us both."

Benedict digested the information. "We need to go to the warehouse first. It's closest and as they wouldn't have time to reach the estate before daybreak, it's the most likely location for them to have taken Miss Masters. It is probably too much to hope that we will find Mary there, as well, but I pray that I am wrong."

"No doubt you are right on the first count. It'd be much harder to explain hauling an unwilling woman around in daylight hours. Perhaps we will be lucky and locate your sister, as well." Middlethorp's expression hardened and he blocked the door. "But before we leave here, I need the truth about you. Who are your parents?"

"I don't know. If you are intending to ask whether or not I believe myself to be the missing Viscount Vale, the answer is simply that I no longer know. A week ago, I would have found it laughable. Two days ago, I found Lady Vale to be pitiable and potentially mad. But at every turn, I am confronted with more coincidences than I can comfortably deny," Benedict answered honestly. For the entirety of his life, he'd imagined that he'd been unwanted, a foundling tossed out to be picked up and carted off by the Masons. That was the version of events they had given him, at least most of the time. Invariably, the truth and the story changed to serve their purposes. That version had been the kindest they'd ever offered.

"And what of Sarah? What happens when she is permitted to continue putting her faith in this only to possibly be proven wrong one day?"

Benedict tossed up his hands. "What do you believe, sir?"

"I believed that my nephew was dead," Middlethorp said. "I have always believed it because I couldn't imagine that anyone ruthless enough to steal a babe directly from its mother's arms would be foolish enough to then leave that child alive."

"Then there you have it," Benedict said. "I am not Viscount Vale."

"I said believed, Mr. Mason... not believe. For the first time since Sarah's son was taken, I am given cause to doubt my assessment. You are so very like her that I cannot think of any other plausible reason for such a similarity. It would help if we could question the couple who adopted you."

Benedict froze. "That is not possible."

"Would they not tell the truth, then?"

"They cannot tell you anything," Benedict said. "They are dead. Both of them."

Middlethorp's eyes narrowed. "An accident?"

"No. It was not an accident... I killed them," Benedict admitted, uttering words that damned him completely.

Middlethorp said nothing for the longest time. He remained completely silent as he surveyed Benedict critically. Finally, he asked, "Did they deserve it?"

"Every single day of our lives," Benedict answered. "My only regret is that I didn't do it sooner."

"Why?"

The question was a simple one, uttered with a complete lack of judgement. Benedict could hear that in the other man's voice. Perhaps it was that lack of judgement that prompted his answer. "To protect Mary from something far worse than simply his fists. We'd both taken our fair share of beatings, but I could see that the way he looked at her had changed. Young as I was, I knew enough to recognize lust when I saw it."

"And did you save her?"

"I did… I began keeping a knife tucked under my bed." The nightmare returned, the horrible memory of their father, drunken and violent, entering the small loft that he and Mary had shared. But he was awake, reliving the memory for once. "I didn't intend to kill him…only to defend her and keep him from—just to stop him. But he was drunk and violent. He began hitting me and her. We struggled and fell to the floor and then he stopped."

Benedict paused and took a deep, shuddering breath. He'd never spoken of it, never said aloud the awful things that had happened that night. "I felt the blade sink into his belly and then the blood. I'd never seen so much of it."

"How old were you?" Middlethorp asked. The question was uttered softly.

"I don't really know how old I am. I was never told what year I had been born in. Birthdays were not marked or even commented upon," Benedict answered striving for an even tone, struggling to regain his composure. "Fifteen years have passed since."

The other man nodded sagely. "If you are, in fact, my nephew, that would have made you thirteen at the time. Not quite a child, but very far still from being a man… and yet you did what men do. You protected those you love from harm. There is no shame in that. No sin in it."

"I murdered my father."

"You killed a man who never deserved the title of father," Middlethorp corrected. "Any man that would beat a child with his fists, or worse, that would look upon a young girl with lust when he was supposed to have been her father, has no right to be called such."

"He didn't die immediately… he lay there bleeding for a long time. Mary wanted to get our mother to help him, but I wouldn't let her. I made her sit there with me and watch him die. That's hardly the hallmark of a brave man, is it?" Benedict argued.

"It's the hallmark of a wise one. Had he survived, he would have killed you and then there would have been no one to protect her," Middlethorp pointed out. "What became of your mother?"

"Mary lured her from the house, saying she'd heard a noise and thought it might be father needing help." Benedict could recall how she'd protested having to lie, how terrified she'd been. He'd badgered her into doing it. More than anything else, forcing her to be a part of his crimes left him riddled with guilt. "While they were out of the house, I set fire to it to hide our crime. When our saw mother saw the flames, she rushed back and ran into the house. We tried to stop her, but she wouldn't listen to reason. She said she wanted to die with him… I didn't mean for her to die. But the simple truth is I'm not especially sorry that it happened. Had she lived, no doubt she'd have either abandoned us or brought in some other man who would have harmed Mary just the same."

"As far as I am concerned," Middlethorp offered, "no crime has been committed. It was an accident. You were defending your sister and his own drunkenness caused him to behave imprudently. Had he not had impure intentions, he would never have been in harm's way to start. You've saved you sister once and you will do so again, but first, let us locate Miss Masters and move forward from there. I have only one request of you, Mr. Mason. Do not make promises you cannot keep."

"I have promised Lady Vale nothing," Benedict insisted.

"And it was not Lady Vale of whom I spoke."

MARY RAN UNTIL her sides ached from the exertion. Her slippers had long since been lost during the days when she'd lain senseless from whatever drug they'd forced upon her. The cold, hard ground had torn at her feet, leaving them aching and bleeding. Still, she trudged on. She had to. It was one thing to await a rescue when others knew where she was and where to look for her. As she herself had no notion of her current location, it seemed more than a little foolish to assume that others would be able to find her.

Branches snagged at her hair and her dress. Every noise made her jump. Had her captor managed to free himself? Had others gone looking for him when he did not return from serving her evening meal? Were they in pursuit even at that very moment?

Every question that circled rapidly in her mind only fed her fear and anxiety. Already at their peaks as she was running through unfamiliar woods in the dark, Mary did her best to force those thoughts aside.

Ahead of her, she could see light through a break in the trees. It was still early in the morning, not quite dawn. Yet in the deep shadows of the trees, even that had been impossible to tell. The opening ahead of her could be either a stream or, God willing, a road. Slowing for just long enough to catch her breath, Mary proceeded cautiously. Once she reached the opening, she sighed in relief. It was, in fact, a road. It posed dangers of its own, she supposed, but at least she felt that she was making progress in her escape.

Turning to her right, she headed in the direction of what she could only hope would be a village or town. If she were lucky, it would be the road back to Bath. She could return to the small room she'd rented from Mrs. Simms and plead with the woman for mercy. Clean clothes, a bath, food she wasn't afraid to eat, and she could send for her brother to come fetch her, if he wasn't in Bath already to look for her.

The rumbling of carriage wheels and the thunder of hooves brought a moment's elation, but it was immediately overshadowed by fear. What if they had employed a carriage in their search for her? What if it wasn't someone who meant to help her, but simply to place her in captivity once more?

It might have been instinct or it might simply have been her traumatized mind prompting such thoughts. Regardless, Mary ducked back into the trees, crouching down and making herself as small as possible.

The carriage slowed and then stopped near her. The driver peered into the shadowy recesses of the woods and Mary's breath caught.

A man's face appeared in the carriage window. "Why have we stopped?" His tone was sharp and impatient.

"I thought I saw somethin', my lord... running alongside the road and into the trees!" the driver explained.

"It was a deer most likely. Drive on!"

"What if she's gotten out?" the driver asked.

The man laughed. "No one ever has, Jones. Drive on."

As the carriage moved forward, the driver still clearly reluctant, Mary breathed a sigh of relief. She had narrowly dodged a miserable fate. What if she hadn't listened to that small niggling voice of doubt? What if she'd been foolish enough to ask them for help?

"How did you know?"

The deep voice whispered from the darkness behind her and it was all she could do to stifle her scream. Whirling, prepared to run again or to fight with everything in her, Mary faced down the person who'd managed to slip up so soundlessly behind her.

She couldn't see anything more than his shadowy silhouette in the darkness. It was enough. He was tall and broad of shoulder. Even without the ability to make out detail, she could feel the power of him.

"I won't go back," she vowed. "You may as well kill me now."

"You will go back," he said softly, but with complete conviction.

He stepped closer, close enough for the moonlight to illuminate the harsh planes of his face. Not handsome, but arresting, he had the bearing of an aristocrat or perhaps a soldier. She knew, of course, that being in possession of a title of honor did not make one an honorable man. "What is your name?"

"Mary Benedict," she lied, not wanting to give her last name. Benedict was wealthy enough that ransom was a genuine fear. At this point, she had no way of ascertaining whether this stranger was a villain in his own right, employed by those who had captured her, or something else altogether.

He smiled as if he saw the lie for what it was. "You're coming with me, Mary Benedict," he said.

No, she wasn't. She'd had more than enough of being bullied and told what to do by men. When he reached for her, Mary did the thing her brother had taught her. Drawing her leg back, she brought her knee up swiftly, catching him squarely between his muscular thighs. When he dropped to the ground with an agonized groan, she turned and fled through woods again.

She could hear him giving chase behind her, the tress thrashing and leaves rattling. Forcing herself to move faster, to increase her speed and put greater distance between them, she ignored her protesting muscles and her heaving lungs. Despite her determination, he appeared to be gaining on her. Stepping off the worn and overgrown path, she dove deeper into the trees. Her foot slipped in the mud and she struggled to regain her balance. A stifled scream escaped her as she fell, the ground rushing up to greet her. Her head struck a large section of the tree roots and the world went completely black.

Chapter Twenty

BENEDICT DUCKED BEHIND a stack of barrels and watched the comings and goings from the various warehouses along the waterfront there. There were small boats coming and going on the canals, mostly hauling goods and passengers between Bath and Bristol. It wasn't difficult to ascertain which one was housing things other than simple merchandise. One building, out of all those he surveyed, remained completely quiet. No one came or went from it and it remained locked up tight.

"That's the most likely location, I think," Benedict said. "This time of morning should be bustling and not a soul is stirring there."

"It's certainly suspect," Middlethorp agreed. "I asked, under the guise of being a merchant looking to expand my operation, who owned it and the gentlemen working in the establishments next door could not tell me. They stated that they've not seen anyone entering or exiting from it in ages. It had belonged to a man by the name of Carstairs but, apparently, he lost it on the turn of a card. No one knows to whom."

"I'm going in... I'll slip through the alley and around to the back. You keep watch on the front door in case someone comes to move her."

Middlethorp nodded his agreement. Benedict remained concealed behind barrels and crates but kept moving forward until, at last, he could duck around the side of the building. There were two windows in the upper part, and someone had, thankfully, left several crates in the alley. Stacking them carefully, Benedict climbed up until he could reach the windowsill. The wound at his shoulder burned like fire, but he ignored it as he pulled himself up and through the narrow opening.

The window itself led to nowhere. There was no floor, no room, only open space, save for a few beams below him. Lowering himself carefully onto one of those beams, he broke out in a sweat as it groaned beneath his weight. There was a small staircase and a single room across the way. The door was shut and barred. Even from a distance, he could see the heavy bar in place. If she was inside the building, that was no doubt where she would be.

Every step across the narrow beam, his booted feet sliding in the dust and grime that had settled there through the years, had him gritting his teeth. When at last he reached the railing at the top of the narrow stairs, he let out a long, slow breath. It hissed between his teeth as sweat dripped from his brow.

As he reached for the heavy bar that held the door fast, Benedict uttered a quick prayer beneath his breath. He didn't know that God had any interest in hearing from him, but he said it just the same. He prayed that he would find at least one of them safe and unharmed behind that door.

ELIZABETH HAD BECOME attuned to every noise, every single creak and groan of the ancient building. She'd known the minute they left her there, when the building had gone eerily silent. She'd heard the rats within the walls. She'd heard the shouts of the workmen in the streets below. For some time, she'd shouted back at them, screaming for help. But no one had heard her or if they had, they had not bothered to answer.

Too afraid to lie down, afraid of falling asleep and terrified of the scurrying sounds within the walls, she'd sat perched on the edge of that dirty mattress for hours it seemed. Of course, the light coming through the small, dirty window high above her showed that it was still only morning. It was fear that made her feel she'd been there so long.

The slight shuffling she heard, followed by the creaking of the beams that extended above her prompted her to leap to her feet. There was little in the room in the way of weapons but a single floorboard she'd managed to pry up with her bare hands. Gripping it with all her might, she braced herself on the other side of the door and waited for whoever was about to come through it.

The grating sound of metal moving signaled that the bar was being lifted. When the door swung inward, she raised the board, prepared to bring it down with all the force she could muster. At the very last second, recognition dawned and she managed to narrowly avoid striking her rescuer.

As she tossed the board aside, Benedict grabbed her, pulled her to him and held her tightly.

"You came," she whispered, her words muffled against his chest. "You came for me."

"Of course, I came for you. Why the devil did you think I wouldn't?"

She looked up at him and the tears she'd managed to hold at bay since being tossed into the back of that wagon began to fall. "Because no one else would have."

He stared at her for a moment, his eyes widening, and then he offered her a vow. "Wherever you are, I will always follow. I promise you that, Elizabeth. Nothing will change that."

It was a promise he could not keep. He meant to, and it was not his sincerity that she questioned, but the reality of their society, because she would never be accepted and never be forgiven for her previous fall from grace. "Even if you are Lord Vale?"

"I'm Benedict Mason. They can tack on any titles and names they like, but I'm still me. I was still raised poor, dirty and hungry, and I still run a gaming hell that not too long ago doubled as a brothel… I'll never be an aristocrat, Elizabeth, no matter what they call me."

He meant it. She knew that he did. Every time she'd questioned his honesty, it had been more about her past than about his character.

He'd been honest from the start.

"What about Mary?"

"She's not here," he said. "There is no other space in this building where a person might be kept. But we have an idea where to find her. I'll get you back to Lady Vale and then I'll set out for her."

A horrible thought pressed in upon her then. Guilt wracked her. "It will be my fault if you don't. If you hadn't been injured trying to save me, if you hadn't had to take yet more time to rescue me again, you might have already found her! Oh, Benedict—"

"If I hadn't rescued you, I wouldn't have found myself in Lady Vale's care. That was a stroke of luck, Elizabeth, not misfortune. I've reconnected with a family that was lost to me before. Whether I find Mary today or not, I know who took her, and that's the first step in tracking her down," he insisted. "And there is only one person at fault here. It's Lord Harrelson. He's behind all of it."

Elizabeth gasped with shock. It was Freddy after all. "Lord Wendell Harrelson?"

Benedict frowned at her. "You know him?"

"When I spoke to you of my indiscretion before… his name was Fredrick Hamilton. His mother is Lord Harrelson's sister," she whispered. "Oh, dear God! I cannot believe that Freddy would stoop to such levels. I suspected it was him because I couldn't imagine it would be anyone else… but I never dreamed… you must be very careful, Benedict. They are ruthless people. I never knew how ruthless until I refused Freddy's offer. He told me that he would see me ruined and he did. There was nowhere I could go that the whispers did not follow me. It wasn't until Mr. Middlethorp that I found an employer who was willing to truly look past them!"

His expression turned grim. "You'll never have to worry about them again. I swear it. Let's get you out of here."

They turned toward the door but never made it out. The same large man who'd locked her in that morning was there. His fist slammed into Benedict's face, sending him sprawling backward. Elizabeth screamed. Scrambling backward, she retrieved the board she'd pried loose earlier. The man looked at it and laughed, thinking it was an ineffectual weapon. From his vantage point, he couldn't see the nails still sticking out of the other side.

Before she could even take a swing at him, Benedict was up. He moved toward the man in a low crouch, slamming his shoulders into the larger man's abdomen. They tumbled backward through the door. Wood splintered. A short, tight scream split the silence.

Elizabeth rushed forward, her heart in her throat, thinking that Benedict had fallen to the hard, stone floor below. But as she stepped onto the landing, he was there, hoisting himself back up onto the wooden planks. She swayed and managed to catch herself, planting her hands firmly on the wall.

"Do not faint," he said. "We haven't time. I can't imagine he's Harrelson's only employee."

They rushed down the stairs. The narrow wooden steps had become even more rickety minus their upper railing and appeared in danger of collapse with each step they took. Rushing outside into the pale morning sunlight, Elizabeth was heedless of the fact that she was in her nightdress and wrapper. She wanted nothing more than to be safely ensconced once more in Lady Vale's townhouse, surrounded by servants and without a moment's privacy to herself.

Mr. Middlethorp was waiting. Somehow, by means she surely did not wish to know, he had procured a small gig for them. Elizabeth let out a mild squeak of alarm as Mr. Middlethorp grasped her arm and hauled her up beside him. Benedict climbed onto the back. Without a word, Middlethorp cracked the lash over the horses with enough skill that it never even came close to touching their flesh. Immediately, the cart surged forward. Behind them, she could hear the commotion and assumed that it probably had something to do with the manner in which he'd obtained the vehicle.

"I don't think you're a gentleman either," she said.

Middlethorp smiled. "That may be the kindest thing any of my employees has ever said of me, Miss Masters. Thank you."

ZELLA HOPKINS OPENED the door to her home and let herself inside. It was dark and cold, as all the curtains were drawn and the day servants had been dismissed. No fires had been laid, no bricks warmed. The house was as silent as a tomb.

Harrelson followed her inside. He intended to lay down the law and she intended to let him or at least grant that illusion.

"I need whiskey," she said abruptly. "If you mean to have this chat now, I need fortification first."

"It's barely past ten," he pointed out.

"I wouldn't care if the rooster had just crowed," she snapped back. Crossing the narrow hall to her small study, she opened the door and stepped inside. Her gaze fell to the desk and her eyes fluttered closed in relief for only a split second. The ledger and the letter had been taken. Providing that information was the only small step available to her to possibly atone for her sins. It wouldn't be enough and hell was surely waiting, but at least she felt better about the going.

Opening a cabinet behind the desk, she retrieved a bottle still sealed with dark red wax. She placed it on the desk and put a glass next to it.

"And why are you not drinking from the bottle that is already opened?" Harrelson asked. He was a suspicious man with a nasty turn of mind that had served him only too well over the years.

"Because it's watered down. I'm not wasting good whiskey on the fools who darken my door. They wouldn't know the difference anyway," she answered evenly as she carefully opened the bottle and deposited a healthy amount in her glass. She lifted it and took a deceptively small amount into her mouth for the long swallow she portrayed. If her deception failed, she'd be free of him regardless. But her plan, all along, had been to take him with her.

He smiled cooly. "Well, now that I can be certain you aren't trying to poison me, I'll take a glass as well."

"But it's barely past ten," she answered in a mockingly sweet tone.

"Surely a gentleman such as you would not indulge in strong spirits so early in the day? Only us lower class folk would be so crude!"

He strode toward her, grasped her wrist and took the glass from her hand. "You forget yourself, Zella. I am not the type to tolerate your word games and sharp tongue. Remember that."

She watched as he took a healthy swallow from the glass. It wasn't enough, but it was a nice start. Retrieving a second glass, she poured another healthy measure into it and began sipping, slow and steady. She didn't mean for either of them to make it out of that room alive but she wanted to watch him shuffle off the mortal coil before giving it up herself.

"I do hope your little Irishman managed to successfully carry out the abduction of Miss Masters this time," Harrelson said, settling himself into one of the chairs. "I would hate to disappoint Freddy again. He's such a dear boy and has never asked a thing of me till this. She fair broke his young heart when she refused him."

"She refused to marry him?" Zella asked in mock incredulity. She didn't care, honestly. Women, in her opinion, had the right to refuse a man anything. They seldom agreed and seldom accepted the refusal in her experience.

Harrelson laughed. "Oh, no! Never that. He has a wife. Quiet, meek, biddable… and an heiress. Miss Masters was his first love, so to speak. He'd thought to keep her as his mistress after he wed but she proved less than amenable to that offer. And while meek, biddable heiresses are certainly a boon for the family coffers, I think they leave something to be desired in the marriage bed."

"There are other women," Zella replied. "Women who would gladly accept his offer. Why torment the girl this way?"

"Because she wounded his pride," Harrelson said. "We are an unforgiving lot. You're very lucky, Zella, that I hold you in such affection. Otherwise, this little escape you planned would have gone very badly for you, indeed."

Zella kept her gaze completely impassive as he raised his glass to her and then took another generous swallow of the liquid it contained.

When he lowered it, the glass was very nearly drained.

"I wouldn't say it went so badly. I'll be free of you soon enough… one way or another." Her expression was calm, her voice utterly serene, but inside she was dancing and shouting with joy.

"What a curious thing for you to say." His voice cracked a bit at the end of his statement and he cleared his throat. When it did not relieve the pressure he was feeling, pressure she recognized because it was beginning to impact her as well, his eyes widened. "What have you done, Zella?"

"Something I should have done long ago… this world is a better place without you in it."

"You drank from the same glass!" Harrelson protested, wheezing as he did so.

"We're both dying, you bastard. I just sipped slower in order to watch you go first," she said.

Harrelson tried to rise from the chair, but he stumbled, pitched to and fro and then sank to his knees on the carpet. His fingers clawed at his neckcloth and collar, pulling them away so forcefully that he drew blood from his own mottling flesh.

"Bitch," he hissed, because his voice had been reduced to little more than that.

Zella said nothing, she simply took another sip and watched him collapse. He writhed there for a few moments, his body convulsing as he tried desperately to draw air into his failing lungs. When at last he stilled, his face pale and lips blue, Zella simply closed her eyes. She didn't fight it. She didn't try to escape what she had come to view as her destiny. The end of her life was a small sacrifice to ensure that his evil was eradicated from the world. There was no more fear. Death could not possibly equal the suffering that he had inflicted on her for so many years.

A gentle smile curved her lips as she thought of Dylan and drew her last shallow breath. She pictured him on a ship, sailing for America and a new life there.

Chapter Twenty-One

UPON HER RETURN to Lady Vale's, Elizabeth was whisked away to her chamber and tucked into a hot bath. Mr. Adler had been there as they arrived and had joined Benedict and Mr. Middlethorp as they headed out toward Lord Harrelson's estate.

Lady Vale entered the chamber just after Elizabeth had emerged from the tub. She had only just donned the wrapper that had been borrowed from Lady Vale for her as her own was too dirty and damaged to be salvaged.

"I trust you were not injured?" Lady Vale asked, once they were alone.

They both knew that injured was merely a euphemism for raped. "I am uninjured," Elizabeth answered as she took a seat on the edge of the bed. She was still unsteady, her nerves frayed and her emotions barely in check.

Lady Vale sighed with relief, tipping her head back and uttering a soft prayer. After a moment, she took the single chair in the room and settled herself into it.

"There is a conversation we must have, and I felt it best to do it with as few prying eyes and listening ears about as possible," Lady Vale stated.

She was being sacked for her inappropriate behavior with Benedict. There was little question of it and, in truth, Elizabeth could not fault her for it. "I will pack my things as soon I have finished here."

Lady Vale tilted her head to one side, a thoughtful expression on her face. "I see. And where is it that you will go, my dear?"

"I have an aged aunt in Derbyshire," Elizabeth answered. "She is a most unpleasant woman, but as she has become increasingly infirmed in the last years, I think she would welcome me." It was a lie, of course. There was an aunt and she would certainly be permitted to reside with her, but to state that she would be welcome was a gross exaggeration. Her Aunt Helene would remind her on an hourly basis of all the various ways in which she had disgraced the family.

"Is that what you wish to do, then?" Lady Vale pressed. "To care for your aged aunt in the wilds of Derbyshire?"

"If there are wilds in Derbyshire, my lady, I have yet to discover them," Elizabeth evaded. "It is an expedient solution to the crossroads we find ourselves at. You do not wish, and rightly so, for me to remain in your employ. And I would not be able to maintain a genteel life in Bath on the meager savings that I possess."

Lady Vale nodded sagely. "Yes. That is a conundrum… but there is one part of it all by which I am still puzzled."

"And that is?"

"At what point, you darling but utterly daft girl, did I or anyone else state that you were no longer welcome in this house?"

Elizabeth gaped at her. "Surely, after my disclosure to you about the nature of my interactions with Mr. Mason—"

"Lord Vale," she corrected. "He is my son. Whatever proof Branson still requires will be addresses to his satisfaction, no doubt. We shall all have to accustom ourselves to addressing him thusly. Perhaps Benedict most of all. As for your disclosure, my dear—we have all, at one time or another, been imprudent. And it was pointed out to me, to my great shame, that I was trying to force my dear son to make the very same mistake that I did."

"I don't understand." Elizabeth was more confused than ever. She had no notion what Lady Vale's current motivation was or what on earth she was getting at, but the entire conversation left her at a distinct disadvantage.

Lady Vale rose and began examining the small selection of gowns that hung on hooks behind the chamber door. "We must introduce some color to your wardrobe, my dear. Quite frankly, these drab browns are more depressing than the black and grey of widow's weeds!"

"Lady Vale!" Elizabeth snapped. Remembering herself, she softened her tone, "Lady Vale, if you'd please explain whether or not I'm to be sacked, I would appreciate it most greatly."

"Oh, you're definitely sacked, my dear. But you're not going anywhere. Not yet. When you and Benedict have decided what it is you wish to do about one another... and I might add that it should be matrimony of some sort, whether it's the reading of the banns and a big ceremony, by special license or, heaven forbid, a common license... it should happen. It's the only way."

"I cannot marry your son," Elizabeth protested. "It would ruin him."

"Why ever not?"

"Because I am not a virgin!"

"I should say not," Lady Vale said, even as she blushed. "He certainly saw to that."

"I was not a virgin when I came into your home, Lady Vale," Elizabeth said bluntly. "While I have tried to behave in the most proper manner since my arrival—until recently, at any rate—I have not always been cautious and circumspect. I have paid rather dearly for it, too. There is scandal attached to my name and I would not bring it to his door!"

Lady Vale was silent for a moment, and then asked, "Do you love him?"

Elizabeth dropped her head. "I do. Of course, I do. I think I have from the moment I first laid eyes upon him."

"That is infatuation, my dear. Love is something else," Lady Vale insisted. "Love means that you want him beside you even when he's so infuriating that you want to throttle him. Love means that you trust him to be there for you and to take care of you regardless of what comes, and the knowledge that you would do the same."

"I do trust him, and I would certainly do anything I could for him… that includes removing myself from his life before I can damage it further!"

Lady Vale sighed heavily. "Do not be so self-sacrificing that you do a disservice to you both. He's been missing for two decades. Half of society will not even accept that he is who we claim him to be. The other half will only want to get a look at him so that they can further aggrandize their *on dits* at other parties. His father died in the arms of his married lover while embroiled in the lengthy process of attempting to annul our marriage. If you think the scandal you bring to him is any more salacious than that which is already attached to his name—let them think what they will and let them say what they will. Live happily enough together for nothing else to matter."

Was it truly that simple? Could she just be with him, assuming he wanted her and damn what the world thought of them? "What if it becomes too much? What if he hates me for it later?"

"And what if his past is too much for you… I believe him to be an honorable man but there is much we do not know of where he's been and what he may have done in his life. Why do you assume your own sins are so great and insurmountable?"

Because they had been to everyone else, Elizabeth thought bitterly. Because her own father had disowned her, because only a handful of relatives on her mother's side even continued to acknowledge her existence and, even then, it was only in letters filled with pious recrimination. There were no invitations to visit, no suggestions of how she might improve her lot in life, not even a letter of recommendation when she'd been searching for a position.

"He hasn't asked me to marry him. I have the distinct impression that marriage is not something he has envisioned for himself… you may very well be pleading his case when that is the last thing he would wish you to do." It was a reasonable argument and one that, if true, would surely break her heart.

Lady Vale nodded. "That is true enough. I am assuming his intentions are honorable. If they are not… then perhaps you are better off not to marry him. All I ask is that you do not run away… that you allow the necessary time to determine what your future with him might be before any decisions are made. Please, just remain here for now."

Elizabeth considered her answer carefully. "I will remain for a while… but I cannot simply stay here indefinitely, especially as you will no longer need my services as a companion… and whether you choose to have a companion or not, I could not remain here after all is said and done. It would be very painful I think to be reminded on a daily basis of both my folly and my dashed hopes."

"If it comes to it, and he is not the man I believe him to be," Lady Vale vowed, "arrangements will be made for you. I will not simply see you tossed into the street or left at the mercy of relatives who, had they possessed mercy at all, would never have seen you here to begin with! Rest assured, Miss Masters, that one way or another, your future will be secured."

BENEDICT WAS SWEATING again, profusely. His shoulder no longer simply ached but blazed as if on fire. No doubt the wound had become fevered. Ripping the stitches out and then taxing those healing muscles as he had would have resulted in significant damage.

The path they followed through the woods on Harrelson's estate was narrow and overgrown, at times disappearing altogether. As he wound his way through the trees, he finally caught sight of what they'd been looking for. He whistled for Middlethorp's attention rather than calling out, the sound mimicking the call of a bird.

The entrance to the abandoned mine was a heavy, wooden door with rusted iron hardware upon it—save for the lock. It had been replaced and was shiny and new. Even more curious, it was unlocked and the door itself was ajar.

As Middlethorp stepped closer, Benedict asked in a low voice, "Why would you go to all the trouble of installing a new lock on an old door if you mean to leave it standing open?"

Middlethorp shrugged. "Perhaps there is someone inside who can answer our questions, then?"

Benedict moved ahead first, pushing the door open cautiously. It was dark inside, cold and damp. No lamps burned and, for all intents and purposes, it appeared to be exactly as reported—abandoned.

Middlethorp entered the chamber behind him, and his booted feet struck an object and sent it skittering over the floor. It rolled to a stop after bouncing off Benedict's own boot heel. Stooping to pick it up, he held it up to the light coming in from the open door. It was a delicately carved wooden button, something that would be sewn onto a woman's pelisse or spencer. In short, it was an item that had no place in their current environment unless Madame Zula's letter had been truthful.

Reaching for his neckcloth, Benedict tugged it loose and draped, then retrieved, one of the torches tucked into a bracket on the wall. He wrapped the cloth around it and Middlethorp produced a small flask from his waistcoat to douse it with, as well as a tinder box to strike the flame.

With torch in hand, they moved deeper into the cavernous space. In the distance, a very small and dim light glowed. As they neared it, it was easily identifiable as a lamp that had nearly burned out. It sat on the floor next to an abandoned tray that had been scavenged by rats. Cursing, Benedict passed the torch to the other man and then lifted the heavy bar that crossed the door.

It opened slowly, grudgingly, the wood scraping over the uneven floor. Inside the chamber a man lay on a small cot. An empty flask was on the floor next to his hand, and he appeared to be passed out in a drunken stupor.

Crossing to him, Benedict slapped him hard. The man sat up sputtering. "What? What? Why'd you do such a thing?"

Speech slurred and nearly incomprehensible, he was obviously not the man in charge of the operation.

"Where is the woman you were holding here?" Benedict demanded.

"She escaped... go ahead and kill me. Best to put a bullet in me now than wait for him to find out I let her get away!" the man groused.

"Your employer is the least of your concerns. Where is she?" Benedict demanded again.

"She hit me on the head with a rock and ran away. Locked me in here and left me for dead," he complained.

Benedict closed his eyes and prayed for the strength not to simply end the worthless bastard right there on the spot. Explaining to him that he had done precisely the same to her was pointless. "What did she look like?"

The man smiled then, grinning toothlessly. "Oh she were a pretty piece! Tiny, little thing with blond curls... I'da liked to teach her a thing or two—"

Benedict hit him then, his fist connecting with the man's nose. The crunching sound of bone on bone echoed throughout the small chamber. The man screamed and cupped his bleeding nose.

"What'd you do 'at for?" he squalled.

"How long ago?" Benedict asked, ignoring his question.

"It was breakfast time! Just 'afore daybreak. I brung her some porridge!"

Benedict looked back at Middlethorp. "That was hours ago. She could be anywhere by now!"

"Would she have gone back to Bath, to Mrs. Simms? Or would she try to return home to London?"

Benedict shook his head. "I've no idea. Who can say what's in her mind after what she has been through?"

"What to do with him?" Middlethorp asked "Should we kill him?"

The man screamed again and Benedict shook his head. "We can't prove he's done anything wrong. There are no other women here."

"Don't kill me!" He dropped to his knees and continued his pleading. "I can tell you who he's sold 'em to. At least some of 'em. I can tell you which abbesses handle the auctions!"

Middlethorp frowned. "Auctions?"

"Yes!" The man rose to his feet, clearly seeing that his information had perhaps spared his life and made him useful. "Some he sells direct to men what ask for certain types or certain girls! But others, he has auctioned off at bawdy houses in London and gives the abbesses a portion of the sale price!"

Benedict swallowed the bile rising in his throat. It wasn't an unheard of practice. But when coupled with the hundreds of dates and locations that Madame Zula had recorded in her ledger, the amount of suffering that he so casually spoke of, as if the women bought and sold like cattle were not even human, turned his stomach.

"We need to get him back to town... I'll not take him to Sarah's. But with a hefty payment to the jailor, I can see to it that our friend is well secured," Middlethorp offered.

"Do that. I'll make my own way back to town. I mean to search the woods in case she's lying injured somewhere," Benedict insisted.

"I'll send men to help, and send a carriage back for your use. You'll need it by the time you're done."

As Middlethorp left, the dirty, drunken sot walking before him, Middlethorp's gun pointed at his back, Benedict left the mine and began traversing the same path they'd taken to get there. He stepped off it frequently, following every offshoot, and examining every potential hiding place, looking for any sign or indication that she'd come that direction. Hours passed and a group of men arrived, servants sent by Middlethorp to assist in the search.

HE'D BACKTRACKED ALL the way to the road before he found it. There was a small bit of cloth, dirty and frayed, clinging to a low thicket. The cloth was embroidered with a delicate Greek key pattern that was one of Mary's favorites.

"Mary!" he called out again and again, until his voice was hoarse. Stepping deeper into the woods there, he saw the dark stain on the white bark of an oak. Kneeling beside it, he touched the spot and his fingertips came away red with blood.

Fear churned in his gut. The other men convened on that area, each of them looking for any sign. One found hoof prints beneath a tree not far from there, indicating that a horse had grazed there for some time. But that was it. Mary was gone once more and with only faint traces left behind. He didn't know if the blood was hers. He didn't know if she was injured or even dead. He only knew that his sister was still missing and he wouldn't rest until he found her.

Epilogue

MARY WAS RUNNING, her legs pumping and lungs burning. The trees that surrounded her were dark and twisted, each one appearing more sinister than the last. Deep shadows seemed to write and move on the ground. Twigs and branches snagged at her hair and clothes as she ran, almost like hands grasping at her. She fought them off, screaming as she did so.

"Stop your wailing or I'll give you something to wail about!"

Mary stopped in her tracks as her father stepped from behind the trees. He looked as he had the last time she'd seen him, drenched in blood, his face pale and eyes clouded by death.

It was not the first time she'd seen him thus, but strangely, for once, it offered her a sense of peace. His presence told her the truth of it, that what she was experiencing was only a dream. Even knowing that, and try as she might, she could not force herself to wake up.

Instead, she stood still, facing the man who'd tortured them both for all of their childhood as the trees twisted about her, their branches curving about her limbs and holding her fast.

"It's all right," a distant voice whispered. "You're safe now. No one will harm you."

That voice penetrated the dream, penetrated the very blackness within her own mind and pulled her back to reality. Her eyes fluttered open and she looked up into the dark visage of a man she did not know.

"Who are you?"

"Ambrose," he replied softly. His large hand stroked her face gently, bathing it with a cool, damp cloth. "You struck your head."

"In the woods," she whispered, her voice hoarse and weak. "It was you."

"I didn't mean to frighten you there," he said. "It's my fault you were harmed."

She tried to shake her head but pain exploded. She cried out from it and then the blackness claimed her once more, sucking her back down into the nightmares she'd only just escaped.

ELIZABETH WAS SITTING in the library. It was well after midnight. Mr. Middlethorp had retired to one of the guest rooms. Lady Vale had given up waiting for Benedict to return and had sought her own bed. Tired as she was, Elizabeth knew she would not sleep until he had safely returned.

When she heard the front door open and close, Calvert speaking in hushed tones, she breathed a sigh of relief. Within minutes, the door opened and Benedict stepped inside. His clothes were dirty and torn, hair mussed. But it was the expression on his face. He looked haunted. Grieved, she thought.

"Is she... I had thought she would be with you," she said.

"I still don't know," he answered, "where she is. Middlethorp told you she'd escaped her guard?"

"Yes," she nodded. "She was apparently quite resourceful."

He smiled sadly at that. "She is, indeed. But not invincible. I found blood... and a scrap of fabric torn from her clothing, probably her petticoat or chemise. It's a pattern I've seen her embroider time and again. It's on every handkerchief she's ever given me."

"It's possible the blood isn't hers," she said. "Even now, she could be on her way back to London thinking to reunite with you."

"I've considered it. I'm praying for it," he said softly. "I mean to leave word with Mrs. Simms and pay her well in the chance that Mary returns there... but I have to return to London, Elizabeth. I need to be there if she arrives."

Her heart stuttered painfully in her chest. "Of course you do. I wouldn't expect you to remain here. And you needn't worry, of course. We've made no promises to one another—"

"We may not have made a promise to one another," he interrupted. "But I made one to myself. You are mine, Elizabeth. You gave yourself to me in this very room and I've no intention of letting you go. Return to London with me?"

"And be your mistress?" She didn't dare hope for more.

"And be my wife," he corrected. "We can be married by common license... as soon as possible."

It was something she hadn't thought about, hadn't let herself consider as an option for her future. But he was offering her the thing she'd always dreamed of, to spend her life with a man who cared for her, who made her heart race and her blood sing. "And Lady Vale? Benedict, every shred of evidence thus far points to the fact that you are Lord Vale. All that's left is to make a case in front of the House of Lords and have it confirmed!"

He frowned at that. "If you want me to be Lord Vale, I'll be Lord Vale, Elizabeth. If you'd be happier for me to remain the lowly owner of a quite successful gaming hell, that is what I will do. Right now, there are only two things I want. You as my wife and my sister safely home with us."

"I want you to have what is yours... a family. A mother who adores you and an uncle who is far more terrifying than I ever realized," she answered.

"Even if that means having your secrets laid bare for all of society... and mine?" he asked.

"It doesn't matter. The only person whose opinion counts for anything is yours." It was true, she realized. He accepted her as she was. He wanted her for who she truly was and not who she had tried to pretend to be. "I know it shouldn't be possible given our short acquaintance, but so much has happened in that time. I love you. I love you and I can't imagine trying to go on with my life without you being part of it."

Benedict felt some of the tightness leave his chest, felt one the fears that had been riding him so hard slip away. Mary wouldn't begrudge him that. She had always fought for his happiness, even when he himself would not. "And I love you. I think I was born loving you. How strange it all is the way our lives have intersected here. It's as if all of this was meant to be. Freddy's connection to Harrelson, Harrelson's connection to my abduction and now to Mary's. We've all come together in this strange manner, like marbles in the corner of a crooked room."

Elizabeth's face tensed, her lips firming into a thin line. "Mr. Middlethorp went back to Madame Zula's this afternoon. She and Harrelson are both dead... and her manservant was there. She'd served Harrelson and herself poisoned whiskey. He'd drank from it but was still alive when Middlethorp arrived."

"So the main players are all dead now... all that is left are the bit parts," Benedict surmised. Whether any useful information would be had from Hardwick and the imbecile who had guarded Mary's tiny cell remained to be seen.

"If I take up the mantle of Lord Vale," he said softly, "I would make it my life's work to track down as many of Harrelson's victims as possible... to give them their freedom and some chance at a normal life. It eats away at me, now. Knowing what he did to them all."

Her head dropped to his shoulder and he pressed a kiss to the top of her head. It was simple acceptance—of him, of what he now saw as his purpose in life. Together, they would attempt to right those wrongs.

"She will come back to you," Elizabeth offered. "I believe that. We will find her and you will be reunited with your sister."

He lifted one hand to her head and stroked her hair as they sat there on that small settee. It was a moment's peace in a storm of chaos, and he had it because she was at his side.

"Do you think Middlethorp will ever profess his love to Lady Vale?" he asked, on a totally different topic. He didn't want to talk about

Harrelson anymore. He didn't want to talk about Mary and where she might be or what might be happening to her. For that moment, he wanted to simply hold the woman who made his world right.

He felt her smile against his chest. "I imagine that he will. The bigger question is whether or not Lady Vale will be willing to acknowledge her own feelings for him."

"Can I persuade you to be utterly scandalous and sneak into my bed?"

She smiled. "As if I require much persuading... will Mary like me, do you think? Or will she be offended that you have shackled yourself to a scandalous woman?"

Benedict smiled again. "Mary has only ever wanted one thing for me, and I for her, and that is happiness. Wherever she is, I pray that we are all together again soon and that someone will care for her as tenderly as you cared for me."

Elizabeth leaned in and kissed him again. "I will pray for the same."

They left the library hand in hand, neither caring if one of the servants saw or was utterly scandalized by it, and retreated to the solitude of his room and the peace they could offer one another.

The End

If you enjoyed *The Vanishing of Lord Vale*,
please take a moment to leave a review.

Also, if you have not yet read the first book in the series,
The Lost Lord of Castle Black, you may find it online.

Also by Chasity Bowlin

THE LOST LORDS SERIES
The Lost Lord of Castle Black
The Vanishing of Lord Vale
The Missing Marquess of Althorn (Coming in February, 2018)
The Resurrection of Lady Ransleigh (Coming Soon)
The Mystery of Miss Mason (Coming Soon)
The Awakening of Lord Ambrose (Coming Soon)

THE DARK REGENCY SERIES, PART ONE
The Haunting of a Duke
The Redemption of a Rogue
The Enticement of an Earl

THE DARK REGENCY SERIES, PART TWO
A Love So Dark
A Passion So Strong
A Heart So Wicked

STANDALONE
The Beast of Bath
The Last Offer
Worth the Wait

About the Author

Chasity Bowlin lives in central Kentucky with her husband and their menagerie of animals. She loves writing, traveling and enjoys incorporating tidbits of her actual vacations into her books. She is an avid Anglophile, loving all things British, but specifically all things Regency.

Growing up in Tennessee, spending as much time as possible with her doting grandparents, soap operas were a part of her daily existence, followed by back to back episodes of *Scooby-Doo*. Her path to becoming a romance novelist was set when, rather than simply have her Barbie dolls cruise around in a pink convertible, they time traveled, hosted lavish dinner parties and one even had an evil twin locked in the attic.

If you'd like to know more, please sign up for Chasity's newsletter at the link below:
http://eepurl.com/b9B7lL

40512642R10124

Made in the USA
Middletown, DE
27 March 2019